Welcome to Montana—a place of passion and adventure, where there is a charming little town with some big secrets…

Frannie Hannon: She was definitely more Hannon than Kincaid, with her flair for the understated. But the evening Frannie dared to replace her bun and twin sets with an outfit fit for a femme fatale, she found herself the recipient of a champion car racer's attention…and amorous *in*tentions…

Austin Parker: He'd never understood commitment …till he met Frannie. Though he could tell *she* was inexperienced, nothing in his past could have prepared him for the feelings Frannie inspired. Especially when he learned she was pregnant with his child.

Gretchen Neal: She was driven to unmask Raven Hunter's murderer. Then another dead body surfaced…

David Hannon: He claimed a holiday motivated his return home, but many people saw Special Agent Hannon digging for clues—when his attention wasn't on Officer Gretchen Neal!

Dear Reader,

Welcome to Special Edition.

This month sees the final instalment of THE STOCKWELLS family saga—Jackie Merritt's *The Cattleman and the Virgin Heiress* allows the amnesia-afflicted Stockwell heiress to experience a very different kind of life...

How about catching the most eligible single dad in town? That's exactly what the heroine of Carole Halston's *Because of the Twins...* attempts to do in our THAT'S MY BABY! mini-series. Of course, another vastly eligible bachelor appears in Diana Palmer's SOLDIERS OF FORTUNE story, *The Last Mercenary*. Her ruggedly dangerous hero needs to deal with his past before he can claim his bride...

For all those who have been reading and enjoying the hugely successful MONTANA BRIDES, we have *And The Winner—Weds!* by Robin Wells which is connected to this series. Look out for *Just Pretending* next month.

Finally, we round off the month with Jean Brashear's super revenge story *Texas Royalty* and *Cowboy's Baby* by Victoria Pade—where a temporary shotgun marriage is beginning to look very permanent!

Enjoy!

The Editors

And the Winner—Weds!

ROBIN WELLS

™ SILHOUETTE®
SPECIAL EDITION™

*First published in Great Britain 2002
Silhouette Books, Eton House, 18-24 Paradise Road,
Richmond, Surrey TW9 1SR*

© Harlequin Books S.A. 2000

*Special thanks and acknowledgement are given to Robin Wells for
her contribution to the Montana Brides series.*

ISBN 0 373 65059 0

23-0502

*Printed and bound in Spain
by Litografia Rosés S.A., Barcelona*

ROBIN WELLS

Before becoming a full-time writer, Robin was a hotel public relations executive whose career ranged from writing and producing award-winning videos to organising pie-throwing classes taught by circus clowns. At other times in her life she has been a model, a reporter and even a charm school teacher. But her life-long dream was to become an author, a dream no doubt inspired by having parents who were both librarians and who passed on their love of books.

Robin lives just outside New Orleans with her husband and two young daughters, Taylor and Arden. Although New Orleans is known as America's most romantic city, Robin says her personal romantic inspiration is her husband, Ken.

Robin is an active member of the Southern Louisiana chapter of the Romance Writers of America. Her first book won RWA's national 1995 Golden Heart Award.

When she's not writing, Robin enjoys gardening, antiquing, discovering new restaurants and spending time with her family. Robin loves to hear from her readers, and can be reached at PO Box 303, Mandeville, LA 70470-0303, USA.

If you enjoyed

MONTANA BRIDES

you'll love to know that it's not over yet...

**The latest Montana Brides
four-book series coming
to you from Silhouette
Special Edition®**

MONTANA BRIDES
THE KINCAIDS

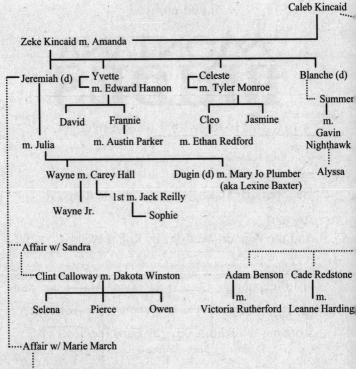

Caleb Kincaid

Zeke Kincaid m. Amanda

Jeremiah (d) — Yvette
m. Edward Hannon

Celeste
m. Tyler Monroe

Blanche (d)

Summer
m.
Gavin
Nighthawk

David   Frannie

Cleo   Jasmine

m. Julia   m. Austin Parker   m. Ethan Redford

Wayne m. Carey Hall   Dugin (d) m. Mary Jo Plumber
(aka Lexine Baxter)

Alyssa

1st m. Jack Reilly

Wayne Jr.

Sophie

Affair w/ Sandra

Clint Calloway m. Dakota Winston   Adam Benson   Cade Redstone

Selena   Pierce   Owen

m.   m.
Victoria Rutherford   Leanne Harding

Affair w/ Marie March

Jennifer McCallum

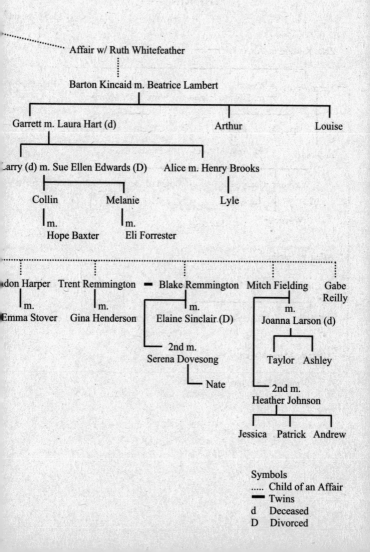

Affair w/ Ruth Whitefeather

Barton Kincaid m. Beatrice Lambert

Garrett m. Laura Hart (d)   Arthur   Louise

Larry (d) m. Sue Ellen Edwards (D)   Alice m. Henry Brooks

Collin   Melanie   Lyle

m.   m.
Hope Baxter   Eli Forrester

...don Harper   Trent Remmington — Blake Remmington   Mitch Fielding   Gabe Reilly

m.   m.   m.   m.
Emma Stover   Gina Henderson   Elaine Sinclair (D)   Joanna Larson (d)

2nd m.   Taylor   Ashley
Serena Dovesong

Nate   2nd m.
Heather Johnson

Jessica   Patrick   Andrew

Symbols
..... Child of an Affair
— Twins
d   Deceased
D   Divorced

To Ken—the winner of my heart

One

"What do you think of Summer's hair?"

Frannie Hannon pulled her eyes away from the computer screen and swiveled around in the wooden office chair to see her two gorgeous cousins, Jasmine and Summer, standing in front of the front desk of the Big Sky Bed & Breakfast. Summer's long, dark hair fell in a tousled cascade of curls to her shoulders, where it lay in dramatic contrast against the red silk of her short chic dress.

"Give me your honest opinion, Frannie." Summer ran a hand through the loose waves in her normally straight hair. "Do you think Gavin will think curls look good on me?"

Frannie pushed her tortoiseshell glasses higher up on her nose, a dry smile curving the corners of her lips. "Your husband would think you looked gorgeous if you shaved your head and painted your skull green. And the annoying thing about it is, he'd be right."

It was the absolute truth. With her beautiful Native American features, deep chocolate eyes and wide, expressive mouth, Summer Nighthawk was breathtaking. But then, so was Jasmine Monroe, with her close-cropped dark hair, delicate features and creamy pale skin. Either woman's face or figure could stop traffic and a man's heart at fifty paces.

All mine could stop is a clock, Frannie thought ruefully. A familiar twinge of inferiority tweaked at her heart.

She'd grown up here in Whitehorn, Montana, with Summer, Jasmine and Jasmine's equally gorgeous sister, Cleo, and she viewed them more as sisters than as cousins. Their mothers, in fact, *were* sisters. Frannie's mom, Yvette, and Jasmine's and Cleo's mom, Celeste, ran a bed-and-breakfast in the rambling arts and crafts-style manor house. Summer's mother, Blanche, had died shortly after Summer's birth, so Celeste and Yvette had raised their sister's daughter as one of their own.

The four cousins had all grown up together. They'd spent summers splashing in the waters of Blue Mirror Lake and winters tobogganing down the foothills of the Crazy Mountains. They'd shared their dreams and their secrets, their toys and their clothes. They were family in every sense of the word, and yet sometimes, when Frannie looked at her cousins, she found it hard to believe she'd come from the same gene pool.

Times like now. Summer was so dark and exotic, Jasmine so fair and fragile. Next to them, Frannie always felt like a little brown mouse.

Well, not little, exactly, she thought ruefully. Tall and gawky was more like it. At five-foot, nine-inches, Frannie's height was the only exceptional thing about her. There was nothing special about her light brown hair except its unruly nature, which was why Frannie kept it clamped back in a tight ponytail. Her skin was clear and fair, but her features were unremarkable. Her eyes were an okay shade of hazel, but she kept them hidden behind her large, tortoiseshell-framed glasses. Oh, she had her own unique characteristics, of course—her nose was faintly freckled, her figure was on the scrawny side, and she grew incredibly clumsy whenever she was nervous—but overall, she was drab, colorless and nondescript.

Which suited her just fine, Frannie reminded herself. It was better to fade into the background than to stick out and be ridiculed. In fact, she deliberately cultivated an inconspicuous look. She dressed to blend in, wearing brown or beige suits for her job at the Whitehorn Savings and Loan, and jeans and shapeless sweaters, like the baggy gray one she was wearing now, on evenings and weekends.

When it came to her appearance, Frannie didn't kid herself. She was plain, and she knew it. She'd made peace with that fact years ago, and now, at twenty-six, she knew there was no point in pretending to be something she wasn't.

"So what do you think?" Jasmine prompted. She waved her hand toward Summer's hair as if she were Vanna White pointing to a grand prize. "Am I a maestro with a curling iron, or what?"

"You are the Queen of Coif." Frannie leaned back in the rolling chair and gazed approvingly at Summer. "You look great. But what's the special occasion? You and Gavin haven't been married long enough to be celebrating an anniversary."

Summer lifted a shoulder. "No occasion. Just a Saturday night date with my husband."

"Who's baby-sitting?" Frannie asked. "Isn't it the nanny's night off?"

"She switched to accommodate our schedules. It isn't often Gavin and I are off on the same Saturday night." The nanny took wonderful care of their toddler Alyssa.

"So where are you going?"

"To dinner at the country club—if he ever finishes up at the hospital. I told him I'd change here instead of driving all the way home." Summer sighed. "I love living in the country, but as many hours as we spend at work, sometimes I think we just ought to live in a room at the hospital."

Frannie nodded sympathetically. Gavin was a general

surgeon at the Whitehorn Hospital, the same place where Summer practiced as an immunologist. Both of them spent most of their waking hours there or at the clinic on the reservation. Since their home was twenty miles away, Summer often used the bed-and-breakfast to change clothes, wait for Gavin, or simply relax between shifts.

"So if there's no special occasion, what's with the snazzy dress and new hairstyle?" Frannie asked.

Summer shrugged. "I just think it's good for a husband to see his wife looking different every now and then. I want to keep the magic in my marriage."

Jasmine and Frannie looked at each other, then simultaneously burst into laughter.

Summer put her hands on her hips and eyed them indignantly. "And what, pray tell, is so funny about that?"

"Summer, your entire life is magic," Jasmine said.

"Yeah," Frannie seconded. "You're beautiful, you have a fantastic career, a beautiful daughter, and you're married to a successful surgeon who worships the ground you walk on."

Summer's hands fell to her sides. "Well, you know the old saying—familiarity breeds contempt. I don't want Gavin to get bored with me."

Jasmine rolled her eyes. "As if that could ever happen."

"Yeah, Summer. Gavin's not fickle like Jasmine here." Frannie grinned at her pixie-faced cousin. Jasmine was hotly pursued by all the local bachelors, but she had yet to get seriously interested in any of them. "Who's the lucky guy you're going out with tonight?"

Jasmine looked down at her neatly buffed nails. "Bill Richards. You know—one of the architectural engineers of the new resort and casino. He stayed here a few weeks ago."

"Oh, I remember him! Broad shoulders, dark hair..."

Summer frowned. "But I thought he left town when the construction halted."

The construction of a casino on the Laughing Horse Reservation and a resort on adjacent private land was the biggest thing to ever hit Whitehorn. The development was supposed to boost the local economy, become a major revenue source for the Northern Cheyenne tribe, and create several hundred jobs for the citizens of Whitehorn. The ground had barely been broken for the project, however, when a skeleton with a bullet in its rib had been unearthed at the construction site.

And it wasn't just any old skeleton, either. Dental records had revealed that the remains belonged to Summer's father, Raven Hunter. Fortunately—well, it wasn't exactly fortunate, Frannie mentally amended, but in view of the discovery of his body, it certainly made the situation less emotionally painful— Summer had never known her father.

The police were conducting a murder investigation, and to the distress of the citizens of Whitehorn, the construction project had been put on hold until the investigation was completed. Rumor had it that the police probe could take months. If it lasted until the onset of winter weather, the grand opening could be delayed for a full year.

"I thought the engineers weren't going to return until construction resumed," Frannie remarked.

Jasmine nodded. "Evidently it has. When Bill called to ask me out, he said they've decided to build the resort's sports complex first. It's being built further to the east, on Garrett Kincaid's property."

"So the project is back on track," Summer said. "Well, that's good news for Whitehorn's economy."

"Not to mention Whitehorn's single women." Jasmine gave a mischievous smile. "The town's probably filling up right now with hunky engineers and contractors and heavy-equipment operators.''

''That's right.'' Summer's gaze fastened on Frannie, one eyebrow arching in mock reproach. ''But in order for a gal to meet any of them, she'd have to get out there and mingle.''

Frannie winced, knowing she was in for another round of the old familiar lecture.

Jasmine quickly picked up on Summer's theme. ''Are you going out tonight, Frannie, or are you going to hole up here like you usually do?''

Frannie swiveled her chair back to face the computer. ''The books are a mess. You know how hopeless Aunt Celeste is with finances, and she's been doing all the purchasing since Mom's been gone.''

''But it's Saturday night,'' Summer scolded. ''Don't you know all work and no play makes you a dull girl?''

Frannie made a face. ''I'm already dull. It's too late to worry about it.''

Summer wagged a finger at her. ''It's never too late to get a life, Frannie. You need to go out and meet some men.''

''It's not as if they're eagerly lining up for an introduction.''

''That's because you're always hiding away here,'' Jasmine insisted.

''That's right.'' Summer nodded. ''You'll never meet anyone if you don't get out and circulate.''

''You two do enough circulating for all of us.'' Desperate for a change of subject, Frannie glanced at her watch. ''Speaking of circulating, when are your guys arriving?''

''Gavin should be here any minute.''

Jasmine glanced at the grandfather clock in the entryway alcove, then clasped a hand to the lapels of her white terry-cloth robe. "Oh, dear. Bill will be here in ten minutes and I'm not even dressed! Summer, come help me figure out what to wear."

"Okay—if you'll let me borrow your new necklace."

"Deal."

Frannie heaved a sigh of relief as her cousins scurried upstairs to Jasmine's room in the back wing of the house. She knew they meant well, but she hated it when they tried to coax her into social situations. The few times she'd allowed them to drag her to the local nightspots, she'd sat on the sidelines as man after man ignored her.

Her cousins refused to accept it, but Frannie knew it was a fact: she didn't have what it took to interest a handsome, successful, desirable man—not for any length of time, anyway. The best she could hope for was a kind-hearted geek, and she had yet to meet one who held the least bit of appeal.

She was better off sticking with the one thing she knew she was good at: numbers. Numbers could always be counted on. There was no guesswork, no wondering if the results would be worth the effort, no question about how things would turn out. Numbers didn't care if they were gussied up in colors and fancy fonts or set down in plain black and white. Unlike men, numbers were solid and reliable and trustworthy.

She plucked a yellow slip of paper off the top of the stack of receipts in front of her, determined to get her mind back on bookkeeping. She'd been managing the books for the Big Sky Bed & Breakfast since she was fifteen, but she still found it a challenge. Aunt Celeste's unorthodox way of operating kept it that way.

She stared at the receipt in her hand and frowned. Whitehorn Cleaners. Was this a bill for laundering business linens or Aunt Celeste's personal clothing? Lately Aunt

Celeste had been even more careless than usual about labeling the receipts. With a sigh, Frannie placed the receipt in the growing stack of items she needed to ask her aunt about and reached for another.

She was inputting information from an itemized grocery list when the bell over the heavy oak front door jangled. Since Summer had said her husband was due any minute, Frannie assumed he'd arrived. "Come on in, Gavin," she called. She heard the door open, but didn't bother to turn around. "Summer's getting ready. She'll be out here in a moment."

"Well, now," said an unfamiliar voice. "I thought summer was already here, seeing as it's the end of June."

It was a low, deep throb of a voice, smoky and unrelentingly masculine. Something about it made the hair on the back of Frannie's neck stand up, as if she'd just entered an electric force field.

She jerked around to find two men standing just inside the doorway. The one on the right was middle-aged and stout, clad in denim overalls, a red plaid shirt and brown work boots. His gray hair was sparse and closely shorn, and he had a face as round and friendly as a pumpkin pie.

But the other one… Frannie tried to swallow, but her mouth was suddenly so dry she felt as if her tongue had melded to the top of her mouth.

The other one… *My, oh, my.*

He was obviously the owner of that seductive voice. Tall, lean, and muscular, he wore jeans and cowboy boots, and held a battered, buff-colored Stetson hat in his hand. Frannie wasn't sure if it was his deep tan or his denim shirt that made his eyes look so blue, but they seemed to jump out of his handsome face like blue flames, blue flames that licked at her very soul. There was a strange heat in his gaze—the heat, Frannie realized with a jolt, of sexual awareness.

He was looking at her in the way a man looks at a woman. Well, of course he was, she thought distractedly—after all, she *was* a woman, and he was most definitely a man. What surprised her was that he was looking at her as if she were a *desirable* woman. His mouth was curved into a small, amused smile, and Frannie realized he was waiting for her to speak.

She started to scramble to her feet, and tipped her chair over in the process. She leaned to pick it up, caught her foot on a chair roller, and toppled into the overturned chair face-first, leaving her bottom in the air.

"Hey, are you all right?" The handsome man quickly rounded the desk and took her arm, helping her pull herself upright.

His hand was warm, and the warmth spread rapidly through her body, causing her cheeks to burn. Frannie smoothed her sweater, embarrassed at her awkwardness. "I, uh, I'm fine. I was, uh, expecting someone else."

"Sorry to disappoint you, ma'am." His low, smoky voice managed to make the word "ma'am" sound like a caress.

His hand was still on her upper arm. Frannie felt as tongue-tied as a schoolgirl. "Oh, I'm not disappointed." The moment she said it, she wanted to bite her tongue. Why did she always manage to say and do the most awkward things whenever she was around a handsome man?

The corners of his mouth curved up further. "Well, good." He dropped his hand and stepped back.

Frannie was certain she'd never met him before, yet something about him seemed strangely familiar. "Do I know you?"

"I don't believe I've had the pleasure. I'm sure I would have remembered."

Frannie gave a wry grin. "Not necessarily. I don't always make such a memorable first impression."

The man laughed, and a fresh tug of attraction pulled at Frannie's chest. Did he look at every woman that way, as if he found her attractive and fascinating? He no doubt did. Most women probably just weren't as susceptible to it as she was. It was probably some kind of subliminal body-language come-on that she ought to know better than to fall for, but she knew no such thing. Whatever he was doing, it was working. Oh, yes, it was definitely working.

She tried to pull her thoughts out of the fog and search her mind for a reason the man looked so familiar. Maybe he was a movie star or a TV actor.

Maybe, she thought as she watched him circle back around the front desk, he was just the man of her dreams. Aunt Celeste believed that dreams were gateways to the soul, that they held clues to both the past and the future.

What on earth was the matter with her? There was no way a man such as this was going to be a part of her future. She was still staring, she realized abruptly.

She pulled her eyes away and tugged at the bottom of her sweater again. "Thanks for the help. Sorry about the klutz attack."

"I'm sorry we startled you."

Frannie was relieved to hear Summer's high heels click on the hardwood floor as she entered the foyer. "Gavin, is that you?" Summer appeared in the doorway, her arms high, her hands behind her neck as she fastened what Frannie recognized as Jasmine's new necklace.

Summer stopped in her tracks, immediately dropping her arms. "Oh, I'm sorry," she said with a smile. "I was expecting my husband." She stepped forward and stuck out her hand. "Welcome to the Big Sky Bed & Breakfast. I'm Summer Nighthawk."

"Nice to meet you, ma'am." The tall handsome man

shook her hand. "I'm Austin Parker, and this here's Tommy Deshaw."

Summer shook hands with both men, then cast a quizzical look at the younger one. "Austin Parker—the race car driver?"

The man smiled sheepishly. "Afraid so."

"My husband is one of your biggest fans." Summer's smile widened. "We'd heard you'd bought some land around here."

"Yes, ma'am. The old Givens ranch."

"That place has a huge house. Do you have a large family?"

"No, ma'am. I'm not married."

"No?" Summer gestured to Frannie. "Well, neither is Frannie here."

Frannie longed to crawl under the front desk.

"I take it you two have met?" Summer continued.

"Yes, ma'am. But we hadn't quite gotten around to introductions." He treated Frannie to a blinding smile.

Frannie had no choice but to reach out her hand. "F— Frannie Hannon." Good grief, she could barely say her own name! It was a good thing she'd managed to spit it out before he touched her, because when his large, warm hand closed around hers, the ability to speak deserted her along with all coherent thought. She felt a sense of both relief and loss when he loosened his grip.

She turned and shook hands with Tommy. The older man smiled warmly. "It's a pleasure, ma'am."

"Frannie, Austin Parker is the hottest ticket on the NASCAR circuit," Summer said.

"How…nice."

"Tommy here's the really hot ticket," Austin said, gesturing to his companion. "He's my pit crew chief, so he's the one who really runs the show. The crew's what keeps a driver on the road."

"We're delighted to have both of you here." Summer's smile included both men. "What can we do for you two gentlemen?"

"I'd like to book a room for Tommy for the next few days, if you've got one available." Austin shifted his hat to his other hand. "He's going to be overhauling the engine on my car. I intended for him to stay out at my ranch, but I'm havin' the place renovated and all the guest rooms are a wreck. Do you happen to have any vacancies?"

"As a matter of fact, we're nearly empty this evening." Summer smiled at Tommy. "We'd be delighted to have you stay with us. Right, Frannie?"

Frannie smiled wanly, edging her way back to the computer. That gleam in Summer's eye meant she was up to her old matchmaking tricks, and Frannie wanted no part of it. Trying to interest Austin in her would be like trying to interest a yacht owner in a rowboat. Turning, Frannie picked up a handful of receipts and lowered herself back into the wooden swivel chair.

"Frannie, would you like to handle the check-in?" Summer prompted.

Frannie froze. "I—I, uh…oh, gee, I really need to get these numbers into the computer. Since Gavin's not here yet, could you go ahead and take care of it?"

Summer had no choice but to graciously nod. "Why, sure." She pulled a large leather book out from under the desk, opened it and angled it toward Tommy. "If you'd just sign in here, Mr. Deshaw."

The look she shot Frannie told her she was in for a lecture as soon as Summer got her alone. Frannie fervently hoped Gavin showed up before that happened.

Frannie had no such luck. Austin had no sooner said his goodbyes and Tommy Deshaw headed to his room than Summer grabbed the back of Frannie's chair and spun her around to face her. Frannie could tell from the way her cousin's lips were pressed in a thin tight line that she was thoroughly exasperated.

"What's the big idea?" Summer demanded.

"Of what?"

"Of ignoring the most eligible bachelor to hit White-horn since my Gavin, that's what."

"Oh, Summer, a man like that's not going to be interested in the likes of me."

"Not if you turn your back to him and act rude!"

"I wasn't acting rude. I was acting busy. Which, it just so happens, I am."

Frannie was relieved to see Jasmine saunter into the front foyer, wearing a striking black pantsuit. Frannie seized on the opportunity to change the subject. "Jasmine, you look great."

"Thanks. What's going on?"

Summer pointed at Frannie. "A wonderful specimen of manhood just walked in here, and our cuz wouldn't even talk to him."

"I didn't have anything to say!" Frannie protested.

"You don't have to *say* anything, Frannie," Summer said. "You just have to *talk*."

"Oh. Thanks for the clarification," Frannie said dryly.

Jasmine laughed. "You know what she means, Frannie. Make small talk. Be pleasant. Show you're accessible."

"Let him know you're interested," Summer added. "Smile. Flirt."

"That's easy for you two to say. I don't know how to do any of that."

"Well, then, it's high time you learned. Jasmine and I can teach you."

Jasmine nodded vigorously.

"Oh, no." Frannie held up her hands, palms out. "No way. No, thanks."

Jasmine's flawless forehead creased in a frown. "Why not?"

"Because it wouldn't work. Besides, I'd feel like an idiot."

"No, you wouldn't. Not for long, anyway." Jasmine circled the front desk and stopped in front of Frannie, her hands on her hips. "Think about it, Frannie. Isn't it better to feel a little silly for a little while than to feel lonely forever?"

Lonely forever—was that what they thought she was destined to be? A sharp little knife of pain sliced into Frannie's heart. "There are worse things than being lonely," she mumbled.

Such as being humiliated. And heartbroken. And feeling like a pathetic fool.

Summer's dark eyes filled with sympathy. "Just because you had a bad experience with one guy in college is no reason to shy away from all other men for the rest of your life."

It wasn't just a bad experience, Frannie thought, it was an amputation of part of her soul. Joe had not only betrayed her; he'd emotionally maimed her. He'd stripped her of her self-confidence and her ability to trust anyone.

Frannie pushed back her chair and rose, wrapping her arms around herself. "I'm not shying away. I'm just minding my own business, living my own life."

"Frannie, you're practically a recluse," Jasmine said softly.

"I'm not!"

"Yes, you are," Summer affirmed. "You never go to any parties or social events. You go to work at the bank, then you come home and work here. And if an attractive man happens to come within a mile of you, you duck your head and avoid making eye contact."

"And then there's the matter of how you dress," Jasmine added gently. "You're hiding all of your best qualities. You have a great figure, but no one would ever know it under the clothes you wear. You have beautiful eyes, but instead of wearing your contact lenses, you hide behind your glasses. I'd love to have thick, curly hair like yours, but instead of making the most of it, you keep it skinned back in a ponytail or a tight little bun."

Frannie was surprised to find herself blinking back tears. "Sorry I'm such an embarrassment to you."

"Oh, Frannie, that's not what we're saying!" Jasmine stepped forward and embraced her in a hug. "We love you and want you to have all the good things in life, that's all."

"That's right. We want you to be happy." Summer placed a hand on Frannie's back and gave her a consoling pat. "I didn't mean to hurt you. I was just trying to jar a little sense into you, that's all."

Frannie sniffed and wiped her eyes, then pulled away. Summer gave her another pat on the back, then pulled herself onto one edge of the computer workstation. "I don't think you realize it, Frannie, but when it comes to men, you're your own worst enemy. You'll never meet anyone if you don't stop hiding."

"I'm not deliberately hiding. I'm just...I don't know. Being self-protective, maybe." Frannie turned away and stared at the large stone fireplace in the living room across the foyer. She took a ragged breath. "If I had one-tenth of the good looks you two have, things would be different. But I don't. I don't want to set myself up for rejection again, that's all."

"You've got everything we've got," Summer said.

"And in some places, more." Jasmine looked down at her own petite chest in such an amusingly wistful way that Frannie had to smile.

"I'm plain as mud," Frannie said bluntly.

"You're not!" Summer said. "You just need a little polishing up."

"That's right." Jasmine nodded. "And attitude."

Frannie gave a tight smile. "Oh, I've got plenty of that."

"Boy, do you ever!" Jasmine grinned. "But that's not the kind of attitude I mean. You need to project more self-assurance."

"Jasmine's right," Summer said. "Your outlook and expectations become a self-fulfilling prophecy. If you think you're unattractive and don't expect anyone to approach you, you're going to act in ways that will make men keep their distance. But if you act confident and look your best and expect men to be attracted to you, that's exactly what will happen."

Frannie wished she could believe them. Something about that race car driver had stirred up longings she'd all but forgotten she could feel. She heaved a sigh. "You make it sound so easy. Too bad it isn't."

"Well, how about giving us a chance to prove that it is?"

If she had any sense, she'd say no right away. But the memory of Austin's touch was too fresh on her mind. "What have you got in mind?" Frannie asked.

Summer grinned. "I just thought of the perfect occasion to prove to you that a makeover of your appearance and attitude can make over your love life."

"And what might that be?" Frannie asked skeptically.

"Yeah, what is it?" Jasmine asked.

Summer paused dramatically. "The Whitehorn Ball. It's the hospital's big annual fund-raiser, and all of the staff is expected to be there. There's this new doctor in radiology. He's single, he doesn't know anyone in town and he doesn't have a date."

Panic welled up in Frannie's chest. "Oh, no. Not a blind date."

Summer raised her hand in a calming gesture. "Just hear me out. The dance is three weeks away. That's plenty of time for Jasmine and me to make you over and give you some pointers."

"Oh, Summer, I don't think this is a good idea...." Frannie began.

"It's not a good idea. It's a *great* one," Jasmine said excitedly. She clasped her hands together. "We could triple date."

"But—"

"But what?"

"But it's a formal dance," Frannie protested.

"So? That makes it all the more fun. We'll turn you into Cinderella for the ball."

"But—" Frannie swallowed around a lump in her throat. "But I was supposed to go to a formal dance with Joe the night after...after..."

"After you found out what a heel he was," Summer finished for her.

Frannie nodded.

Her gaze was soft and warm. "That was what? Five years ago?"

"Six."

Summer gently placed her hands on Frannie's shoulders. "Can you look me straight in the eye and honestly tell me you don't ever want to go to a formal dance again the rest of your life?"

Did she really want to limit her life in that way? Frannie sighed. "I guess not."

"Well, then, it's high time you got back in the saddle."

"But the idea makes me so—so *uncomfortable*."

"Frannie, sometimes we have to move outside our comfort zone in order to move forward. We have to face our fears in order to get over them.'' Summer's tone was calm and authoritative, the tone that Frannie secretly called her doctor's voice. ''This is a great opportunity for you to put the past behind you, once and for all, and start a new chapter in your life.''

Jasmine nodded earnestly.

''Besides,'' Summer continued, ''what have you got to lose? It's just one night out of your life. For just one night, try things our way. If you don't like the results, you can always go back to the way things are now.''

A car pulled up in the drive and killed its engine. The hum of another engine rapidly followed. A wave of relief washed through Frannie. ''Sounds like both of your dates are here. Too bad we'll have to discontinue this fascinating discussion.''

Summer rose and straightened her skirt, her lips curved in a smile. ''Don't worry. We'll continue it later. In the meantime, will you promise to just think about it?''

It would be a disaster. She was awful at making small talk. She would make a fool of herself. She was nuts to even consider it.

But she *was* considering it. Heaven help her, she was. Meeting that race car driver had made her realize how much she longed for male companionship. More than anything, she wanted a husband and a family.

Her cousins were right, Frannie thought ruefully. She wasn't likely to meet any prospective mates sitting at home in front of the computer.

Frannie sighed and reluctantly nodded. ''Okay. I'll think about it.''

Two

Frannie thought of little else for the rest of the evening. She was still thinking about it the next morning when she strode into the large sun-filled kitchen, where Aunt Celeste was fussing over the stove.

Frannie smoothed a wayward strand of hair back into the tight bun she'd coiled at her crown, thinking how different her own drab coloring was from her vivid aunt's. A natural redhead, Celeste had russet hair that became progressively brighter over the years as she fought off the signs of aging. Her current shade was called Autumn Flame, and she'd evidently taken the theme to heart, because she was dressed in a loose yellow shirt over a filmy orange and yellow gypsy-style skirt.

"Ouch!" Celeste dropped a heavy skillet back onto the stove with a loud clatter, then stuck her index finger into her mouth and dashed to the sink, her bangle bracelets jangling.

Frannie hurried forward. "Are you all right?"

Celeste flipped on the faucet and stuck her right hand under the running water. "Depends on your definition of 'all right.' That's the second time I've burned myself this morning, and the third skillet of scrambled eggs I've nearly ruined."

"Where's Jasmine?" Jasmine normally did all the cooking at the B and B.

"That nice young man she went out with last night came by and wanted to take her fishing this morning,"

Celeste said. "I told her to go ahead, that I'd enjoy taking a turn in the kitchen. I didn't know I was going to be all thumbs this morning."

Frannie frowned. Aunt Celeste might be less than careful when it came to bookkeeping and paperwork, but she was usually the very picture of efficiency in the kitchen. Celeste's personality was as warm as her hair color, and she was just as nurturing as she was warm. She loved cooking and baking, and was as comfortable around the stove as Frannie was around the computer.

Frannie stepped closer. Her aunt's complexion seemed paler than usual this morning, and the delicate skin under her eyes was etched with deep blue shadows.

"Are you feeling ill?"

Celeste brushed a strand of hair away from her forehead with her left hand and sighed. "I'm fine, dear. Just tired. I didn't sleep well again last night. I kept having those awful dreams."

Celeste had been plagued by nightmares for the past two weeks. All of them involved members of her family, and most of them centered on her sister, Blanche. In one particularly vivid dream, Blanche had warned that the past was about to rise up and greet her. She'd also cautioned Celeste be careful to make the right choices.

"Have you had any more dreams about Blanche?" Frannie asked.

"All of them seem to involve her." Celeste stared out the kitchen window at the forest. "A couple of them last night were about my brother, Jeremiah. He was angry— horribly angry—but I don't know why or at whom or what was going on. Another time I woke up with my heart racing, and I'd been dreaming about Blanche. I could see her in the distance."

Celeste shut off the faucet and reached for a paper towel. "She was trying to tell me something, but for the life of me, I couldn't understand what it was. She was too far away. I could see her lips moving, but I couldn't hear what she was saying."

Frannie reached for a clean cloth and filled it with ice. She gave it to her aunt. "You've been having a lot of bad dreams lately."

Celeste put the ice pack on her injured finger. "Just about every night. I'm sure it's a sign."

"Of what?"

"I don't know. Blanche keeps trying to tell me something. I keep thinking back to the dream where she told me the past was about to rise up. Something's about to happen. And whatever it is, it's important."

Celeste was a deeply spiritual person, but she harbored some odd notions about dreams and ghosts and the afterlife. She'd lived in Louisiana for a year with her late husband, and she'd brought back some strange beliefs from the bayou.

"Sometimes a dream is just a dream," Frannie commented.

"And sometimes it's not." Celeste shook her head. "You know, dreams are nothing to dismiss lightly. Sometimes they contain messages from the other side. The problem is, the messages are often hard to read." Celeste inspected her finger. "They're like smoke signals—they can drift away before you get a chance to understand them."

An acrid odor reached Frannie's nose. She sniffed, then looked at Celeste in alarm. "Speaking of smoke, is something burning?"

"Oh, dear!" Celeste dashed across the kitchen, grabbed an oven mitt and yanked open the oven door, then reached inside. "Ouch!" she exclaimed, waving her hand.

"Did you burn yourself again?"

"Yes, dadblast it! Frannie, come and take these cinnamon rolls out of the oven before they burn to a crisp."

Frannie patted her aunt's back. "Why don't you go sit down and relax? I'll get breakfast for our guests this morning. We only have three, don't we? Mr. Deshaw and that nice couple from Washington?"

"Four. Mr. Deshaw's friend came by to pick him up, and I invited him to stay for breakfast. I believe Mr. Deshaw said he's a race car driver, of all things."

Frannie's heart unaccountably picked up speed. She pulled on the oven mitt her aunt had abandoned and retrieved the burned rolls from the oven.

"The couple ate an hour ago. They're out on the lake in the rowboat, fishing."

"Well, then, I'll get breakfast for the gentlemen."

"Why, thank you, dear." Celeste smiled at her niece. "I believe I'll take you up on that offer."

"Are you serving breakfast on the back porch?"

Celeste nodded. "It was too beautiful a morning to stay inside. Since the rolls are burned, why don't you make some toast? You can serve it with the scrambled eggs. I made enough to serve an army."

Celeste made her way upstairs and Frannie bustled around the kitchen. In a matter of minutes she'd prepared two attractive plates garnished with sliced cantaloupe and fresh strawberries. She loaded them onto an antique silver tray, her stomach fluttering nervously. Taking a deep breath, she headed out of the kitchen, through the den and onto the screened-in back porch.

The porch overlooked Blue Mirror Lake and Frannie usually found the view breathtaking, but she was too distracted by the sight of the tall, handsome man to notice the scenery this morning. Austin was settled in a rustic twig chair at a wooden table, deep in conversation with Tommy, and he looked even more handsome than she remembered. Her pulse fluttered wildly when he looked up at her and smiled.

He rose as she approached the table. "Good mornin'. May I help you with that?" He gestured toward the tray.

Frannie hesitated, completely flustered. She wasn't accustomed to guests standing and offering to help when she tried to serve them. "Oh, no. Please take your seat." She lifted a hand from the tray and gestured toward his chair.

She immediately knew she'd made a mistake. The tray tipped and the plates slid. She watched in horror as they headed toward him, as if in slow motion. Trying to correct the slant of the tray, she jerked it upward, but overcompensated.

"Oh, no!" Frannie gasped. A plate of scrambled eggs hit Austin full in the face, then landed back on the tray with a loud clatter.

Frannie stared, too aghast to move. Scrambled eggs dripped from his forehead, from his eyebrows, from his nose. "Oh, I'm so sorry!"

Austin ran his fingers across his eyes, clearing a path through the yellow blobs. Setting the tray quickly on the table, Frannie grabbed a blue cloth napkin and handed it to him. He used it like a washcloth, completely covering his face and wiping the egg away.

Frannie watched helplessly, dying a thousand deaths. "I'm so very, very sorry! Are you all right?"

He pulled the napkin away and opened his eyes. "Fine." Turning the napkin, he took another swab at his forehead. The corners of his mouth turned up in a wry grin.

"It's not the first time I've had egg on my face, is it, Tommy?"

The large man across the table slapped his knee and

chortled. "No, sirree. But usually you're the one that put it there."

"I'm *so* sorry," Frannie repeated. She grabbed another napkin and began dabbing at his shirt. His chest beneath the blue cotton knit was disconcertingly hard and warm. "Oh, dear, you've got it on your jeans, too." She lifted the napkin, ready to attack his crotch, then froze as she realized what she was about to do.

His hand closed over hers, stopping her. The heat from his hand radiated up her arm, through her shoulder and straight through her chest. She stared up into blue, blue eyes.

His grin was blinding. "I think I'd better take over the clean-up operation."

"I'm so sorry," she repeated, her voice a low, mortified whisper.

"It's all right. It's no big deal." Releasing her hand, he took the napkin from her and brushed off his lap. "Looks like you took a bit of a hit yourself." He reached out and brushed a blob of egg from her cheek.

The intimacy of the touch sent a shock wave curling through her. She jumped away as if he'd gigged her with a cattle prod, only to immediately realize the absurdity of her reaction.

"I didn't mean to startle you."

"You didn't," she lied.

"Well, there's a little more egg right..." He reached out his hand again. Once more she reflexively jumped back. Something about this man's touch made her feel hot and bothered and breathless.

"I'm, uh, ticklish," she lamely explained, vigorously rubbing her cheeks. "Is my face clean now?"

He seemed to be looking at something over her head. He pulled his eyes down to meet her gaze. "Your face? Uh, yeah."

"Good. Well, I'll…I'll go fix you another plate, then come back and clean all this up."

She fled to the kitchen, feeling as awkward as a three-legged chair. Quickly she made more toast, sliced more melon and plated up two more servings of eggs.

"Here you go," she said a few minutes later as she hurried back to the porch. She set down his breakfast and backed away from the table, unreasonably worried about getting too close to Austin. "I'll just go get a broom and dustpan and—" She stopped short and stared at the spotless wooden floor. "You cleaned it all up!"

Austin shrugged. "We found a roll of paper towels by the serving bar in the corner."

Frannie frowned in dismay. "But you're guests, and I'm the one who made the mess, and—"

Austin waved away her objections. "We're used to cleanin' up crank cases and oil pan spills. This was nothing."

"That's right." Tommy smiled, his widely spaced teeth giving his round face the appearance of a friendly jack-o'-lantern.

But it was Austin's amused expression that held her gaze. He was looking at her in such a strange way, as if he found her intensely interesting.

Frannie felt her pulse race. She was used to being ignored by men, not treated as an object of endless fascination—especially not by the likes of Austin Parker. She was drab and colorless and average. She certainly wasn't dressed to rate any undue attention; she was just wearing a faded brown sweatshirt and loose-fitting khakis. She wasn't wearing any makeup, her hair was wound in a bun at her crown, and her glasses were firmly in place on top of her nose. Austin's intense scrutiny rattled her down to her toenails.

"Well, uh, thanks for the help. Can I get you anything else?"

"I think we're all set."

She beat a hasty retreat to the kitchen, where she tried to drown out her clamoring thoughts by loading the dishwasher and vigorously mopping the floor. She was nearly finished when Austin stuck his head inside the door fifteen minutes later. "Breakfast was delicious. Thanks. And give my thanks to your aunt."

She heard the men's footsteps retreat down the hall, then heard the front door close behind them. She leaned against the kitchen wall and inhaled a deep breath, her hand on her stomach.

Thank goodness they were gone. Austin made her feel as if her lungs were too small to draw enough air. And the way he looked at her! His gaze went so...so *deep,* as if he were seeing things in her that no one else had ever seen.

"You're being ridiculous," she muttered to herself. Instead of standing around mooning over an unattainable man, she needed to march herself back to the computer and finish the bookkeeping. She started through the dining room on her way to do just that, then jerked to a halt as she caught sight of her reflection in the mirrored china cabinet.

"Oh, dear," she murmured.

There in the mirror, staring back at her from between plates of flowered Franciscan china, was the reason Austin had regarded her with such fascination: a giant glob of scrambled egg was perched atop her head like a yellow rubber tiara, supported by the bun she'd pulled her hair into that morning.

"Great. Just great."

Striding back into the kitchen, she held her head over the sink and dislodged the enormous lump of egg. She pulled a paper towel off the holder and rubbed her hair, heaving a sigh of disgust. Austin was the sexiest man she'd ever set eyes on, and what did she do? She acted like a hopelessly tongue-tied klutz, so skittish that the poor guy didn't dare tell her that the top of her head looked the inside of an egg salad sandwich.

Summer and Jasmine would never have been behaved so clumsily. They would have known how to talk and behave and flirt. Summer and Jasmine never would have thrown a plate of eggs in a guest's face in the first place, and they certainly wouldn't have ended up walking around all morning looking as if an airborne goose had just used them for target practice.

Maybe she should take them up on their offer to make her over. She had no expectations of being as glamorous as her cousins, but maybe, just maybe, she could gain a little of their self-assurance. Maybe Summer was right. Maybe if she quit feeling like such a nerd, she'd stop acting like one.

"What the heck," she muttered, heading upstairs to wash her hair for the second time that day. It was worth a try. When Jasmine got home, Frannie would tell her she'd agreed to the makeover.

Frannie was still burning with mortification over the egg incident when the bell over the front door jangled thirty minutes later. She looked up from the computer to see a tall man in a tan uniform stroll into the foyer, accompanied by an attractive blond woman dressed in jeans and a white cotton shirt with a large black tote bag over her shoulder.

Frannie rose from her seat and smiled. "Sheriff Rawlings, good morning!"

Rafe Rawlings's rugged face creased in a friendly

smile. "Good mornin', Frannie. I'd like you to meet my new detective, Gretchen Neal."

Frannie stepped forward and shook the blonde's hand. "Nice to meet you." The woman's handshake was as sturdy as her tall, athletic build. With her milky skin, light blond hair and blue eyes, she reminded Frannie of the movie star Gwyneth Paltrow.

"Gretchen just moved here from Elk Springs," Sheriff Rawlings said. "But before that, she worked on the police force in one of the toughest neighborhoods in Miami. We're lucky to have someone with her experience join our force."

"We sure are. Can I offer you two breakfast?"

"No, thanks. I'm afraid we're here on business today, Frannie."

Frannie raised her brows in surprise.

Rafe's dark eyes grew serious. "Gretchen's heading up the investigation into Raven Hunter's death. I need someone who can devote one hundred percent of their time to the case, and Gretchen's got the background to handle it."

"I...see." Although she didn't. Not really. That still didn't explain why they were here on a Sunday morning. "Do you have any other suspects? Other than Uncle Jeremiah?"

"No one." The sheriff adjusted his holster, his expression uneasy. He cleared his throat. "We're still investigating your uncle."

Frannie nodded slowly. Her mother's brother had died before Frannie was old enough to remember him, but she'd heard plenty of tales about him. According to her mother, Jeremiah had been cold-hearted, bigotted and controlling. Based on what she'd heard about him, Frannie wasn't at all surprised that he was a suspect. Jeremiah's hatred of Raven Hunter was well known.

"We'd like to talk to your mom and your aunt again,

to see if they remember anything else about the night Raven disappeared," Rafe said gently.

"I'm afraid Mom's in Minnesota. Dad's mother just had hip replacement surgery, and so Mom and Dad went to stay with her for a while while she recovers."

"When will they get back?" Gretchen asked, pulling a small notebook out of her tote bag.

"I don't know exactly. But I can give you a phone number where you can reach them."

"Thanks. I can take her statement over the phone."

Rafe glanced at Gretchen. "And if need be, we can get the police in Minnesota to take a deposition from them."

Frannie rounded the front desk, flipped through a Rolodex file and located the number. She wrote it on a slip of white paper. "Here it is." She handed the number to Gretchen. "I'm afraid Mom won't be much help to you, though. As she told Rafe, she was in Bozeman when Raven disappeared."

Gretchen tucked the number into a pocket of her folder. "Well, we'll give her a call and get an official statement."

"What about Celeste?" the sheriff asked, leaning on the front desk. "Is she around?"

"Yes. She's upstairs, resting."

Rafe's brow pulled together. "I thought she was always up at the crack of dawn."

"She usually is. But she hasn't been herself lately. She hasn't slept well for the last couple of weeks."

The sheriff glanced at Gretchen. "That's about how long it's been since we found Raven's skeleton."

Gretchen nodded, then turned to Frannie. "Could I talk to your aunt?"

"Of course." Frannie motioned toward to the large silver coffee urn that sat on a sideboard in the hall, next to a stack of cups, spoons and cloth napkins. They always kept it filled in the mornings for the convenience of their guests. "Help yourselves to some coffee. I'll go get her and we'll join you in the living room."

Frannie climbed the winding staircase, headed down the long hall, then turned right at the end, where it intersected a shorter hallway. She stopped at the second door and knocked softly. "Aunt Celeste?"

"Come in, dear."

She found Celeste sitting in a rocker by the window, her eyes closed. Frannie paused. She was used to seeing her aunt bustling around the house, full of energy and vitality, tending to everyone else's needs. It was disturbing, seeing her so still in the middle of the day.

"Aunt Celeste?" She hesitantly stepped into the room, closing the door behind her. "Rafe and a new detective are here. They want to ask you some more questions about the night Raven disappeared."

Celeste opened her eyes and gave a long, deep sigh that sounded as if it came from the depths of her soul. "Fine. I'll talk to them." She got up from the rocker. "But I've already told Rafe what I know."

The forlorn, troubled look on Celeste's face touched Frannie's heart.

At least Rafe was an old family friend, she thought as she followed her aunt downstairs. That should make the interview process easier on Celeste.

The sheriff stood as they entered the room.

Celeste mustered a warm, hospitable smile and kissed him on the cheek. "Hello, Rafe, dear. It's good to see you again."

"It's a pleasure to see you, too, ma'am."

"How are your lovely wife and child?"

The lawman's face softened. "Raeanne's just fine. And Skye keeps us plenty busy."

Celeste smiled. "I bet she does. You'll have to bring her by."

"I'll do that." Rafe turned and gestured to Gretchen. "Celeste, I'd like you to meet Gretchen Neal, my newest detective. Gretchen, this is Celeste Monroe."

Celeste nodded. "It's a pleasure." She shook Gretchen's hand, then waved her palm toward one of two mission-style sofas that faced each other in front of the massive stone fireplace. "Please have a seat."

Rafe and Gretchen lowered themselves onto one of the sofas. Frannie sat beside Celeste on the opposite one, across the heavy oak coffee table.

Rafe leaned forward, resting his forearms on his thighs. "I suppose Frannie told you I've put Gretchen in charge of the investigation into Raven Hunter's death."

"Yes."

"I'm sorry, Celeste, but she'd like to ask you some questions you and I have already discussed."

Gretchen pulled a small tape recorder out of her black leather tote bag. "Do you mind if I record our conversation?"

Celeste looked questioningly at Frannie, her green eyes round. Frannie nodded encouragingly.

"I—I suppose that would be all right," Celeste conceded.

Gretchen punched a button on the machine and placed it on the coffee table, then opened her notebook and pulled out a pen. "Let's start at the beginning, then, Mrs. Monroe. Would you please describe the relationship between your brother Jeremiah and Raven Hunter?"

Celeste eyed her warily. "What do you mean?"

"Were they friendly? Did they get along?"

Celeste wound her fingers together in her lap and stared down at them. "No. Not at all."

"Why not?"

Celeste took a deep breath and exhaled it in a sigh.

"My sister Blanche was in love with Raven. She wanted to marry him, but Jeremiah wouldn't hear of it."

"Why not?"

"Well…" Celeste looked at Rafe pleadingly. "I hate to speak ill of the dead. We don't know if they can hear us."

Rafe's eyes were sympathetic, but his tone was firm. "You need to tell us everything you know, Celeste. We need all of the facts."

Celeste nodded, her lips pressed tightly together. She took another deep breath. "Well, I'm afraid Jeremiah was something of a racist. He didn't want a Kincaid from our side of the family to marry an Indian. And Raven, of course, was Cheyenne."

"Did Raven and Jeremiah have an argument about it?"

"Oh, many. Jeremiah forbade Blanche to see Raven."

"Did Blanche routinely do what Jeremiah told her to do?"

"Oh, yes, indeed. We all did—me, Blanche, and Yvette. After our parents died, Jeremiah ran the family. He was very strong-willed."

"You and your sisters lived with Jeremiah at that time?"

"Yes. In the old house."

Rafe turned to Gretchen. "Garrett's Kincaid's place now. It was boarded up for years until he moved in a couple years ago."

Gretchen jotted the information down in her notebook, then looked at Celeste. "Did your brother own a gun, Mrs. Monroe?"

Celeste's fingers tensed in her lap. "Yes. He had a whole collection."

"Did he have a pistol in his gun collection?"

"Several."

"Where did he keep that gun collection?"

"In his study. He had a glass case built into the wall for it. He was very proud of it."

"What happened to those guns?"

"I—I don't know. I imagine they're all still in the house."

Gretchen and Rafe exchanged another look, and Gretchen scribbled another notation. At length she looked back up at Celeste. "I'd like to get back to the topic of Blanche and Raven. Did Blanche follow Jeremiah's orders to stay away from Raven?"

The older woman stared down at her hands. "No." She shifted uneasily and plucked at the fabric of her skirt. "She continued to see him. And she became pregnant with his child." Her eyes took on a gentler look. "With Summer."

"What was Jeremiah's reaction to that?"

"Oh, my." Celeste's fingers twisted and untwisted the fabric. Her forehead creased in a frown. "Oh, dear. I—I really don't remember. I know he was upset. I know Blanche and Raven planned to run away and elope. But my…my memory about those days is all kind of a blur."

"Do you remember when Blanche told him she was pregnant?"

Celeste shook her head. "Blanche didn't want to tell him. She kept putting it off. But as time went on, it became impossible to hide her condition. And when Jeremiah found out, he—" Celeste broke off.

"He what?"

Celeste pressed the back of her hand to her forehead. "I'm not really sure. Everything about that time gets all jumbled up in my mind."

Gretchen leaned forward. "This is really important, Mrs. Monroe."

"I—I'm afraid I'm getting a terrible headache. Everything is all mixed up and confused."

"Take your time, Celeste," Rafe said soothingly. "Do you remember anything at all about that time?"

Celeste leaned her head back against the sofa and wound the fabric of her skirt around her index finger. "Let me see... Well, I remember Summer's birth. I was there, you know, when Blanche gave birth. And I was there when she died of complications, a week afterward." Celeste grew silent. "I promised her that Yvette and I would raise her baby. Jeremiah didn't want us to, but we did."

"You and Yvette did a fine job of that," Rafe said softly.

Celeste smiled. "We did, didn't we?"

"Yes, indeed. And I'm sure Gavin agrees." Rafe returned her grin. After a companionable silence, he pressed forward. "Do you remember anything about Jeremiah's reaction to Blanche's pregnancy?"

"No. But I remember something Blanche told me about it after Raven was gone."

"What?" Gretchen took over the questioning.

"She said that Jeremiah tried to pay Raven to leave town."

"Did she think Raven took the money and left?"

"Oh, no. Raven had told her about the offer. He said at first he thought it would be best if he accepted it—that Blanche and the baby would have a better life without him. But when push came to shove, he couldn't do it. He couldn't break Blanche's heart like that. He loved her—everyone knew that. He told her he was going to give back the money...."

"So he'd taken the money?" Gretchen asked.

Celeste massaged her right temple. Her eyes looked dazed and confused, and her face had grown pale. "I—I guess. I don't know. I—I really can't remember."

Gretchen glanced at the sheriff.

"Do you remember the night Raven disappeared?" Rafe asked.

Celeste shook her head.

"When was the last time you saw Raven?" Gretchen asked.

"I—I don't know. I'm all confused. And my head…" Celeste pressed her palm against her forehead.

Frannie noted with alarm that Celeste's hand was trembling. She put an arm around the older woman. "She hasn't been sleeping well," she said apologetically to Rafe and Gretchen. "I think she needs to go back upstairs and lie down."

"Yes. I think I should. I—I'm sorry I can't be more help," Celeste said weakly.

Gretchen and Rafe exchanged a meaningful glance, then both simultaneously rose from the sofa. Celeste and Frannie rose, as well.

"Thank you for your time, Mrs. Monroe," Gretchen said. "I hope you get to feeling better."

"Me, too." Rafe studied the older woman, his dark eyes thoughtful. "Give me a call if you remember anything you think might help us, all right?"

"I will."

"I'll see our visitors out, Aunt Celeste," Frannie said. "You go on upstairs."

"All right. Goodbye." Celeste shuffled from the room, looking old and wan.

Rafe gazed after her for a long moment, then turned to Frannie. "Thanks for the coffee."

"You're more than welcome." Frannie smiled at Gretchen. "It was nice meeting you, Gretchen."

"Nice meeting you, too."

"Good luck with your investigation."

"Thanks. With a thirty-year-old murder case, we're likely to need it." Gretchen tucked her pen and notebook into her tote bag, then looked at Frannie. "Has your aunt ever told you anything about that night?"

Frannie shook her head. "She never talks about Jeremiah."

"Doesn't that strike you as odd?"

Frannie lifted her shoulders. "Celeste is very superstitious. She used to live in Baton Rouge, and she picked up a lot of Cajun beliefs about spirits and such. She's probably afraid Jeremiah will hear her talking about him. My mom said all of them were afraid of Jeremiah. He evidently had quite a temper."

"Hmm," Gretchen murmured. "Well, I'm sorry if we upset your aunt."

Rafe followed the detective out the front door, then paused on the porch. He turned to Frannie. "Have a good day. And thanks for your time."

"Any time."

The sheriff paused, his hand on the door. "We'll probably need to come back and question Celeste again."

"I understand."

Frannie leaned against the door as soon as she closed it behind the sheriff. Aunt Celeste was one of the kindest, warmest, most helpful women she'd ever known. She was a natural-born nurturer, and she'd always been open and straightforward.

Her reluctance to talk about Jeremiah and her inability to recall the events surrounding Raven's death struck Frannie as highly unusual. The sheriff and his new investigator seemed to think so, too. There was more to the story than Celeste was telling, and Frannie couldn't help but wonder what it was.

Three

Frannie looked up from a stack of loan applications late the next morning to see a familiar figure in a white physician's coat approach her desk at the Whitehorn Savings and Loan. "Summer! What brings you here?"

"You do." Summer sat in the armchair across from the desk and grinned at her cousin. "Jasmine tells me you've agreed to let us give you a makeover."

Frannie shifted uneasily in her desk chair. She'd told Jasmine yesterday that she'd go along with Summer's plan, but now she was having second thoughts. "Well, I've been thinking about that, and—"

"Oh, no," Summer broke in, lifting her hands in a stop gesture. "We're not going to let you back out now. I've already told Kyle that his date with you is confirmed."

"Confirmed!" Frannie's eyebrows flew up. "What do you mean, confirmed?"

Summer's mouth curved into a small smile. "Gavin and I ran into Kyle at the country club Saturday night, and I asked if he'd be interested in having me fix him up with you for the dance. He seemed quite eager."

Probably because he thinks I look like you. Frannie eyed her cousin suspiciously. "Saturday night? But how did you know I'd agree?"

Summer didn't even pretend to look apologetic. "I didn't." She reached into her pocket and pulled out a newspaper clipping. "Anyway, here's your first assignment."

"Assignment?"

Summer nodded. "Jasmine and I are going to give you assignments, and you're going to follow them exactly."

Oh, dear, what had she let herself in for? Summer's take-charge attitude and sense of initiative had served her well—it had helped her work her way through medical school, and she'd used it to see her husband through a difficult episode when he'd been falsely accused of a crime—but sometimes Summer could make Frannie feel as if she'd been hit by a steamroller. She eyed her cousin warily. "What kind of assignments?"

Summer handed Frannie the clipping. Frannie glanced down at it, then looked up quizzically. "This is an ad for Kiss of Dew makeup and skin care products."

Summer nodded. "A representative is giving free facials and makeup lessons at Kaylor's Drug Store today. I want you to go on your lunch hour."

Summer read the clipping more closely. "It says you have to call and schedule an appointment."

"I've already done it for you. I know you take a late lunch, so your appointment is set for one."

"Summer, I usually eat *lunch* on my lunch hour."

"As a physician, I'm fully aware of your nutritional needs." Summer took out a packaged sandwich from her purse. "That's why I brought you this from the hospital vending machine."

Frannie sighed as Summer set the sandwich on her desk. "You're a real piece of work, Summer. You know that, don't you?"

Summer flashed a blinding smile. "So I hear." She glanced at her watch and rose from the chair. "I have to get to the clinic. I'll stop by the Big Sky on my way home this evening to see how your makeup looks." She hoisted her large purse on her shoulder and raised a hand as she walked away. "Ta-ta!"

Frannie watched her go, a sinking feeling in her stomach. Why had she ever agreed to this silly plan? She'd be better off taking an assertiveness training class—or lessons in basket weaving or tea cozy knitting or trapeze flying. Then, at least, she'd stand a ghost of a chance of succeeding.

"We need the smoothest skin possible under our foundation, so we're going to start with this lovely kiwi avocado skin mask."

The Kiss of Dew cosmetics representative evidently spoke of everything in terms of "we." She'd already told Frannie that "we" had beautiful skin. All the same, she'd spent the past five minutes preparing it for a beautifying skin treatment.

Frannie winced as the stocky middle-aged woman poured a mound of green slime into her palm and picked up a cotton ball. "Is this really necessary?"

The heavily made-up lady nodded, jiggling her well-powdered multiple chins. "Oh, yes. Absolutely. Why, it's part of our Essential Exfolliants and Emollients Kiss Kollection."

Frannie glanced at the bottle and wondered if it was merely a coincidence that the initials spelled out EEEKK. That was certainly her reaction to the prospect of having the green goo slathered all over her face.

Especially in such a public setting, Frannie thought morosely. Right in the drugstore window.

Oh, well. Frannie had already endured having her face cleaned and swabbed with two different potions while passersby stopped and gawked. Wearing the green goop couldn't be too much more humiliating. Folding her arm under the black cosmetics cape, she closed her eyes and resigned herself to the inevitable.

The woman began dabbing the cold, gooey substance on her face. "There. Doesn't that feel refreshing?"

It felt like having a mixture of gelatin and undiluted pea soup globbed on her skin. Frannie pulled her lips into an expression simulating a smile and tried not to cringe as the woman smeared the thick paste across her forehead, over her nose, on her cheeks and down her chin.

"There! We're all done." The woman held a mirror up to Frannie's face.

She looked as if she'd just stepped off a space shuttle from Mars. The only parts of her face that weren't vivid green were her eyelids and her lips.

"Now all we have to do is sit and wait fifteen minutes while the mask works its magic," the woman said perkily, batting her false eyelashes. "Then we'll sponge it off and apply your makeup."

Great. Fifteen minutes of sitting in the front window of Kaylor's, looking like Swamp Thing. The only good thing about it was that nobody would be likely to recognize her under all that gunk.

Frannie pulled on her eyeglasses and stared out at Main Street, noting that there seemed to be more traffic than usual. Three yellow dump trucks cruised slowly past in single file, heading toward the resort and casino construction site.

She was following their progress when a small black-and-white object on the sidewalk across the street caught her eye. It was a dog, Frannie realized—an adorable, tiny dog with a puglike face and long, fluffy hair, probably a Shih Tzu. As Frannie watched in horror, the little dog wandered into the street and narrowly missed being hit by a passing blue van. The animal headed back to the curb, but a white Chevy cruised by, forcing the dog into the center of the road. Turning, the little dog skulked down the yellow line in the middle of the street, its tail tucked between its legs.

Frannie tensed. The dog was in front of the drugstore window now, directly in her line of vision. Judging from the rhinestone-studded collar and red bow, it was obviously someone's pampered pet.

The little animal timidly started across the street again, heading right into the path of a red sports coupe. Frannie gasped as the driver swerved and honked. She didn't realize she'd shut her eyes until she opened them a second later to see the little dog cowering in the street, its tail tucked, as the red car zoomed past.

Before she had time to consider her actions, Frannie flew off the stool, dashed through the drugstore and ran out the door. She stood on the sidewalk for a second, scanning the street for the little dog, then spotted it standing in the middle of the eastbound lane. The creature's big brown eyes gazed at her pleadingly as it cringed in the road, directly in the path of a sleek black Jaguar rapidly barreling toward it.

"Stop!" Frannie yelled, waving her arms and stepping toward the road. The car showed no signs of slowing. The driver honked, but continued to speed toward the little dog.

"Don't hit the dog!" Frannie screamed. The driver either didn't hear or didn't care.

There was no time to waste. Frannie dashed into the street, the black plastic cape flapping wildly around her. She threw herself headlong at the little dog, clutched it to her chest and rolled onto the pavement, praying she was rolling out of harm's way.

She heard the squeal of brakes and smelled the burn of rubber. When she opened her eyes, she was facedown on the pavement, so close to the concrete that the pebbles in it looked like boulders.

She slowly lifted her gaze to see the bumper of the Jaguar less than a foot away. It was a good thing she was lying down. Otherwise, she surely would have fainted.

The driver's door jerked open, and an angry man climbed out. His face was so mottled with rage that it took her moment realize that it was Lyle Brooks, the owner of the Whitehorn-based construction company building the resort and casino.

"What the hell do you think you're doing, running in front of my car like that?" Lyle demanded.

Frannie gazed down at the black and white dog wriggling in her arms. "I was saving this dog."

"To hell with the dog! He's not big enough to have caused any damage to my car. You, on the other hand, are a different story. Do you have any idea what it would have done to my insurance premiums to have an accident like that?"

Frannie gasped. She knew who Lyle was—his picture had been in all the papers when he won the contract for the casino and resort—but she'd never met him before, even though he was a distant Kincaid cousin. She'd heard he was callous and hard-hearted, but she'd always figured the stories were exaggerated. She was beginning to think differently.

"Your insurance premiums wouldn't have been nearly as high as your court costs and bail bond," said a low male voice from behind her, a familiar smoky voice, full of unfamiliar, barely controlled anger. "I saw the whole thing, and it looked to me like you were speeding. And I'd testify to that in a court of law."

Frannie turned to see Austin Parker behind her, his eyes narrowed and his lips set in a hard, ungiving line.

The woman on the pavement stared up at him, her strangely familiar hazel eyes huge in her bright green face.

Under any other circumstances Austin was sure he'd be amused, but what he'd just witnessed left him too shaken and angry to feel any sense of humor.

"Are you all right?" he asked.

"Yes."

He reached down a hand and helped her up. The moment he touched her, he knew why she looked familiar. This was the woman from the bed-and-breakfast—the one who'd fallen over her chair when he first met her, then spilled egg all over both of them. He peered at her curiously.

"Frannie?"

"Yes?"

How the devil had her face gotten in that condition? "You didn't just try to serve someone something green, did you?"

She looked at him blankly, then pulled her hand away to get a better grip on the dog, who was licking her cheek with gusto. Comprehension dawned. "Oh. N-no. I was having a facial."

Austin turned back toward the driver of the Jaguar, a feeling of distaste rising in his throat. Even if he hadn't just seen the man nearly run down a helpless animal with what looked like cold-blooded deliberation, he was certain he would have disliked him on sight. His lips were set in what looked like perpetual disdain, and he had a foppish, overly groomed look that spoke of self-absorption. His perfectly combed hair was so heavily moussed and gelled that the wind lifted it as a single unit. He wore a Rolex watch on his left wrist and a pinky ring on each hand. A gold chain was visible at the open neck of his custom-made shirt.

Austin looked him dead in the eye. "Looked to me like you were aiming for that dog."

"It had no business being on the street." Lyle glared at Frannie. "And the same goes for you."

Austin took a menacing step forward. "Well, now, I believe you have that all wrong. Frannie here has as much right as anyone to be anywhere she pleases. You're the one who was out of line. You owe Frannie an apology, and I'd like to hear you make it."

"I'll do no such thing. I had the right of way. I was driving along, minding my own business, when she recklessly threw herself in front of my car."

"There's no such thing as 'your own business' when you're behind the wheel of a car," Austin said sharply.

The man stared at him coldly. "I know who you are. You're that racing hotshot that just moved here, aren't you?" He pulled himself up to his full height, but Austin still towered over him. The man puffed out his chest and scowled. "Maybe you don't know who you're dealing with here. I'm Lyle Brooks, the owner of one of the biggest construction companies in Montana, and I don't need lessons in how to drive a car."

Austin glared at the man. "Well, then, maybe you need lessons in how to read street signs, because you were clearly exceeding the speed limit. You were racing down Main Street as if it were the final lap at Winslow, and I'll have no problem telling that to the police."

"The police?" Lyle's eyebrows shot up. His brow furrowed, and his eyes widened in apprehension. "Hey, now, there wasn't an accident. There's no reason to get the law involved."

Austin took another step forward, enjoying the fact that it forced Lyle to back up. "Not if you apologize to Miss Hannon."

The man's eyes narrowed.

Austin rubbed his chin. "If you have a problem with that, well, then, I'm afraid I'll have a problem letting this matter go without filing a report. And Miss Hannon, here, is likely to want to press charges for reckless endangerment.''

Frannie looked at him wide-eyed. Austin was pretty certain she'd never do any such thing, but he was thankful she kept silent.

''If we all stand here blocking traffic much longer, the police are likely to show up whether we want them to or not,'' Austin added.

Lyle's eyes were small, hate-filled slits. With an impatient sigh, he turned toward Frannie. ''Sorry.''

He hardly sounded sincere, but Austin decided not to push it. He watched the man stalk back to his expensive car, climb in and peel rubber as he drove away.

''What a charmer,'' Austin muttered. He looked at Frannie, and the absurdity of her green face made him smile. ''We'd better get out of the street.''

He took her arm, started to the sidewalk, only to realize she was limping. ''Are you hurt?''

She winced in pain. ''I think I skinned my knee.''

''I've got a first-aid kit in my car. Let's get you to that bench on the sidewalk, then I'll go get it.''

They'd made it to the sidewalk and had nearly reached the bench when an elderly woman rushed up to Frannie, all out of breath. ''Snook'ems!'' Her wrinkled face beaming, she clasped her hands to her chest. ''Oh, you found my Snooky-Wook'ems! Oh, how can I thank you?''

The fur ball in Frannie's arms thumped its tail madly. Frannie passed the dog to the woman's outstretched arms.

The woman joyfully kissed the animal on its wet black nose. ''I've been looking everywhere for her.'' The little dog nearly knocked off the woman's glasses in its effusive expression of delight. ''Where did you find my angel?''

''Wandering around in the middle of the street,'' Frannie said.

"Oh, dear! I'm glad she wasn't hit by a car. I don't know what I'd do without my Snooky-Wook'ems!"

Austin fixed her with a stern look. "You'd better keep her on a leash, then. Frannie risked her life to save your dog."

"Oh, my! Oh, I'm so sorry!" The woman's gray eyes were round and earnest behind her thick trifocals. "I left Snooky in my car while I ran into the drugstore to get my heart medicine. I put the window down so she wouldn't get hot, and well, she must have jumped right out." The woman held the little dog up to her face and spoke in a high-pitched, babyish voice. "You were a naughty girl, weren't you, Snook'ems? You gave Mommy quite a scare."

"Scared me pretty good, too," Frannie said dryly.

They weren't the only ones, Austin thought. His heart had nearly jumped out of his chest when he'd seen a woman—Frannie—dive in front of that car.

"I don't know how to thank you, dear." The woman kissed the dog again, then turned to Frannie. She peered over the top of her thick lenses. "It just goes to show, you can't judge a person by the way they look. I never knew you punk rockers cared about animals."

"Punk rocker?" Frannie's eyes were shocked. " I'm not a punk rocker!"

Austin leaned toward the old woman conspiratorially. "She's very sensitive about her skin condition. I keep telling her its nothing to be ashamed of. Anyone can pick up a fungal condition."

The old woman's eyes flew wide. "You mean, that's fungus? Is it contagious?"

Austin nodded somberly. "I'm afraid so. The only antidote is to cover your entire body in peanut butter for twenty-four hours immediately after exposure."

"Oh, dear!"

"I suggest that you and Snooky go right home and get started."

Wearing a look of horror, the woman hurried down the sidewalk, clutching the little dog to her ample chest.

Frannie convulsed in a fit of laughter. It took her a minute to regain her ability to speak. "You're as naughty as Snook'ems," she finally gasped.

Austin grinned. "Served the old biddy right."

She grinned at him, her smile so warm and bright he practically reached for his sunglasses. A jolt of attraction zapped through him despite her green face.

He cleared his throat, disconcerted. "Let's take a look at your knee." He gestured to a wooden bench under the green-and-white-striped drugstore awning. Frannie sat down, lifted the cape and pulled up the long tan skirt of her gabardine suit to reveal long slender calves.

Her right knee was scraped and bleeding. Austin felt a rush of empathy. "You sit right there, and I'll go get my first-aid kit."

"Okay. Thanks." He could feel Frannie's eyes on him as he sprinted across the street. Opening the door of his black pickup, he pulled out a box from under the seat, then strode back across the street.

She looked so ridiculous, sitting on that wooden bench in that ridiculous cape, with that goofy green face and those enormous eyeglasses. Something inside of him went warm and oddly mushy.

"Are you okay?" He squatted in front of her and opened the box.

"Yes. But you might as well go ahead and say it."

"Say what?"

"What you're thinking. That it was stupid of me to run out in the street like that."

Austin pulled out a cotton pad and squirted it with disinfectant. "Why do you think that's what I'm thinking?"

"Because it *was* stupid. I acted before I thought. But that little dog looked so scared and helpless, and that car was coming so fast. I knew if I was going to try to help it, I had to act fast."

"Well, I gotta say, you nearly gave me a heart attack."

"I did?"

Austin nodded. "I was just coming out of the automotive store when I saw you flying across the street. You looked like Batman, swooping into the street in that cape."

He was glad to see that he'd made her grin.

"I didn't see the dog at first, but I heard you yell, and I saw the Jag speeding toward you. When I saw you take a tumble right in front of it, well, my heart was in my throat."

"It was?"

"Dang right. No one knows better than me the damage an automobile can inflict on the human body."

"I'm sorry. I'm not usually so reckless."

Something about the chagrin on her green face made him smile. "Hey, I said you scared me. I didn't say I wouldn't have done the same thing."

Her hazel eyes fixed on him in a way that made him forget all about her green face.

"Come to think of it, I *have* done the same thing," Austin found himself saying. "I nearly got trampled by a stallion once, trying to get a sick colt out of a herd back when I was breaking horses."

"You used to break horses?"

He grinned. "Well, it's debatable who got broken more, the horses or me." He set the bottle of disinfectant on the sidewalk and lifted the soaked pad. "This is likely to sting, but I need to clean the wound."

"Okay."

He dabbed at her left knee. She bit her lip, but didn't cry out. Once again he felt that odd, mushy feeling.

"Did you work with horses here in Montana?" she asked.

He shrugged. "Among other places. My father never stayed in one place for long."

"Because of his job?"

Austin gave wry smile. "Not really. Because of his lifestyle."

Frannie tilted her head quizzically, and looked at him, really looked at him, in a way he hadn't been looked at in a long time. She wasn't just looking at him; she seemed to be really seeing him.

"What do you mean?" she asked.

Austin lifted his shoulders. "He didn't want to put down any roots, didn't want to get attached to anyone or anything." Including me, Austin thought bitterly. "We moved a lot."

"What did he do?"

"He was a ranch hand. Had a real talent with cattle. Me, I always preferred horses."

"Is that what you're raising on your ranch?"

Austin nodded. Why was he telling her all this? It wasn't like him to gab about his personal life with someone he'd just met. It must be that sincere way she looked at him, as if she were somehow connecting with him.

Austin picked up a Band-Aid strip and peeled the paper away. He gently set it on her knee, covering the wound, then found himself oddly reluctant to take his hand from her leg.

It was a very nice leg. Her skin was warm and smooth and lightly tanned. Her calves were well-shaped and slender. It was a shame that a woman with legs like that would hide them under such a long skirt.

"There." He pressed down the edges of the Band-Aid

strip, then pulled back his hands. He had the oddest urge to bend down and kiss her knee.

But that made no sense—no sense at all. He clicked the metal box of bandages closed and straightened.

She stood, as well. "Thanks. I really appreciate your help."

"My pleasure."

His gaze fell to her lips. They were moist and pink, and they stood out in sharp contrast to the green on the rest of her face. In fact, she seemed to be all eyes and lips. Beautiful hazel eyes. Plump, luscious-looking lips—lips that parted slightly as he stared at them. A rush of heat coursed through him. How he'd like to press his mouth to those lips, to draw that pouty bottom one into his mouth, to slide his tongue right between her lips....

The inappropriateness of his thoughts jarred him. He shifted the first-aid kit to his other hand. "Well, I'd better get back to the ranch. Tommy needs these parts for the car."

"And I'd better get back inside and get this goop off my face."

"Right." Austin nodded curtly. "Well, see you later."

"Okay." Those tempting lips curved into a smile. "And thanks. For the first aid, and for stepping in with Lyle." Her hair had come loose from the low ponytail she wore, and she brushed a stray strand behind her ear.

"My pleasure." But it was pleasure of an entirely different kind that he was thinking about as he watched her turn and scurry back into the drugstore.

I must have taken one too many knocks to the head in race collisions, Austin thought as he strode to his car. *Why else would a woman covered in a shapeless plastic cape who looked as if she'd fallen face-first into a bowl of puréed spinach turn him on more than any woman had in a long, long time?*

*   *   *

Lyle Brooks gunned the engine of his expensive car as he tore down the dirt road leading to the resort construction site, still fuming over his near accident in town.

Who the hell did Austin Parker think he was, telling him what to do? He might be a hotshot on the NASCAR circuit, but that didn't mean he was anyone here in Whitehorn.

Around here, Lyle thought heatedly, *he* was the hotshot. After all, he was the owner of the construction company building the resort and casino, the biggest thing to ever hit this one-horse town. The complex was going to put Whitehorn on the map. Even more importantly, it was going to make Lyle richer and more powerful than ever.

Lyle braked as he approached the construction trailer, pulling into the spot directly in front of the door. His foreman had suggested that they reserve the spot for the handicapped, but Lyle hadn't cared for the idea. It was *his* construction company, by damn. If anyone was going to get the best parking spot, it was going to be him. He wanted the best out of life, whether it was parking spots or cars or cigars or women. He wanted it, he deserved it, and he intended to see that he got it.

Slamming the door of the Jag, he strode up the wooden steps into the luxury trailer to find his secretary, Pam, on the phone. "Oh, he just walked in, sir," the attractive blonde said into the receiver. "Just a moment." Pam punched a button and looked up. "It's your grandfather."

So the old goat finally decided to call me back, Lyle thought. He'd been trying to reach Garrett Kincaid all morning, but all he'd got was the old man's answering machine. Lyle didn't know why his grandfather didn't just get a cell phone. Garrett said he didn't need one, but Lyle was certain he was just being stubborn. It was awfully hard to get the old man to change his mind about anything once his mind was made up about it.

But Lyle was working on it. Oh, yes, he was working on it. "I'll take the call in my office," he said, stalking past the secretary and closing the door.

He lowered himself into the tall cordovan leather chair. It was a custom-made chair Lyle had ordered from a furniture company in North Carolina, stately and large, with an extra-high back. Even with the two-inch lifts in his shoes, Lyle was only five-foot-nine, and he liked to make an imposing impression.

He picked up the phone and punched the button, forcing a warmth he didn't feel into his voice. "Hello, Granddad. Thanks for calling me back."

"What can I do for you today, Lyle?"

"I was, er, wondering if you've given any more thought to what we were discussing yesterday. "

He heard his grandfather sigh. "Lyle, we've been all through that, and you know how I feel about the matter. That land is reserved for Gabriel, and I'm not going to swap it for yours. There's no point in discussing it further."

"I'm not asking for a straight trade. I'm willing to offer a considerable amount of money in addition to my land. For the sake of fairness, I don't see why you can't at least consider the possibility of selling it to me."

"I've been more than fair with you, Lyle." Garrett's voice was as hard as steel. "It's my land, and I'll do what I damn well please with it."

"But two years ago, you didn't even know about Larry's brood of bastards!"

"I won't have you talking about your cousins that way." The steel in Garrett's voice sounded razor-sharp.

"Cousins." Lyle spit the word out, derision dripping from his voice. "I don't understand how you can consider those illegitimate whelps as family.'' As far as Lyle was concerned, they were nothing but unfortunate reminders of his uncle Larry's philandering ways.

''Because that's what they are, whether you like it or not.'' Garrett's voice cut sharply through the phone line. ''They're Larry's sons. They're as much my blood as you are, and I suggest you start accepting that fact.''

Lyle stared out the window at the Crazy Mountains, their tops rugged and craggy above the timberline. They looked just like his grandfather sounded, tough and indomitable and unmoving. No, his grandfather was tougher than the mountains, Lyle thought ruefully. If a mountain was in his way, he could always blast through it with dynamite. With his grandfather, he'd have to find a way around.

The old man was completely intractable when it came to this topic. Ever since he discovered two years ago that his late son, Larry, had fathered seven illegitimate children, Garrett had refused to listen to reason. The old man had not only welcomed the bastards into the bosom of the family, but given them all large chunks of the Kincaid ranch, as well. Land that should have been split three ways—between Lyle and his two legitimate cousins, Melanie and Collin—was now going to be split among the bastards.

And that wasn't even the worst of it. The piece of land the old man had given Lyle was a worthless parcel abutting the Laughing Horse Reservation up north. The land the resort was being constructed upon, however, was being saved for Gabriel Reilly Baxter, Larry's youngest illegitimate child who'd been adopted by Jordan Baxter. Adding insult to injury was the fact that the little bastard was probably still in diapers.

Lyle's grandfather refused to see the injustice of it all. Lyle had tried to reason with the old man. He'd tried wheedling and logic. He'd even had his mother intercede on his behalf. She'd manage to convince Garrett to give Lyle an extra piece of the Whitehorn property, but it had been more of that useless tract next to the reservation. He'd even offered to buy the land the resort would be built on from the stubborn old mule. The only concession he'd gotten was that Garrett had agreed to let him represent the land in negotiations with the Indians, and he'd made sure that Lyle's construction company got the contract to build the casino and resort.

"You've gotten a huge real estate commission from acting as my agent, and you stand to make a fortune from this building contract," Garrett had told him. "You're making out a like a fat cat on this deal."

That was true. Lyle had also made a few under-the-table deals his grandfather didn't know about that would make him plenty more money once the complex was completed. But that wasn't enough. Lyle wanted more.

Lyle wanted it all.

But it was clear he wasn't going to get it from his grandfather. Not this way. Not today.

He took a deep breath and forced a conciliatory tone to his voice. "You're right, Granddad. It's your land, and you're free to do as you wish."

"Well, I'm glad you're finally starting to see reason."

It wasn't so much reason as the writing on the wall, Lyle thought dourly, turning his Mont Blanc pen in his hand. The harder he pushed, the deeper the old man dug in his heels.

"I know you don't share my view of things, but I want to put the past behind us. All of us," Garrett continued.

Lyle sighed. His grandfather was getting on his soap box again. This might take all day.

"This family has been divided too long," Garrett was saying. "I want us all to make peace and get along. I want us to be a real family." There was a long pause. Lyle realized his grandfather was waiting for him to say something.

"We *are* a real family, Granddad."

"No, we're not. Want me to tell you what a real family's like?"

As if I could stop you. "Sure, Granddad."

"Well, son, in a real family, the members look out for the best interests of each other and not just for themselves."

"I see." Lyle saw, all right. He saw that the old man had just slapped him on the wrist, and he didn't appreciate it, not one little bit. Gritting his teeth, he forced a pleasant tone into his voice. "That's a good definition."

"Glad you think so. Guess that means I won't be hearin' any more nonsense from you about tryin' to get your hands on Gabriel's property, then."

Lyle's fist clenched around the phone, but he carefully kept his tone light. "I only want what's best for the family, Granddad."

"Good to hear it. Well, you have a nice day." The phone clicked in Lyle's ear.

Lyle slammed down the receiver, pushed back his chair and rose to his feet. Muttering a low oath, he shoved his hands into his pockets and strode to the large window that looked out at the mountains behind him.

Damn, but the old man was a stubborn cuss! It had been a tactical error to keep pushing for him to trade the land. Instead of trying to convince his granddad to give him that property, he should have been working harder to convince the Indians to move the resort site up north to his land.

He'd tried to get them to move the whole project—the resort and the casino—to the north earlier, but it was a hard sell. The casino had to be built on Indian land for legal reasons. The land that abutted Lyle's property was so mountainous and rocky that it would take a small fortune to just level it enough to lay a foundation. The land adjacent to Gabriel's property was already level. Since the Indians wanted to locate the resort as close as possible to the casino, they'd naturally selected Gabriel's property instead of Lyle's.

When the construction project was halted after the discovery of a skeleton, Lyle had tried again to convince the Indians to move the resort site to his land, but they'd stuck with their original decision. The tribe's lawyer, Jackson Hawk, had suggested that Lyle's company begin construction on the resort's pool and sports complex while they waited for the murder investigation to be completed. Lyle couldn't argue with the logic of the suggestion. In fact, his company had dynamited a forty-five-foot hole for the sports complex foundation just yesterday, and workmen were clearing away the debris now.

Maybe he'd tried the wrong approach, Lyle thought now, staring out at the mountains. Since he couldn't outsmart the Indians with logic, maybe he should have tried appealing to their superstitious nature. He probably could have frightened them away with stories about a horrible curse.

Lyle's dark thoughts were interrupted by a knock on the door. "Who's there?" he growled.

"Peter Cook," came the answer.

"Who?"

"Pete Cook. I operate one of the earth movers."

Where the hell was his secretary? At lunch, Lyle supposed. Heaving a sigh, he strode back to his desk and lowered himself into his massive chair. Damn, but he hated having to deal with all the daily headaches of the construction business. The way he saw it, he shouldn't have to. His role was to figure out the money-making angles. The day-to-day work was the problem of his construction foreman.

Lyle picked up a stack of papers. "You're supposed to report to Hank," he called.

"He went into town to get a part for a broken backhoe. Besides, this is somethin' I think you might want to know about person'lly."

Hell. Lyle rubbed his chin and sighed. "Come on in."

A man about Lyle's height stepped into the room. Clad in jeans and a dirty gray T-shirt, the thin, middle-aged man held an orange hard hat in one hand and what looked like a chunk of rock in the other.

"Yes?"

"Sorry to bust in on ya like this, Mr. Brooks, but I found somethin' just now at the construction site that I thought you'd want to know about."

Lyle closed his eyes and rubbed his forehead. "I hope it's not another damn skeleton."

"No, it's not that."

"Well, then, what is it?"

Peter's neck moved as he swallowed. "I'm no expert, but I hit somethin' that looks an awful lot like a vein of sapphire."

Sapphire! Lyle's pulse began to race. He'd heard rumors about a sapphire vein hidden in the mountains, but he'd always thought it was nothing more than an old prospector's tall tale. He leaned back in his chair and gave the man his full attention. "Where?"

"At the south end of the project, about forty feet down. I've brought you a piece of it."

Peter handed him the rock. Lyle turned it in his hand. The back of it looked like ordinary granite, but a thick vein of deep blue shot through the center. Excitement mounted in Lyle's chest.

Don't give away your hand, he cautioned himself. Play

it cool. "Hmm. Well, it's interesting, but I don't know that it's sapphire."

"I don't, either. But I know a little about stones— I like to collect 'em—and this darn sure looks like the real thing. These hills are rumored to have a sapphire vein in them somewhere, and, well, I just figured you'd want to know."

Lyle nodded, trying to remain calm. "You did the right thing, bringing this to me. I'll send it off and have it analyzed." Lyle's mind worked fast. He turned the chunk of rock in his hand, then looked up at the older man. "Does anyone else know about this?"

Peter shook his head. "I just found it, and I came right here."

"And you didn't tell anyone else?"

"No one else was around. The rest of the crew is at lunch. No one knows but you and me."

"Good. Let's keep it that way." Lyle rose from his chair and circled his desk. He placed his hand on the man's shoulder. "After all, you don't want to have to share your finder's fee, do you, Pete?"

The man's brow knit quizzically. "Finder's fee?"

"Sure. If this is real sapphire, why, you should get a nice chunk of change for being the first to spot it."

Pete's face lit up. "What kind of money are we talking about?"

Lyle raised his shoulders. "I don't know. Depends on whether or not this is real and how much there is of it."

The man's eyes lit in a way that told Lyle he had him in the palm of his hand. "But if it's real, I'll get some money?"

Lyle nodded. "Absolutely. I'll see to it personally. Provided you don't tell anyone just yet." Lyle turned the rock in his hand. "I'll get this tested. In the meantime, don't breathe a word of this to anyone." He looked at Pete closely. "No one. No girlfriends, no buddies, no bartenders. Not even your wife, if you've got one."

"I won't tell a soul," Peter promised.

"Good." Lyle strode across the lush burgundy carpet to the door of his office. Pete followed. "We're going to shut down the digging operation for the day."

"What'll I tell the foreman when he gets back?"

"Tell him I came out and told you to stop. Something about not having the right permits. Have him come see me. I'll tell him we have a paperwork hassle to straighten out before we can proceed." Lyle pulled his lips back in a smile. "Don't you worry about a thing. Not a thing, except keeping your mouth shut."

Lyle could practically see the dollar signs in the man's eyes. The poor fool was probably buying a new double-wide trailer in his mind's eye right now.

Pete touched his fingers to his forehead in a snappy salute. "Don't you worry, Mr. Brooks. I'll be quiet as a mouse."

Lyle closed the fist of his left hand possessively around the rock and extended his right hand to the construction worker. "I'm counting on it, Pete. I'm counting on it."

Lyle waited until the foreman returned, then took the rock into Whitehorn and over-nighted it to a mineralogist in Seattle. He didn't dare send it to anyone within the state; he didn't want to risk word getting around that sapphire had been discovered near Whitehorn. To further insure secrecy, he even enclosed a note saying that he'd found the stone in North Dakota.

If this really was a sapphire vein, Lyle intended to keep it to himself—all to himself.

He was at his desk signing payroll checks the next morning when his phone intercom crackled. "Mr. Jasper with Seattle Mineral Testing is on the line," Pam said.

"All right. Thanks." Lyle's hand was shaking when he picked up the phone. "This is Lyle Brooks."

"Andy Jasper here," said a cordial voice. "I have some interesting news for you."

"You do?"

"Yes. That specimen you submitted for analysis—it's sapphire, all right. High-quality stuff, too. Top notch."

Lyle tamped down the urge to let out a whoop of victory. "What's it worth?"

"Well, the gem in that rock would retail for around fifteen or twenty thousand dollars, depending on how it was cut."

Fifteen or twenty thousand, for a rock small enough to hold in his hand—and there was whole mountain of the stuff, just sitting out there! Lyle's heart pounded like a jackhammer. He fought to keep his voice calm. "Is that a fact?"

"Yes, sir."

"Any guess how much sapphire's likely to be at the site where I found that?"

"Well, it's anyone's guess. But usually these gems run in veins. When conditions are right for creating some of the stone, they're right for creating a lot of it. Judging from the size of the gem in this rock, I'd say that most likely, you've stumbled onto quite a windfall."

Lyle swallowed, his mouth dry.

"You say you found this on your vacation property in North Dakota?" Mr. Jasper asked.

Lyle immediately grew wary. "Uh, yeah. That's right."

"Well, I'd say you're a mighty lucky man." Mr. Jasper chuckled. "You don't happen to want a partner, do you?"

"No. I'm afraid I don't."

"Well, I knew you were anxious for the report. Do you want me to send the rock back to you by special courier?"

"No. I don't want to call undue attention to it. Just

insure it and send it back by overnight mail.'' Lyle gave the man his home address, then switched the phone to his other ear. "And, Mr. Jasper, I trust you'll adhere to your company's confidentiality policy."

"Oh, yes, sir."

"You'd better. Because if you leak anything to anyone about this, my lawyers will be on you like ticks on a bloodhound."

Lyle hung up the phone, then rose from his chair and pumped his fist victoriously in the air. He was sitting on a dad-blasted gold mine!

Or rather, Gabriel Reilly Baxter was. The thought made his exuberant mood sputter and die.

Lyle knotted his hands into fists. "Well, not for long," he muttered. His mind churning, he paced the floor in front of his office window.

If he could get the Indians to move the resort site to his property up north, his grandfather would probably agree to the property swap. After all, the old man's only concern was insuring that his precious bastard grandchild had a valuable piece of real estate.

Lyle's face broke into a smile. Oh, this was ingenious. Why, Lyle would look downright generous if he gave his little cousin the more valuable land! His sudden big-heartedness might be a little hard to explain, though. He'd have to come up with a story about how he was sentimentally attached to this particular piece of property. Granddad had always been a sucker for an emotional story.

Lyle smacked a fist into the palm of his hand. Oh, but he was brilliant! He grinned broadly as he stared out the window. Just think—a whole mountain of sapphires sitting out there, and only he knew about them.

He—and Peter Cook. Frowning, Lyle rubbed his jaw.

He couldn't let a small-time wage earner like Cook interfere with his plans. No, sir.

Cook was an obstacle that could easily be eliminated. All it took was the guts to do it. And the sooner he did it, the better.

Striding to his desk, he picked up a piece of notepaper and scrawled a note:

Pete—
I have news about that rock you found. Meet me at the construction site tonight at 10:00 p.m. and I'll fill you in. Tell no one.

Lyle signed his name with a flourish, then riffled through the paycheck envelopes on his desk until he found the one marked Peter Cook. He stuffed the note inside, licked the flap and sealed it closed.

He was smarter than all of them, Lyle thought smugly. Smart enough to know exactly what he wanted and smart enough to figure out how to get it. And no one—not his grandfather, not his bastard cousin, and certainly no one the likes of Peter Cook—was going to stand in his way.

Four

"So how's it going?"

Frannie looked up from the container of yogurt she was eating to see her pixie-faced cousin lowering herself into one of the chairs across from her desk at the Whitehorn Savings and Loan.

"What are you doing here, Jasmine?"

"I came downtown to pick up a few things for Mom at the drugstore, and I thought I'd stop in and see how you're doing."

"I'm doing fine."

"I didn't mean *you*. I meant the flirting. How's it going?"

The flirting, Frannie groaned. That was today's assignment from Summer and Jasmine. Wearing her contacts, which she hated, and mascara, which she loathed, she'd been instructed to make eye contact with a man and give him "the treatment"—whatever that was. And it didn't end there. She had to wear these blasted four-inch heels that looked like radio towers. All designed to make her legs look shapely.

Frannie tossed the empty yogurt container into the wastebasket, avoiding her cousin's eyes. "I thought I didn't have to report back to you two until tonight."

Jasmine folded her arms across her chest and eyed her accusingly. "You haven't tried it, have you?"

"Not yet." Frannie straightened a pad of forms on the

corner of her desk. "I happen to be on the payroll here to work, not to pick up men."

Jasmine glanced at her watch. "I thought you were on your lunch hour."

"Well, I technically am, but I have a lot of work to do, so—"

"So come on." Jasmine rose and motioned for Frannie to follow her.

"Where are we going?"

"To the ladies' room to put on more mascara. Then you're going to march back to your desk and give the eye treatment to the next man who walks in here."

"Ah, Jasmine, I don't think I can bat my eyelashes like Summer said."

Jasmine eyed her sternly. "You agreed to let us make you over, and this is an important part of the process."

There was no point in arguing with Jasmine when she got that determined look in her eye. With a sigh, Frannie rose and followed her cousin.

She returned to her desk a few minutes later, her eyelids feeling unnaturally heavy. "I think you overdid the mascara," she grumbled to Jasmine.

"With the lighting in here, it takes more makeup to do the job. But don't worry. You look great." Jasmine smiled at her. "Now, I want you to give the eye treatment to the next man who walks through that door. I'm going to go stand on the other side of the lobby and watch."

Frannie knew Jasmine was as tenacious as a bulldog. Unless she wanted her cousin standing around watching her all afternoon, she'd have no choice but to go ahead and get it over with. Frannie heaved a sigh. "All right. The very next man who walks through the door—provided he's not old enough to be my grandfather, someone I work with or a man I know is married."

"I know you'll be great." Jasmine flashed an encouraging smile, then sauntered to the far side of the lobby.

With her luck, Frannie thought, the next man to walk through that door would look and smell like Sasquatch.

Her shoulders tensed as the door opened. A blue-haired old lady in a lavender dress toddled in. Frannie was just inhaling a breath of relief when the door opened again and Austin Parker strode into the lobby.

Great. Just great. Frannie cast a desperate look across the room to see Jasmine nod her head in Austin's direction.

Oh, dear. Why did she have to practice this silly technique on *him?* He no doubt already thought she was mentally deranged. With a last desperate glance at Jasmine, Frannie took a deep breath and looked directly at Austin. To her surprise, he looked back and smiled.

Frannie's pulse pounded in her throat. She glanced away, only to see Jasmine wildly blinking her eyes in a silent command. Frannie gulped, turned her gaze back to Austin and blinked rapidly.

Oh my stars—it was working! Austin was heading to her desk. Frannie frantically busied herself, gathering pieces of paper on her desk into a senseless pile.

"Good afternoon, Frannie."

"G-good afternoon."

"I hardly recognized you without your glasses."

Frannie continued to collect the papers into a haphazard stack. "Sometimes I wear my contacts."

"Well, you look very nice. Are they new?"

"No. I've had them for a while."

"Oh."

Behind Austin, Frannie saw Jasmine point to her eye. Frannie looked up at Austin and repeatedly blinked.

He frowned. "Do you have something in your eye?"

"What?"

"I notice you keep blinking."

"Oh. No. I'm okay." Oh, dear, just as she'd feared. The blinking made her look like a nutcase. To make matters worse, she suddenly did, indeed, have something in her eye. All that blinking seemed to have dislodged a fleck of mascara, and it hurt like the dickens. She blinked some more, trying to get it out.

"Well, good." Austin looked her uncertainly, the way one might look at a dog suspected of having rabies. "I came by to open a savings account. Can you help me with that, or do you only handle loans?"

She closed the afflicted eye, wanting to ease the pain, only to realize in horror that it must look as if she was winking at him. "I—I do it all." Oh, heavens, that hadn't come out right. It sounded alarmingly suggestive. "I mean, I can handle anything. I mean, everything."

Her eye was twitching now. This was going from bad to worse. "I—I'll do anything you want."

Austin studied her, his brow furrowed. To her distress, Frannie realized that now her eyes were watering. Not just watering—gushing.

Through the wet blur, she saw Austin lean across her desk. She couldn't make out the expression on his face, but his voice was concerned. "Have I said something to upset you?"

"Of...of course not." Frannie tried to act normal, but it was hard, what with her eye twitching and her face feeling like Niagara Falls. She could barely see him through the haze of tears. She did her best to sound nonchalant. "Why would you think a thing like that?"

She couldn't see well enough to be sure, but she thought his lips quirked upward in a grin. "No reason. Except I'm not really used to having bankers cry when I try to open a savings account."

It was time to cut her losses and run. Frannie rose from

her chair. "I—I'm sorry. I seem to have something in my eye, after all. If you'll excuse me for a moment, I'll be right back." She rounded her desk, wobbling on her unnaturally high heels.

Austin moved to steady her. "Are you all right?"

"I'm…"

Oh, dear, she was losing it—her poise, her vision, but worst of all, her balance. She tried hard to regain it. "I'm…"

She toppled forward and grasped at Austin, pushing him into the chair. She fell hard on top of him. The next thing she knew, she was perched atop his lap. "…I'm fine," she finished weakly.

"Fine" didn't begin to describe it. His thighs were hard and warm beneath hers, and his chest was solid under her hand. She could feel his heartbeat through the cotton of his burgundy sports shirt. Her face was pressed to his cheek, which smelled deliciously of soap and shaving cream, and his freshly shaven skin against hers sent goose bumps skittering all over her.

One of his hands rested on her arm, the other on her hip. "Are you okay?" he asked.

Her voice didn't seem to work. She numbly nodded.

"My goodness, Frannie—what's going on?" asked a deep, raspy voice.

Frannie abruptly looked up. Her vision was cloudy, but she could make out the heavy jowls of the bank manager over Austin's shoulder. She struggled to sit upright, her face burning heat. "I—I lost my balance and fell."

"On a *customer?*"

Frannie nodded. Clearly nonplussed, the large man looked at Austin. "Well! I don't know what happened here, but on behalf of the Whitehorn Savings and Loan, I'd like to apologize for—"

"No apology needed," Austin said quickly. "I happen

to like a bank with friendly, personal service." He tightened his grip on Frannie's hip and angled a smile down at her. "Why, the last place I opened a savings account, all I got was a toaster."

Frannie couldn't help it. The ridiculousness of the situation, the banker's befuddlement and the outrageousness of the remark made her burst into laughter. Even with her tear-impaired vision, she could tell that Austin was grinning at her.

The bank manager looked from her to Austin, his lips stretched in an uncertain smile. Recognition suddenly poured over his face. "Say, you're that race car driver, aren't you?"

Austin nodded. "Austin Parker." He stuck out his right hand, his left one still firmly planted on Frannie's hip.

The banker pumped his hand. "I'm a big fan. Here, let me get Miss Hannon off your lap."

"No hurry." Austin's fingers surreptitiously caressed her hip.

Heat flared through Frannie. Her face flaming, she took the bank manager's proffered hand and rapidly struggled to her feet.

But the banker's attention was focused on Austin. "Tell me about that car you drive. Does it have a V-8 engine?"

"Well, it's a converted Chevy Monte Carlo, and…"

While the two men talked cars, Frannie circled back behind her desk, pulled her lens case out of her purse and quickly removed her contacts. Oh, that felt so much better! She rubbed her eyes in relief. Her near-sightedness allowed her to see things at close range, but she could no longer tell if Jasmine was still watching from across the room.

"…So now my pit crew chief is at my ranch, fine-tuning the transmission," Austin was saying.

"He's here in Whitehorn?"

Austin nodded. "He's staying at the Big Sky. That's where I met Frannie."

"Oh, so you and Miss Hannon had previously met?"

"Oh, sure." Austin smiled at Frannie. "We're old friends. In fact, I decided to move my savings account to your bank because of Frannie."

The banker's face creased in a pleased smile. He nodded at Frannie approvingly. "Frannie is one of our finest employees. Our satellite office in Billings has been trying to hire her away from us for years, but fortunately for us, she's too fond of Whitehorn to move. I'm sure she'll take good care of you."

Austin gave Frannie a slow grin. "That's what I'm banking on."

His eyes were warm, and Frannie felt a jolt of sexual awareness as she met his gaze. The bank manager waddled off, and Frannie looked down at her lap, nervously twining her fingers together. "That was kind of you."

"What?"

"Telling him I'm the reason you're opening an account here."

"You are."

"Oh, come on." Frannie opened her file drawer, trying hard to hide her racing pulse. "You didn't even know I worked here."

"Not at first. But after you landed in my lap like that, well…" He lifted his shoulders. "Where else am I going get a dividend like that?"

The fact that he was being so nice about her clumsiness only increased her embarrassment. "I'm usually not such a klutz, but my cousin talked me into wearing her shoes today, and I'm not used to high heels, and, well…"

"What are you apologizing for? I liked it."

Even without her contacts or glasses, she could see an unmistakable light in his eyes. He was flirting with her!

Her palms began to sweat, and she suddenly felt as unsure as a twelve-year-old girl.

Which was ridiculous, she sternly told herself. A man like Austin probably flirted with every woman he met. She'd be an idiot to think he meant anything by it. She'd treat him as if he were any other customer, she decided. In fact, she probably ought to redouble her efforts to appear professional, considering how unprofessionally she'd acted when he'd first come in. All the same, her face began to burn.

Austin watched her cheeks flame and grinned. Lord, but she was a mess! Black streaks of mascara ran from her eyes to her chin, and her eyes were ringed like a raccoon's. And now the rest of her face was turning as red as a Stop sign.

For reasons he couldn't begin to fathom, he felt a stir of arousal. He shifted on the chair. "Do you, uh, still need to go fix your eyes?"

She shook her head. "I took my contacts out while you were talking to my boss."

"Oh." He started to tell her about the condition of her makeup, then changed his mind. If she knew it looked like an eighteen-wheeler had laid rubber all over her face, she'd want to go to the rest room to clean up, and he didn't want her to leave.

His lips curved in a grin. "You know, you look different every time I see you."

She rummaged through her file drawer and gave a dry smile. "That's because I don't have egg or green stuff on my face today."

He rubbed his chin, trying to repress his smile. She was going to die of embarrassment when she discovered what she *did* have on her face, but Austin wouldn't be the one to tell her.

Frannie plucked a sheet of pink paper out of a file

folder and handed it to him. "If you're interested in opening a savings account, you'll want to look over this form."

I'd much rather look over yours. The thought surprised him. Racing fans and groupies were constantly throwing themselves at him, but Austin hadn't had much interest in women lately.

Heck, he hadn't had much interest in *anything* lately. The past few months, he'd been feeling burned out and restless. Which was one reason he'd bought the ranch. He used to have a passion for horses, used to dream of one day owning a ranch like the kind he'd worked on in his youth. As so many of the dreams that he'd achieved, though, the ranch hadn't lived up to his expectations. He still felt as if something were missing, as if some essential key to satisfaction was eluding him.

"That sheet explains the different type of accounts we offer." Frannie tapped her pen on the desk. "I'll need you to fill out an application, once you decide what you want."

Oh, I already know what I want.

He rubbed his jaw and frowned at the wayward thought. After a long, slumbering hiatus, why had his libido suddenly decided to return with such force? And why on earth had it settled on this unlikely woman who seemed to specialize in wearing the mess du jour?

Part of it had to do with the way she'd felt in his lap, he decided. She was hiding one heck of a shapely body under that baggy tan suit. Her bottom was firm and round, her waist was small, and the breast she'd unknowingly pressed against his arm had felt surprisingly full and lush.

He realized she was waiting for him to select an account. He pointed his finger to the top listing. "I'll take this one."

"Fine." She slid a yellow paper in front of him. "Here's the application."

There was something about the way she acted so stiff and professional, as if she were wary of him, that turned him on, too. He was accustomed to women throwing themselves at him. At every race, there were beautiful, Barbie-doll-shaped women scheming to meet him. Some of them bluffed their way through racetrack security, some approached him in bars and restaurants, some even stalked him to his hotel room. He thought he'd seen it all—but he'd never seen anything quite like Frannie Hannon.

"Do you need a pen?"

He realized he was staring at her, gazing deep into her black-ringed eyes. "Yes."

She handed him the pen in her hand. His fingers deliberately brushed hers as he took it. She pulled back, cleared her throat and spun toward her computer so abruptly that she nearly hurled herself out of her swivel chair.

Austin grinned. No, sirree. He'd never met anyone quite like Frannie.

He quickly filled out the form while she pulled a program up on the computer. When he finished, she entered the information into her computer, printed out a paper and handed it to him.

"I need you to check this over and make sure all the information is correct, then sign it."

"All right." He glanced over the page, scrawled his name on the line at the bottom and pushed the paper across the desk toward her.

Frannie opened a side drawer and pulled out a small packet. "That takes care of the paperwork. Here's your account number and passbook, along with some checks and deposit slips. How much would you like to deposit?"

Austin rubbed his chin. "Oh, I don't know. About a hundred grand, I guess."

Frannie's blackened eyes widened. "You want to deposit one hundred thousand dollars?"

Austin nodded. "If that's all right."

"Well, yes, of course. But most people would want to put that kind of money in one of our higher interest-bearing accounts."

Shucks, honey, if my interest were much higher, I'd have a hard time walking out of here.

Austin ran a hand down his face. Good grief, what was the matter with him? Hell. He ought to just ask her out and be done with it. Once he got to know her and the newness wore off, he was sure he'd lose interest, just like always.

He opened his mouth, ready to ask what she was doing Saturday night, but she was leaning across her desk, her ridiculously streaked face frowning with seriousness.

"It's your decision, of course." Her eyes were earnest in that burglar's mask of mascara. "But we have some excellent rates on our C.D.s. You really ought to consider a long-term investment."

"I'm not much for long-term arrangements." *But I bet she is,* came a wayward voice from inside his head. The thought hit him like a splash of cold water.

Hell, he had no business getting involved with a woman like Frannie. He wasn't a long-term kind of guy, and it didn't take a call to the Psychic Hotline to figure out that a buttoned down, serious-eyed gal like Frannie wasn't one-night-stand material. In fact, it was a pretty sure bet that she didn't take anything—including dating—lightly. Which was exactly the reason he needed to keep his mouth shut, leave the lady alone and haul his tail out of there.

"Long-term investments pay the highest returns," Frannie insisted.

He shoved back his chair. "Sorry, but that's not my

style. I prefer to take my chances in the stock market. This account is just to have some money handy in case I need it.'' He pulled a checkbook out of his pocket and rapidly filled out a check. Pushing it across the desk, he rose to his feet. "It's been nice doing business with you. Stay out of traffic and don't rescue any more dogs, you hear?''

And stay off of men's laps, unless you want to deal with the consequences.

The annoying thing was, he wasn't altogether sure she didn't. She sure sent out a lot of mixed signals. He turned and strode out of the bank, wanting to put some distance between them before he was tempted to try to figure out exactly what her signals meant.

Five

"I looked like I'd gone six rounds with Mike Tyson," Frannie moaned that evening after work as she sat at the kitchen table of the B & B with Summer and Jasmine. She stared down at her glass of iced tea. "When I looked in the restroom mirror, I wanted to sink right through the floor."

"Well," Jasmine said defensively, "I tried to signal you to wipe your face."

"Without my contacts or glasses, I can't see across the room. Why didn't you come over and tell me?"

Jasmine lifted her shoulders and grinned sheepishly. "I didn't want to interrupt you and Austin. He was staring at you as if you were the most fascinating creature he'd ever seen."

"Creature's the word for it," Frannie mumbled.

Jasmine grinned. "Well, I told you about your makeup as soon as he left."

Frannie squeezed a slice of lemon into her glass. "I just wish you'd come over and told me when things first started going downhill."

"You mean when *you* went downhill—into Austin's lap?" Jasmine asked.

Summer snorted.

Jasmine grinned impishly. "Gee, I thought that was when things really started to pick up."

Both cousins snickered and Frannie shot them a disgusted look. "I'm glad you're both amused."

Jasmine reached out and patted her hand. "Oh, come on, Frannie. You've got to admit, it was awfully funny."

"Depends on your perspective," Frannie replied. "I'd be a lot more inclined to laugh if I weren't dying of embarrassment."

Summer raised her hands in a placating gesture. "Well, it seems to me that we're overlooking the really important thing here."

"Oh? And what's that?" Frannie asked.

"That the flirting technique was successful. Austin came over when you made eye contact. We just need to send you out to practice it some more."

Frannie shook her head. "Oh, no. I'm through with making a fool of myself in public."

Jasmine and Summer looked at each other and frowned.

"Well, then, we'll just have to coach you in private," Summer said decisively. "That's how beauty contestants do it." At Frannie's inquisitive look, she explained, "A lot of contestants have behind-the-scene coaches who work with them on their posture and facial expressions and body language."

"Let me see if I've got this straight." Frannie looked from Summer to Jasmine, then back again. "You two would be my coaches?"

Summer and Jasmine both nodded.

"And as my coaches, you'd criticize everything I do, every minute that I'm awake?"

"Pretty much," Summer admitted.

"Oh, gee. Excuse me if I'm not jumping up and down with enthusiasm."

Jasmine laughed. "I know it sounds unpleasant, but Summer's right. The key to sending out the right vibes to a man is body language."

"And what's wrong with my body language?" Frannie asked.

Jasmine looked at her, her eyes narrowing thoughtfully. "Well, right now, for example, you're slumping in your chair and wearing a woe-is-me expression. Your body is saying 'Go away. Leave me alone.'"

"So can't you guys take a hint?"

Jasmine went on, undaunted. "You send out signals that tell men to keep their distance. Instead of crossing your arms and looking all shut down and inaccessible, you ought to sit up, lift your head and smile."

Frannie shifted uneasily. "I don't want to be a phony."

"This isn't about being phony. It's about being smart." Summer's voice was matter-of-fact. "It's about being your best self. If you become aware of what you're doing, you can start behaving the way you want, instead of just acting out of habit."

Frannie hated to admit it, but Summer's words made sense.

"You agreed to this whole makeover idea in the first place because you wanted to be more confident," Jasmine chimed in. "Well, the key to feeling more confident is to start acting as if you already are."

"I don't know..."

"Well, I do," Summer said adamantly. "I wouldn't be married to Gavin right now if I hadn't changed my ways."

It was true, Frannie realized. Summer had made a deliberate effort to change her studious, bookworm persona, and it definitely had paid off. Frannie was now so used to thinking of Summer as charming and gorgeous that it was hard to remember how she used to hide her beauty.

Of course, Frannie thought, Summer's beauty had been there all along. All she'd had to do was let it shine.

Was the same thing possible for her? A ray of hopefulness lit up her heart. She couldn't expect to be a raving beauty like Summer, of course, but maybe she could stop being such a plain little mouse.

"We're right, and you know it," Jasmine said.

The bell over the front door jangled. Frannie pushed back her chair, relieved at the interruption. "I'll get it. That's probably the couple with reservations for tonight."

Jasmine glanced at her watch. "Oh, dear, look at the time! I need to run by the dry cleaner's before they close."

"And I'd better get home," Summer said, rising from her chair.

"You all get going, then. I'll go take care of the guests."

"Stand up straight and pull up your chin," Jasmine called.

Frannie made a face as her cousins headed out the kitchen door, but she did straighten her back as she pattered barefoot across the waxed wood floor to the entry foyer.

Instead of the elderly couple she was expecting, Frannie found Whitehorn's newest police detective standing at the front desk.

"Gretchen, hello. It's nice to see you again."

The attractive blonde smiled. "Good to see you, too."

"How's the investigation going?"

"We're making a little progress, thanks to your aunt." Gretchen tucked a strand of blond hair behind her ear. "Actually, much as I hate to upset her, I wondered if I might speak to her again and see if she's recalled anything further."

Frannie's stomach tightened uneasily. The previous visit by the sheriff and Gretchen had left her aunt more troubled than ever. Celeste's nightmares had worsened, and she'd grown even more distracted and jittery.

All the same, Frannie couldn't very well refuse the detective's request. "She's on the porch with some guests.

I'll go and get her.'' Frannie gestured toward the front room. "Why don't you wait in the parlor?"

Gretchen placed her hand on Frannie's arm as she turned to go. "Before you go, let me ask you something."

Frannie hesitated. "Sure."

Gretchen's expression was warm and concerned. "How is your aunt's memory? In general, I mean. Does she usually have trouble recalling things?"

"Not usually, no."

Gretchen looked at her thoughtfully. "You know, sometimes people repress memories that are extremely traumatic. I can't help but wonder if your aunt has blocked something out that is just too awful to face."

Frannie had been wondering the same thing. And if the memory was so terrible that Celeste had buried it for thirty years, how would she deal with it if it resurfaced now?

Five minutes later Celeste clutched the upholstered arm of the leather chair in the parlor and told herself to breathe. Sometimes she forgot to do it automatically. She had to concentrate, to consciously make an effort, just to take in air. It was a feeling she often got in her dreams—those dark, swirling, awful dreams that tangled her up like sea grass, holding her down, winding around her. The harder she struggled to get free, the more tightly bound she became.

She looked over to the matching armchair, and Frannie gave her a reassuring smile.

The detective seated on the sofa leaned forward. It was the same one who had come the other day with Rafe— the pretty young woman with the shiny hair and the intelligent eyes, the woman who looked far too nice to be investigating something as dark and evil as murder.

"Tell me, Mrs. Monroe," the detective said, "have you

remembered anything further about the night Raven disappeared?''

''No. I...'' Celeste made herself take another breath, then briefly closed her eyes. She felt as if she were floating down a river, floating away, away from herself. And yet part of her was standing on the riverbank, watching. She opened her eyes and reminded herself to exhale. ''It was all a very long time ago.''

Why couldn't she remember? Why was that time so fuzzy and gray in her memory? A whole piece of her life was missing. She'd tried and tried to remember it, but it only brought headaches and a sad sense of shame. She ought to be able to do better than this.

She saw the look Gretchen shot Frannie. The lady policeman thought she should be able to do better, too. Inadequacy, heavy and smothering, wrapped around her like a thousand grasping tentacles.

''We followed your advice and went out to the old Kincaid mansion yesterday. We found two guns in Jeremiah's collection that could have been used in the shooting,'' Gretchen said. ''It's looking more and more like Jeremiah was the murderer.''

''No,'' Celeste breathed.

The detective's brows shot up. Celeste found herself as surprised as the blond woman looked.

''You don't think he did it?'' Gretchen asked.

''No.''

''Why not?''

Celeste didn't know. She was bewildered at her own response. ''I—I just don't feel right about Jeremiah being blamed for this,'' she mumbled.

''The evidence all points to him, Mrs. Monroe. He disliked Raven and didn't want his sister to marry him, so he had a motive. And now it looks like he owned the murder weapon.'' Gretchen's eyes settled on Celeste, warm and understanding. "It's always hard for family members to accept that someone they knew and loved was capable of murder."

Oh, Jeremiah was capable, all right—Celeste had no trouble believing that. Yet somehow, the whole thing just didn't seem right. It was like a piece in a jigsaw puzzle that had the right shape and the right color, but just didn't fit.

The room felt as if it had started spinning. That sometimes happened in her dreams, too—the room would spin faster and faster, like the ballerina in the music box she'd owned as a child. She'd loved that shiny wooden box, loved its lilting music, loved to watch the beautiful, twirling, porcelain ballerina. Her parents had given her that box, and when she was ten years old, she liked to think of them smiling down from heaven as she danced to its music, danced a private pas de deux with the ballerina, just for them.

Jeremiah had smashed that box against the wall in a fit of anger one afternoon, because the music had interrupted his viewing of a football game.

Celeste closed her eyes and gripped the arm of her chair as the room spun faster and faster.

"Mrs. Monroe?"

She opened her eyes to find Gretchen looking at her quizzically. "If you remember anything, please give me a call." She pulled a card out of her black bag and held it out to Celeste. "Anything—even something small, something you might think couldn't possibly be significant—might be a help."

Celeste nodded. "All right." She cautiously let go of the chair arm long enough to take the small white card, then gripped it again.

"What happens now?" Frannie asked the detective.

"Well, we wait for the ballistics report on the guns,"

Gretchen said. "And we're trying to locate Raven's brother, Storm Hunter, to see if he can shed any light on the events of that night."

"Where is he?"

"We don't know. Jackson Hawk, the attorney for the Laughing Horse Reservation, is helping us look for him."

"So you're in a holding pattern for a while."

"On this case." Gretchen tucked a strand of hair behind her ear. "But I've got plenty to keep me busy. Another body was found at the resort construction site this morning."

"Another body!" Frannie gasped.

The words echoed in Celeste's head, circling around and around, making her feel as if she were trapped inside a bad dream. Another body, another body, another body...

Gretchen nodded grimly. "This one's recent. It appears to be an accident or suicide."

"Who was it?" Frannie asked.

"A heavy equipment operator named Peter Cook. He evidently fell to his death."

Another death, Celeste thought. So much death. It was everywhere—hiding, lurking, biding its time, just waiting to strike. Life was so short. So short and so precious.

And yet she'd lost a part of hers. There was a void in her memory, a missing part of her life.

Frannie rose and saw the investigator out. Celeste leaned her head back against the chair and closed her eyes, listening to the creak of the door opening, the murmur of soft goodbyes, the thud of the door closing. Soft footsteps told her Frannie had returned to the room. With an effort, she opened her eyes.

"Are you all right?" Frannie asked.

"Yes. But that detective's on the wrong track."

"What do you mean?"

"I don't know." Celeste rose from the chair. She was

tired, so very tired, yet she could no longer sit still. "But I feel it in here." She touched her chest. "It just doesn't seem right that Jeremiah should take all the blame for this."

Frannie put a hand on Celeste's arm. "Like Gretchen said, I'm sure it's hard to accept that your brother could do such a horrible thing. But the evidence all points to Jeremiah, Aunt Celeste."

"The evidence is only physical." Celeste brushed a strand of hair from her forehead. A need, a compulsion, was growing inside her. She needed to do something. She could no longer sit idly by. She needed to take some action. "Sometimes things aren't as they seem. I've got a feeling—a strong feeling—that there's more to this than meets the eye."

And I intend to do a little investigating of my own, she suddenly decided. The truth was there, somewhere inside her. It was swirling around in her dreams, skirting the edges of her nightmares.

What was that line from the Bible? "The truth shall make you free"—that was it.

She needed freedom. She needed truth. She needed to reclaim her memory—for the sake of Blanche, the sake of Jeremiah, the sake of Raven.

But most of all, she thought with a twinge of desperation, for the sake of her own sanity.

Six

"Oh, Frannie, you look like a princess!" Summer finally found a moment at the festive, elegant Whitehorn Ball to speak with Frannie and Jasmine.

"I *feel* like a princess." Frannie touched the fabric of her sleek red gown that her cousins had helped her find in a marathon shopping expedition in Bozeman. Her hair, thanks to a new stylist, was swept up into a tousle of loose, elegant curls.

In the past week, her cousins had put her through the equivalent of beauty boot camp. They'd taught her how to apply makeup, drilled her on posture and body language, and made her walk in heels for hours. They'd helped her pick out shoes, a matching purse, and face-flattering rhinestone earrings. They'd insisted she get a manicure and pedicure. They'd even made her select a new perfume.

And it had paid off. Frannie looked better than she'd ever dreamed possible. "Is this really me?"

"It's you, all right." Summer beamed like a proud mother. "I wish that slug Joe who dumped you in college could see you now."

Joe. For years, the mention of his name had conjured up the image of his face, complete with painful details such as the cowlick in his hair, the paleness of his lashes, the cleft in his chin. Most painfully of all, it reminded her of the way he'd dumped her for her college roommate.

For the first time, Frannie realized she couldn't recall

exactly what Joe looked like. Her stomach didn't knot at the thought of him, she didn't ache with loneliness, and his memory didn't stir up the old, awful feelings of inferiority that used to grip her like a bad cold whenever he came to mind.

He'd lost his power to hurt her. She was over him. Her lips curved in an enormous grin.

"Kyle seems floored," Summer said.

"Kyle?"

"Your date," Summer said dryly.

Frannie blushed. She knew it was silly, but throughout this whole night the man she kept thinking about was Austin. She couldn't seem to get him off her mind. She kept thinking about the way he'd come to her rescue with Lyle, the way he'd gently bandaged her knee, the way he'd felt when she'd fallen in his lap. The smell of him, the warmth of him, the feel of his hand on her hip—the thought of it sent hot shivers racing all over her body.

Summer leaned across the linen-draped bistro table in the dimly lit hall. "So what do you think of Kyle?"

Frannie saw the tuxedoed back of her date disappear into the crowd as he and Gavin and Jasmine's date headed to the bar to refresh her and Summer's drinks. "He's very nice."

"Uh-oh." Summer looked at her closely. "I hear a 'but' in your voice. But what?"

Frannie hesitated.

"But you don't find him attractive?" Jasmine prompted.

"No, he's very nice-looking. But..." Frannie's voice trailed off.

But he's not Austin. It was ridiculous and Frannie knew it, but she couldn't help it. "Kyle's very nice," she said, "but I just don't feel any chemistry."

"Well, that's certainly not the case on his part," Summer said. "He hasn't taken his eyes off you." Summer looked around and smiled. "But, then, neither have most of the men in this room. You're the belle of the ball." She looked out of the corner of her eye and lowered her voice. "Don't look now, but here comes another admirer."

Frannie glanced up to see a stocky man with a brown mustache standing behind her chair. The man nervously cleared his throat. "Would you like to dance?"

"Go ahead," Summer urged. "I'm sure Kyle won't mind."

Frannie rose and smiled. She *did* feel like the belle of the ball. She felt attractive and feminine and sought-after. Instead of wasting the evening mooning over someone unattainable like Austin Parker, she told herself, she ought be enjoying the attention of all the men who *were* interested in her.

Her cousins were right, she decided as she stepped onto the dance floor. It didn't hurt to live a little.

It didn't hurt a bit, she thought when the orchestra played its last song two hours later as she danced with Kyle. "Is it already over?"

Someone turned up the lights. Kyle looked at her, his pale eyes shining hopefully in his even paler face. "It doesn't have to be. We could go somewhere else."

"Oh, let's!" Frannie looked around the table. "I still feel like dancing. Why don't we all go to the Hot T?"

Summer and Jasmine exchanged amused glances. Frannie smiled sheepishly, realizing that the suggestion was completely out of character. But she *felt* out of character tonight. Just for tonight, she felt as if she were living a fairy tale.

"That's a great idea," Jasmine said.

Summer turned to her husband. "I think that sounds like fun, don't you, Gavin?"

Gavin glanced longingly at Summer and sighed, then smiled gamely. "Whatever you say, sweetheart."

Loud country-western music spilled out of the wooden door into the night air as Frannie followed Summer into the Hot T honky-tonk thirty minutes later. It took a moment for Frannie's eyes to adjust to the dim lighting. When they did, she saw that several couples in the casually clad crowd were wearing formal attire. Evidently a few other people attending the ball had decided to prolong the evening.

"There's an empty table against the wall." Gavin had to shout to be heard above the music and the noisy crowd. He steered Summer toward it. Jasmine and her date followed, and Frannie and Kyle brought up the rear. His hand was on the small of her back when Frannie suddenly froze in her tracks.

"Is something wrong?" Kyle asked.

Just that my heart stopped beating for a moment, and now it's going a thousand beats a minute. "I—I'm fine," Frannie managed to say.

"You look like you've seen a ghost."

He's not a ghost, but he's been haunting me all the same. There, on the far side of the tavern, stood Austin, as handsome as the devil in jeans and a Western-cut blue shirt. He was leaning against the pine-paneled wall, his head inclined politely, smiling at a busty blonde in tight jeans and an even tighter halter top who was talking to him in an animated fashion. He looked over as Frannie stared at him, and his gaze collided with hers like a semi-trailer in a head-on crash.

Frannie couldn't breathe. She couldn't move. She could only stare as Austin stared back.

"Frannie?" Kyle asked, his forehead wrinkled with concern. "Are you feeling all right?"

"Huh? Oh, yes." Frannie knew she should pull her

eyes away from Austin, but she couldn't seem to make herself. As she watched, Austin's lips curved in a sexy smile, and he lifted his can of beer in a silent salute. Frannie unfurled her fingers in a weak wave, then hurried to the table to join Summer and Jasmine, feeling oddly shell-shocked.

Kyle pulled out a chair and Frannie lowered herself into it, letting the conversation at the table buzz around her. The waitress came and took their order. Frannie tried not to look at Austin, but she seemed unable to help herself. She watched the blonde hand him a piece of paper. She saw him scribble something on it, then hand it back to her. Probably a phone number, Frannie thought. A hot poker of jealousy burned in her chest.

Kyle leaned toward her, blocking her view. "I think I can handle this song, if you'd like to dance."

Frannie realized the band was playing a slow ballad. After urging everyone to continue the evening because she felt like dancing, she couldn't very well refuse. "Sure."

She rose from the chair and let Kyle lead her to the dance floor, but she was no longer interested in dancing. She was only interested in the tall man across the room with the vivid blue eyes that seemed to follow her every move.

"Say, aren't those two of the gals from the bed-and-breakfast?" Tommy Deshaw angled his bottle of beer toward the table with Summer and Jasmine.

Austin took a swig of his beer. "Yep."

"Wow, they sure look swell. Musta been some kinda fancy shindig somewhere in town tonight. I wonder where their cousin is. You know—the one who threw egg on your face and tumbled into your lap at the bank and nearly got killed savin' a dog in traffic." Tommy chuckled and shook his head.

"She's out on the dance floor."

"She is?" Tommy craned his head. "Where?"

"There. In the red dress."

"That's her? *That's* Little Miss Hap?" Tommy stared, bug-eyed, then let out a low, appreciative whistle. "I wouldn' have recognized her. Man, she sure cleans up nice."

"No kidding."

"Wonder who she's dancin' with?"

Austin was wondering the same thing. He didn't like the way the man's hand rested on her waist, or the goofy grin on his face as he looked down at her. He didn't like the man at all, for no other reason than the fact that he was dancing with Frannie.

"I don't know who it is right now," Austin said, thrusting his beer into Tommy's hand, "but it's about to be me." Striding purposefully onto the dance floor, Austin dodged his way through the crowd and tapped the tuxedo-clad man on the shoulder.

Frannie's dance partner turned around, his expression startled. Austin looked past him to Frannie. Her eyes were wide, her lips slightly parted.

"Mind if I cut in?"

"Well, uh…"

Before the man could form a response, Austin swept Frannie into his arms and guided her to the far side of the dance floor. "Hey, there."

"Hey, yourself."

It was there again, that sharp, electric attraction he'd felt when she'd landed on his lap that day at the bank—an attraction so keen that everything else receded into the fuzzy distance, everything but the warmth of her skin and the glow of her eyes.

The scent of her perfume invaded his senses, curling around him like a magic spell. "You look gorgeous."

Frannie's lips curved up. Austin found himself staring at them in fascination, wondering how they would feel under his.

"You're just saying that because I don't have any goo on my face. Or do I? Maybe I should go check."

Austin tightened his hold on her. Damn, but she felt good—warm and soft and silk-covered. The desire to get closer pulled at him like undertow. "I don't want you to go anywhere."

He heard the little hitch in her breath, felt her fingers clutch at his back, and it struck him as intensely erotic, the kind of response she might make during lovemaking. Arousal, strong and hot, flamed within him. He moved his hand low along her spine, aligning her body more closely with his.

She sighed and shifted, pressing her breasts against his chest.

Oh, criminy. This was torture—hot, sweet torture. He swallowed, his mouth suddenly dry, and searched for something to say, for something, anything, to divert his attention from the entirely inappropriate response his body was having to her. "So what's the special occasion?"

"Hmm?" Her eyes held a dark, desire-dazed look. A fresh flash of heat flared inside him. So she felt it, too.

"You're all dressed up."

"Oh. We went to the Whitehorn Ball. It's an annual benefit for the hospital."

"Who's your date?"

"Kyle Johnson."

"Are you two serious?"

"Oh, no." Frannie's hair brushed his cheek as she shook her head. "He's a blind date my cousin fixed me up with. They're both doctors."

An irrational sense of relief filled his chest. "Well, it's good to know there's a doctor in the house." *Because the way you're affecting me, sweetheart, I'm likely to need one before this dance is over.*

"So what about you?" she asked. "Who are you with?"

The warm weight of her breasts against his chest made it impossible to think coherently. "Tommy."

She lifted one eyebrow. "I meant, the woman."

"What woman?"

She pulled back and looked at him archly, as if she thought he was trying to pull a fast one. "The blonde you were talking to when I came in."

"Oh, her. I don't even know her name. She just wanted an autograph."

"An autograph," Frannie repeated softly. "Do a lot of people ask for one?"

Austin lifted a shoulder. "A lot more than I'd like."

Frannie's eyes rested on him. "Sounds like you're not all that comfortable with your celebrity status."

He lifted a shoulder. "I don't like folks to make a big fuss."

"You don't like being the center of attention?"

"Not unless it's from someone I want attention from." He pulled her closer. "Like you."

He wasn't sure, but he thought he felt a shiver pass through her. He definitely heard her sigh, because he felt the warmth of her breath on his neck. She rested her cheek against his chin and let him rock her to the music, which ended all too soon.

He reluctantly pulled back as the last note faded and the crowd applauded.

"I'll walk you back to your table," Austin said.

Frannie could tell by the tight look on Kyle's face that he wasn't happy to see Austin accompany her back to the table, but he was too much of a gentleman to make an issue of it. With a forced smile, Kyle stood and pulled out her chair as she and Austin approached.

Austin stuck his hand out to Kyle. "Thanks for letting me cut in on you out there. I'm Austin Parker."

"So I've heard." Kyle gestured to Gavin. "Seems you've got a big fan here."

Gavin was immediately on his feet, his hand outstretched. "Gavin Nighthawk. Around here I'm better known as Summer's husband." Gavin grabbed an extra chair from the next table. "Please, have a seat and join us."

"Well, all right, if you'll let me buy you a round."

Austin sat between Frannie and Gavin. Kyle placed his arm territorially around the back of Frannie's chair.

"I saw the TV coverage of your race in Atlanta," Gavin said, leaning forward. "Man, that was something, the way you pulled into the lead at the last moment."

The conversation was off and running as if a checkered flag had been dropped. Frannie was relieved, because she felt far too rattled to speak.

Never in her life had she felt anything like the surge of attraction she'd felt in Austin's arms on the dance floor. He made her feel weak-kneed and foggy-headed and incredibly, meltingly aroused. Even now, it was hard not to gravitate toward him, like metal shavings to a magnet.

Frannie realized she was actually leaning toward Austin. She started to straighten, but as she pulled away, the hard, warm weight of his thigh against hers under the table made her freeze. The next thing she knew, his hand rested on her leg, just above her knee. Shock waves of pleasure rolled through her. The secret, unexpected intimacy was like forbidden fruit, delicious and irresistible.

She suddenly realized Kyle's hand had slid from the back of her chair to her neck.

"I got shortchanged on that last dance," he said. "Don't you think you owe me another?"

On the other side of her body, Austin gave her leg a little squeeze. A shiver of pleasure coursed through Fannie. It was hard to act normal as she turned to Kyle and forced a smile. "Sure. And I'm ready to pay up."

Austin's hand slipped slowly off her leg as she rose. She could still feel the heat of his hand as she stepped into Kyle's arms and let him lead her in a two-step. She couldn't help but compare the difference in the way it felt, dancing with the two men. She tried to make casual conversation, but her eyes kept drifting to the table. Austin was watching her, his eyes licking over her like blue flames.

The other two couples were on the dance floor when Kyle and Frannie returned to the table. The prospect of sitting alone between Kyle and Austin made her palms begin to sweat. With a quick, "Excuse me," she grabbed her small beaded bag and fled to the safety of the ladies' room.

She hid out until she heard the song end. Hoping that either Summer or Jasmine would have returned to the table, she stepped out of the restroom door—and ran smack into Austin.

Her heart pounded hard as he took her arm and began steering her toward the wall. "What are you doing?"

"I need to talk to you for a minute."

"I—I really ought to get back to the table."

He stopped at the end of the small hallway that housed the restrooms. "It's okay. The doc's outside, returning a call from his answering service." Austin placed his hands on her upper arms. His fingers were warm, his touch gentle, yet Frannie felt as if he left a burning trail of heat as his fingers slid down her bare skin. "Look, I know you're here with him tonight, so I won't try to horn in, but I want to take you out. What are you doing tomorrow night?''

Frannie's heart pounded hard. Something about Austin scared her to death. The way she responded to him was so out of character, so strongly emotional, so completely illogical. ''I don't know...''

What she didn't know, she realized, was *herself* when she was around him. He brought out a side of her she'd never known, a sensual side so intense and compelling that she couldn't trust her own judgment.

''Well, then, I'll tell you what you're doing.'' He trailed the back of his curved finger gently down her cheek. ''You're having dinner with me at the Lakeside Inn. I'll pick you up at seven.'' His finger continued its erotic path, trailing down to her mouth. He gently traced the outline of her bottom lip, then gave a slow smile and walked away.

Frannie leaned against the wall, both terrified and thrilled. How in the world was she supposed to hold her own against a man like Austin?

Seven

Jasmine leaned over the front desk the next evening and tapped her wristwatch. "Frannie, it's ten minutes until seven. Why on earth aren't you dressed?"

Frannie glanced up from the stack of receipts she was sorting, then looked down at her jeans. "I *am* dressed," she said calmly.

Jasmine rolled her eyes. "You know what I mean. Dressed for your date with Austin."

Frannie turned back to the receipts. "I'm as a dressed as I'm going to get."

"Are you out of your *mind?* You're wearing your oldest jeans and a baggy gray sweater, you don't have on a lick of makeup, and you're hiding behind your glasses again."

"This is me. This is how I am. If Austin doesn't like it, well, that's just too bad." She entered the information from a pink receipt into the computer, trying to act more confident than she felt. "Besides, I'm not sure I'm going."

"Of course you're going!" Circling the front desk, Jasmine charged toward her.

"I never said I would. Austin didn't actually ask." Frannie clicked the computer mouse, pretending not to notice that her cousin had pulled up a stool, plopped herself at her elbow and was staring at her in disbelief.

"And why on earth wouldn't you? What possible objection could you have to Austin Parker?" Jasmine placed her hands on her hips and frowned indignantly. "Is he too nice, too charming, too famous, too wealthy or too good-looking?"

"Yes."

"*Yes?*" Jasmine's voice was an incredulous shout.

Frannie raised her finger to her mouth. "Keep it down, Jasmine. You'll disturb the guests and Aunt Celeste."

"What's with you, Frannie?" Jasmine grabbed the arms of Frannie's chair and swiveled her around to face her. "Summer and I spent a lot of time making you over so you'd have some confidence and get a social life, and it worked better than any of us dreamed. The sexiest man ever to hit the state of Montana asked you out, and now you're telling me you don't think you're going to go?"

"That's just it. Last night wasn't me." Frannie's hand swept from her glasses to her jeans. "*This* is me."

"That was you last night, too." Jasmine's eyes flashed hotly, and her voice held a hard edge of insistence. "The only difference is, last night you were making an effort."

Frannie sighed. "Don't you see, Jasmine? I can't sustain that kind of effort, that kind of illusion, for long. I'm not a graceful, glamorous, outgoing person. I'm a shy, awkward, number-crunching bookworm. And sooner or later, any man who spends any time around me will discover that. And when he does, he's bound to dump me for someone more exciting. I think it'll hurt a whole lot less if it happens sooner rather than later."

Jasmine placed a hand on Frannie's arm, her brow creased in concern. "Oh, Frannie, I can't believe how you underestimate yourself! You're letting one bad experience warp your outlook."

Maybe so, Frannie thought, but it was the self-protective thing to do. A man such as Austin Parker was not going to be interested in someone like her for long. And judging from the intensity of emotions he stirred inside her, he had the potential to break her heart ten times worse than Joe ever did.

The loud chime of the doorbell broke her thoughts. Both Frannie and Jasmine turned in the direction of the front door.

"That must be Austin. Everyone else just walks in," Jasmine said. "Aren't you going to answer it?"

Obviously Jasmine had no intention of doing so. Frannie took a deep, steadying breath and rose from the computer. Despite her determination not to fuss with her appearance, she couldn't keep from tugging at her sweater and smoothing her ponytail as she walked to the door.

The sight of the tall, handsome man standing on the porch hit her like a blow to the solar plexus, knocking most the air out of her. "Hi."

"Hi." He grinned, revealing a dimple on his right cheek. "May I come in?"

Frannie realized she was just standing there, staring at him. She stepped back out of the way. "Of course."

He waved a greeting to Jasmine, who was standing behind the front desk, then settled his gaze back on Frannie. "Am I early?"

Frannie hoped she didn't look as nervous as she felt. Her heart was pounding and her palms were damp. "No. I think you're right on time."

"Great." He shoved a hand into the pocket of his khaki slacks. "So, are you ready?"

Was he asking because he didn't think she was? Frannie tugged at the sleeve of her sweater and eyed him suspiciously. "I never actually said I'd go out with you, you know. You didn't exactly ask."

He grinned. "That's because I didn't want to give you an opportunity to say no."

Good heavens, but he had sexy eyes. It was hard to think when he turned them on her that way.

He flashed that dimple again. "If you want to just stay here, though, that's fine with me. We could order in a pizza, and just sit and talk."

Frannie pushed her glasses up higher on her nose, trying to decide what to make of him. Was he suggesting that they stay in because he didn't want to be seen in public with her? Maybe he thought being seen with someone so ordinary would be bad for his image, as Joe had thought all those years ago. The thought roused a stubborn streak within her.

"No. Since you're here, we might as well go ahead and go out."

"Okay." He looked at her curiously, then gestured toward the door. "Well, then, shall we?"

"You two have a good time," Jasmine called.

Frannie stiffly walked beside Austin out the door and across the porch. Part of her was thrilled to be with him, but another part, a self-protective part, was scared to death and wary. What on earth would they talk about?

He led her to a black pickup truck parked in the drive, and she seized on it as a topic of conversation. "I thought you'd be in a racy red sports car," she said as he opened the passenger door.

He lifted his shoulders. "I get my fill of racing on the track. This is a lot more practical for running a ranch." Slamming the door closed, he circled the truck and climbed in the driver's seat. Frannie half expected him to lay rubber as he backed out of the drive, but he drove slowly and carefully.

Frannie felt a disconcerting pull of attraction as she glanced at his profile. She was curious about him, curious why he'd moved here. "Tell me about your ranch. You said you raise horses?"

He nodded. "Quarter horses."

"I would have expected a race car driver to raise Thoroughbreds."

"Nah. Too temperamental. Quarter horses are big, strong and smart. When they race, they run on a straightaway. It's the horse that wins or loses a race, not the skill of the jockey."

"How many do you have?"

"Just six right now. Three brood mares, two foals and a stallion. I'm trying to start a breeding operation. When I retire from racing, I'll expand it into a training facility."

Frannie looked at him in surprise. "You're thinking about retiring from racing?"

Austin shrugged. "Every driver thinks about it, and sooner or later, most of them do. I've told myself a dozen times that I'll quit after the next race. But then there's another one, and, well..." He lifted his shoulders. "I know the smart thing to do is to quit while I'm ahead, but so far I just haven't been able to bring myself to do it. I love the challenge of the sport. I'm beginning to think I probably won't quit until I'm too old to handle the pressure."

"The pressure must be pretty intense. It's an awfully dangerous sport, isn't it?"

His head bobbed in a single nod. "One mistake out there and it's all over."

"Aren't you afraid?"

"Nah. Not for myself. I've got nothing to lose."

"Right," Frannie said dryly. "Just your life."

"Well, yeah, I suppose there's that." Austin shot her a rakish grin. "Or my mind. A few more head injuries, and there won't be enough brain cells left to worry with."

Frannie felt a surge of alarm. "You've been injured?"

"Oh, sure. I don't think there's a serious racer out there that hasn't hit the wall or had a bad crash or two. It happens."

"Doesn't that worry you when you get behind the wheel?"

Austin shook his head. "Once I strap on that helmet, there's no room for worry. There's no room for thinking about anything but driving. It takes total concentration. That's the thing I like best about it, I guess."

"But while you're concentrating, you still have to be aware of the risks."

"Well, sure, but I don't dwell on them. Like I said, I've got nothing to lose—no family to worry about, no wife, no kids. Aside from my pit crew, no one in the world is depending on me. And my crew could find other jobs in a heartbeat if something happened to me."

The flat, matter-of-fact tone of his voice sent a chill up Frannie's arms. "I can't believe you can talk about your life like that."

"Like what?"

"Like it's expendable."

Austin shrugged. "Well, I guess it is. It's of no value to anyone but me. And I like it that way."

She knew she shouldn't ask, but she couldn't help herself. "Why?"

"I don't have to worry about hurting anyone else."

"You could hurt another racer."

Austin nodded solemnly. "Yeah. But I try to look at it this way—out on the track, it's an even playing field. Everyone knows the odds. Everyone's taking the same risks. So I just show up and do my best, and so far, my luck's held out."

"Sounds like an awfully lonely life."

"It's all I've ever known. Besides, having nothing to lose gives me a winning edge."

Frannie gazed at him, trying to fathom the emptiness of a life that wasn't connected to anyone else's in any profound kind of way. "I can't imagine living that way."

Austin shrugged. "It's easy when you're accustomed to it."

Frannie gazed at him. "What happened to your family?"

"I never had much of one. I was an only child, and my mother left when I was six."

"What do you mean, left?"

"Left. Went away."

Something hard in his tone of voice warned Frannie not pursue the line of questioning. She decided to take another tack. "What about your dad?"

"He died when I was sixteen." Austin squirmed on his seat and cut a glance at Frannie. "So tell me about your family. Do your parents live at the Big Sky?"

It was an obvious ploy to change the subject, but Frannie decided to go along with it. Maybe she could get him to tell her more about his family later. "No. My folks have a house about a mile from the bed-and-breakfast, but right now they're out of town. My dad's mom had hip replacement surgery, and they're in Minnesota helping her get back on her feet."

"Do you have any brothers or sisters?"

"One older brother. David's with the F.B.I. in Atlanta. And I have three cousins who seem like sisters."

"I've met Summer and Jasmine."

Frannie nodded. "And the other one is Cleo. She runs the day care center in town. She just got married, so she's off on an extended honeymoon with her new husband and his little boy."

Austin shot her an interested glance as he turned the truck onto a side road. "Must be nice, having a large family. What are your parents like?"

Frannie grinned. "A couple of overgrown kids."

"Yeah?" Austin's eyes were amused. "In what way?"

"Oh, they're outgoing and fun-loving and free-spirited.'' Frannie smiled. ''Sometimes I used to feel like our roles were reversed, like I was the parent and they were the children. They were always trying to get me to go out and have fun. I've always been kind of quiet and reserved and serious.''

''What line of work are they in?''

''Dad is an architect, and Mom helps Aunt Celeste run the B and B. Despite their careers, though, they're both really spontaneous and adventurous. They're a perfect match. They have a really close, loving marriage—the kind I hope to have some day.''

''How did you come to live at the B and B?''

''I spent so much time there when I was growing up that it felt like a second home. In fact, I started doing bookkeeping for the place when I was fifteen. After I graduated from college, Celeste offered me free room and board in exchange for continuing to keep the books. I didn't like living alone and I was spending all my free time there anyway, so it was a perfect solution.''

''It's a grand old house. Has it been in your family long?''

''Quite a while. Aunt Celeste and her late husband bought it before any of the kids were born. She and Mom ran it, figuring it'd be a good way to earn a living while raising a family—which it was. In addition to their own children, Aunt Celeste and Mom raised Summer, their late sister's child.''

''Sounds like your family is awfully close.''

Frannie grinned. ''We are. We're like a big wooly blanket—large, close-knit and warm.''

''When I was a kid, I used to like to pretend I had a family like that,'' Austin said. ''I never could really picture it, though.''

The wistfulness in his voice struck a chord within Frannie, a chord that reverberated right to her very soul.

The pickup slid to a halt, and Frannie was surprised to realize that they'd already arrived at the restaurant. "Stay put," Austin said. "I'll come around and get your door."

Frannie watched him circle the truck, a single word echoing in her head: *lonely*. For all of his success, Austin Parker was a deeply lonely man.

And he seemed to prefer it that way. What was it he'd said? *Having nothing to lose gives me a winning edge.*

She walked beside him across the parking lot, wondering why she was so attracted to a man who'd clearly stated he didn't want a deep relationship. And why was she so talkative around him? She was usually closedmouthed and bashful around people she didn't know well, yet she'd talked a blue streak on the drive to the restaurant.

They were thoroughly unsuited for each other, complete opposites. She wanted a home and family, and he wanted the freedom of being unattached. He belonged to an exciting world of fame and fast cars, while she craved anonymity and quiet.

So why did she feel more drawn to this man than to anyone she'd ever met?

The restaurant hostess seated them beside a window overlooking a portion of Blue Mirror Lake. The water was calm and dark, and the sky held a slight cast of purple as the sun sank into the horizon.

"What a wonderful view," Frannie sighed.

"I was thinking the same thing." She looked up to find Austin's gaze fastened on her face.

Frannie felt her skin heat, and she suddenly wished she'd taken more pains with her appearance. The amazing thing was that Austin seemed to think she was just fine the way she was. He was looking at her with a light in his eye, with real interest, as if he saw beyond her glasses, beyond her casual clothes, beyond her skin.

A warm shiver chased over her.

"Tell me about yourself, Frannie. Have you always lived in Whitehorn?"

Frannie nodded. "Except when I went away to college."

"Where did you go?"

"Montana State University in Bozeman." Frannie looked at him. "How about you?"

Austin shook his head. "After my old man died, I had to go to work to support myself. I didn't even finish high school. I took correspondence courses and earned my high school diploma, but college wasn't in the cards for me. I've always admired people with a lot of education." He leveled his eyes at her, and she felt another thrill of attraction. "What did you major in?"

"Mathematical sciences and literature. I had a double major."

Austin let out a soft whistle and shook his head. "You must be a real brain."

Frannie shrugged. "I've just always loved math and reading."

"Lots of folks love reading—I'm one of them—but I don't know that I've ever heard anyone say they loved math before."

Frannie smiled. "I know. I've always been something of an oddball. My parents used to fuss at me about it."

"How?"

"Oh, when I was a kid, they were always pushing me to get my head out of my books and go outside and play. When I was a teenager, my mother lectured me about not being sociable enough."

"You seem pretty sociable to me."

It was true. Around him, she even *felt* sociable. It was odd, how he made her feel both unsettled and at ease. She shrugged her shoulders. "I've always found it hard to make small talk. I never much saw the point in it. I guess

I like my connections with people to be deep instead of plentiful.''

"I was kind of a loner, too. But I can't say that I enjoyed math.''

"People think math is hard, but it's not, not really. It can be fun, like doing puzzles or riddles. In fact, I've always wanted to write children's books that illustrate that.''

"So why don't you?''

"Actually, I have.'' Frannie twisted the napkin in her lap, immediately embarrassed. Why had she told him that? No one else knew about the stack of papers stuffed in her bedside drawer.

"You've written some books?''

"Well, they're not books, exactly. I mean, they're not published. They're just some pages I've written down.''

"What are they about?''

"Oh, nothing. I mean, they're silly.''

Austin regarded her solemnly. "I promise not to laugh.''

"Well, actually, they're supposed to be funny.''

"Then I'll laugh like a hyena.''

Why had she ever opened her big mouth? Now she had to tell him or appear rude. "Well, they're a series of stories about a baby kangaroo. He and his koala bear buddy make up games about numbers and fractions and percentages, games that the reader can play along with.''

"Are they illustrated?''

Frannie nodded, her face growing warm. "I'm no great artist, but I can draw cartoon figures. Like I said, the books are pretty silly.''

"Are they finished?''

"As finished as I can make them. I have three of them.''

"Have you sent them to any publishers?''

Frannie shook her head.

"Why not?"

"Oh, I'd be embarrassed. They're really not all that good."

"How do you know?"

"Well, they're just something I've been playing around with. I'm not a professional."

"No one is when they first start out. Everyone has to begin somewhere." Austin leaned forward. "What's the worst that can happen if you send it to a publishing house?"

Frannie shrugged her shoulders.

"They can tell you no, that's what. And then you could turn around and put those manuscripts right back in the mail and send them somewhere else."

Frannie gave a sardonic smile. "So another publishing house can tell me no, too?"

"Maybe. But then again, they might just tell you yes." Austin leaned back in his chair. "In order to have a chance of winning the race, Frannie, you've got to show up at the track."

"But what if every children's book publisher in the country tells me no?"

"Well, then, you use all the information you've gained and you try again. You write another book." Austin looked at her intently. "What do you have to lose, except a few dollars on postage?"

Frannie felt her chest tighten. "My dream," she said softly. "I could lose my dream."

"But by not taking action, you're losing the chance of ever making it a reality."

There was no arguing with his logic. Still, a part of Frannie resisted. "It's just..." She took a deep breath and slowly let it out. Her finger toyed with a loose thread on the tablecloth. "I hate to be rejected."

Austin's hand covered hers, enveloping her with warmth. "Everyone does. And sooner or later, everyone is."

An edge to his voice made her look up. His smile had faded, and his eyes held an intensity she hadn't seen before.

"You sound like you've had personal experience with rejection," she said softly.

"I have."

"By whom?"

"Oh, no one important." His mouth quirked into a mirthless smile. "Just my mother."

Frannie's heart turned in her chest. She wanted to ask him more, but he cut her off by picking up her menu and handing it to her. "The waiter is heading our way. We'd better decide what we're going to eat."

They'd just placed their order when Austin waved at someone in the doorway. Frannie turned to see a familiar man with handsome Native American features walking toward their table. "Hi, Austin," the man said, extending his hand. "How's it going?"

Austin stood and shook the man's hand. "Great. Frannie, this is Jackson Hawk, the attorney for the Laughing Horse Reservation."

"We know each other," Frannie said, shaking the man's hand. "Jackson is a good friend of Gavin's."

"Nice to see you, Frannie."

"Good to see you, too." Frannie looked from Jackson to Austin, then back again. "How do you two happen to know each other?"

"Austin came to the reservation and spoke to our boys' club last week." Jackson turned to Austin. "I can't thank you enough, either. You made a big impression on some kids who were veering off in the wrong direction."

Austin shrugged modestly. "Glad I could help."

Frannie looked at him, her heart growing warm. The more she learned about him, the more she found to like. And it scared her to death.

"What did Austin talk about?" she found herself asking Jackson.

"The importance of hard work and goal-setting," Jackson replied. "He gave a really inspiring speech."

Frannie grinned. "Why, that's the very same speech he was just giving me!"

Austin laughed, but he shifted uncomfortably.

Jackson smiled. "The kids listened to him in a way they won't listen to other adults. Austin's a great role model."

Austin gazed at the tabletop. It was funny, Frannie mused, the praise seemed to embarrass him. Who would have guessed that a man in such a high-profile profession would be so modest and unassuming?

"Are you meeting someone here?" Austin asked Jackson, as if he were eager to change the topic.

Jackson nodded. "Lyle Brooks. To discuss some business."

"On a Sunday night?"

Jackson nodded and heaved a sigh. "Afraid so. Lyle is the contractor building the casino and resort, and he wants to talk about moving the location to a piece of land he owns further north."

"I've met the illustrious Mr. Brooks," Austin said. "He left me with a bad taste in my mouth."

Jackson's lips tilted in a dry smile. "He seems to have that effect on people."

Austin's brow pulled into a frown. "You say he wants to move the site? I thought he'd already begun construction on the resort."

"He has. He's blasted and cleared a forty-five-foot-deep construction pit."

Frannie leaned forward. "That's what the equipment operator fell into, isn't it?"

Jackson nodded somberly. "It's a real tragedy, and it's bringing a lot of unfavorable publicity to the project. That's what Lyle says he wants to talk about. Because of that man's death and an old skeleton that was found earlier on a nearby site, he thinks the land is cursed. He says it'll bring the tribe bad luck if we build there."

"Won't it be expensive to move the site now?" Austin asked.

Jackson's head bobbed again. "That's the oddest part. Lyle said he'd absorb the cost for any extra work involved. Says it won't cost the tribe a penny." Jackson shook his head. "I don't know what he's up to, but he tried to wring every last nickel out of us when he negotiated the contract. It's hard to believe he's suddenly willing to swallow tens of thousands of dollars out of the goodness of his heart."

"From what I saw of the man, it's hard to believe he even *has* a heart," Austin remarked. "He didn't strike me as the kind of person likely to look out for anyone's interests but his own."

Jackson grinned. "I'd say you're a shrewd judge of character, Austin." He winked at Frannie. "Not to mention of women." Jackson glanced toward the restaurant entrance. "There's Lyle now. I'll steer him toward the bar and see if a little bourbon will flush out his real motives." He gave a little salute. "You two enjoy your dinner."

Frannie watched Jackson head across the room. "I wonder what Lyle is really up to."

"My guess is it's some kind of scheme to pad his pockets."

"Well, I hope he's more careful in his business dealings than he is at driving."

"I don't think our little encounter with Lyle was a matter of carelessness. I think he was acting with cold-blooded deliberation.''

''What do you mean?''

''It looked to me like he was deliberately aiming for that dog.''

Frannie's eyes widened. ''Why would he do a thing like that?''

Austin shrugged. ''For the sport of it. Some men have no conscience.'' He leaned across the table. ''I gotta tell you, you scared me to death when you dashed out in front of his car.''

A wave of warmth rushed through her. *Don't take it personally,* she warned herself. Austin was the kind of man who would be concerned about anyone in harm's way. For some reason, though, the realization didn't kill the tenderness that was taking root inside of her.

''I guess it was a pretty foolish stunt,'' Frannie conceded.

''You *guess?*''

''Oh, all right,'' she said grudgingly. ''It was.''

''No kidding.'' Austin's eyes warmed her as they slid over her face. The hint of a smile curved his lips. ''But you know what else it was? One of the kindest, bravest things I've ever seen.'' He reached out and covered her hand with his. His thumb moved over the tops of her knuckles, leaving a trail of heat that raced straight up her arm into her chest.

Frannie gazed at Austin, and his gaze held hers, just as surely as his fingers did. Her eyes dropped to his lips. What would it be like to kiss a man like Austin, she wondered. A man so thoughtful and sexy and...

''Here you go,'' the waiter said, interrupting her thoughts as he set down their salads.

Here I go, all right, Frannie thought grimly. Jumping in too deep, too fast. She had no business letting Austin touch her, physically or emotionally. There was no future in a relationship with a man who was not only out of her league, but not interested in commitment.

She pulled back her hand, but it was too late. The heat of his touch had already burned its way inside of her.

The sky was deep blue, almost black, when Austin opened the door from the restaurant for Frannie an hour and a half later.

"That was delicious," she said.

Austin nodded. "The best meal I've had in weeks." The best conversation, too, he thought. They'd talked about music and work and movies, about politics and racing and art. He'd found Frannie bright and witty and amusing. He smiled as she stepped out the door. "The company was good, too."

"You're just saying that because I let you do most of the talking."

"Ow!" Austin placed a hand over his heart, as if he'd been shot. "Well, that's what you get for telling me you wanted to know all about racing."

"But I did. And it was fascinating." She reached out and touched his arm, her lips curved in a smile. "I was teasing you just now."

You've been teasing me all night, Austin thought. Her whole buttoned-down appearance was a tease. All evening long, he'd been itching to take off her glasses, to loosen her hair, to touch the lovely body he knew was hidden under her bulky sweater. "Do you want to go somewhere else? To a movie, or maybe out for a drink?"

She shook her head. "I have to be at the bank early in the morning. I'd better be getting back."

But Austin didn't want the evening to end. Not yet. "It's such a beautiful night. Why don't we walk down by the lake? I saw a path earlier."

"All right."

He led her to the edge of the parking lot, where a trail headed through the forest toward the lake. He fell into step beside her. About a hundred yards from the restaurant, the path twisted to follow the shoreline, and the restaurant was obscured by the trees. The sounds of the night enfolded them. A soft breeze rustled the leaves overhead, stirring the water just enough to make little lapping sounds against shore. A bullfrog croaked, and a chorus of crickets sang backup.

Frannie wrapped her arms around herself and gazed out at the night. "It's so beautiful here."

"Seems like we're miles away from the rest of the world."

Frannie nodded. "It's so unspoiled. Just think—we're looking at exactly the same view Indians saw centuries ago."

"Not exactly the same," Austin found himself saying. "Nothing stays the same for long."

Frannie looked at him curiously.

"Everything is always in a state of change." It was a fact he knew all too well, a fact he'd learned as a boy. And because nothing lasted forever, it was best to not get attached to people or to places or to things. "Better to move on while things are good than to hang around and wait for them to turn sour," his father used to say. So every few months, Austin would stuff all his belongings into his small, brown duffel bag and leave whatever place had come to feel like home. He used to look out the back window of his father's old truck and cry as they drove away. By the age of ten, he'd learned it hurt less to never look back.

"If you mean the seasons, well, yes, of course," Frannie was saying, "But the basic landscape is the same."

"Nah. Even that has changed. I'm sure there have been

floods and fires. A bolt of lightning hits a tree, then—zap!'' He snapped his fingers. ''An entire forest is burned down.''

''Yes, but given enough time, it grows back just as it was. It won't be exactly the same—not tree for tree, not exactly identical—but the basic character of the land is the same.''

Austin looked at Frannie. ''Like you, huh?''

''What do you mean?''

''Well, you're the same person with the same character, but every time I see you, you look different.''

Frannie shot him a teasing smile. ''That's because some days I wear an egg beret, and other days my face is green, and sometimes I have raccoon rings around my eyes....''

''...And sometimes you're so drop-dead gorgeous you nearly stop my heart.'' He turned toward her and lifted her hand. It felt small and warm, and the softness of it wrapped around him like a spell. ''I had trouble sleeping last night, and it was all your fault. I just lay there, picturing the way you looked in that red dress.''

Frannie's smile faded. She stepped back and pulled away her hand. ''Last night wasn't me.'' She made a sweeping gesture toward herself. ''*This* is me.''

Her mood had abruptly darkened. He tried to lighten things up. ''So who was the girl I danced with last night? Your secret twin?''

Frannie's spine straightened. Her eyes grew serious, her mouth unsmiling. ''That was an illusion my cousins created. They wanted to make me over for the evening and I let them, but this is the real me. This is how I usually am.''

She sounded so defensive, so prickly. Combative, almost. Austin frowned, wondering what he'd done to cause her reaction.

''I, uh, get the feeling I said something wrong.'' He

rubbed his chin. "I was just saying you looked great last night. I didn't mean to offend you."

She seemed offended nonetheless. "Well, don't get the idea I'm that way all the time."

Austin's frown deepened, along with his confusion. "What do you mean, 'that way'? Attractive?"

Her eyes flashed. Her chin tilted up defiantly. "If your idea of attractive is someone who's all made up and manicured and teetering around on high heels, well, then, yes, that's what I mean."

What was with her? She acted as if he'd insulted her, when he'd been trying to give her a compliment. "Hey, I don't think it takes any of that stuff to make a woman attractive."

"Hmm." She arched a disapproving eyebrow. "Well, that figures."

What had he done now? He stared at her blankly. "What figures?"

"That you'd prefer the natural beauty type."

He was damned if he did and damned if he didn't. He pulled his brow into a hard scowl. "What's that supposed to mean?"

She pulled herself so straight and taut she looked in danger of snapping in two. "Well, you obviously prefer the kind of woman who wakes up in the morning looking fresh as a daisy without so much as brushing her teeth. Believe me, there aren't very many women who can pull that off."

He'd obviously said something to upset her, but he was damned if he knew what it was. The infuriating part was that she seemed determined not to tell him. "What in blue blazes are you talking about?"

She blew out a huffy breath. "There's no point in pursuing this conversation. I'd like for you to take me home." She turned and started up the trail.

''Sorry. No can do.''

She whipped around and glared at him, her eyebrows high. ''You won't take me home?''

Austin took two steps forward, stopping just inches from her. ''I'm not taking you anywhere until you tell me what the hell is going on.''

''Nothing's going on!''

Austin's frustration had built to the point that by all rights, steam should be shooting from his ears. He stuck his face close to hers and scowled. ''Damn straight. And I want to know why not.''

Now she was staring at him as if *he* were the one who'd lost his mind. ''What do you mean, why not?''

''I brought you out here to kiss you, and we're arguing instead. And I want to know why.''

He wanted to kiss her? The concept made Frannie's head spin. She realized she was staring at him, slack-jawed, and abruptly closed her mouth. ''We're...we're not arguing,'' she finally stammered.

''Well, we're damn sure not kissing!''

They glared at each other, each breathing hard.

Austin raised both his hands. ''Okay. If you say we're not arguing, I won't argue with you about whether or not we're arguing. But would you mind telling me just what the hell it is we're supposedly discussing?''

He wanted to kiss her because he'd liked the way she looked last night, she reminded herself. He was attracted to a bunch of cosmetics, not to her. ''Your male chauvinism.''

Austin's fingers clenched, then unclenched at his sides. His voice was low and calm, but that probably had something to do with the fact that he was speaking through gritted teeth. ''Perhaps it would help if you told me exactly how I'm chauvinistic.''

''You said I looked beautiful last night.''

"And that somehow makes me chauvinistic." He rubbed his head, shaking it at the same time. "Well, at the risk of offending you further, I've got to admit, sweetheart, I still don't know what I did wrong."

"Last night was smoke and mirrors. This is me." Frannie gestured toward herself. "The real me. I'm sorry to disappoint you, but this is what I look like without all the artifice."

Comprehension broke over his face. "And you think I was just attracted to the trappings?" His eyes glittered with something far more dangerous than his earlier anger. "Well, now, Frannie girl, you've got it all wrong."

"No, I don't."

"Oh, yes, you do." His voice was low and silky, and it made her breath catch in her throat. He took a step toward her. "Besides, it looks to me like you've still got a little artifice going there."

Frannie nervously backed up. "What are you talking about?"

"Well, something artificial seems to be holding your hair back." He took two steps forward, invading her personal space, then reached behind her head and pulled the clip out of her hair. Her hair tumbled around her shoulders. His fingers sifted through it, arranging it on her shoulders. A shiver of pleasure shot through her. "There. That's better. Much more natural."

He inched even closer, until she could feel his breath on her face. "And about those glasses— I'm sure you weren't born with them. If you're going to be without any artifice, we'd better get rid of them, too." His fingers brushed her temple as he gently removed them. "Hmm. Well, now, look at that."

He was so close she could smell the faint scent of his shaving cream. It smelled clean and intoxicatingly masculine. "Look at what?" Her voice was a hoarse whisper.

"You. Now you look exactly like the woman I fantasized about last night."

He'd fantasized about her? Frannie's heart pounded hard against her ribs as he slid her glasses into his back pocket, then placed both hands on her upper arms. His touch was warm and electric. He shifted closer until his nose was less than an inch from hers and she could see the facets in his blue, blue eyes.

"Your eyes are incredible," he murmured. "So beautiful, so talkative. They're talking to me right now."

Frannie swallowed, her mouth dry.

"Can you see at close range?"

The ability to speak had deserted her. She nodded, her head bobbing as jerkily as a cork on a fishing line.

"Good. Because I want you to see how very, very much I want to kiss you. Right now. Just the way you look, at this very moment."

His eyes were hot and hungry, and she melted under the warmth of his gaze. Her skin ached to be touched. Her lips ached to be kissed. Her fingers ached to feel his skin. Oh, mercy, she was aching all over. Aching of want, of need, of impatience.

He moved with exquisite, torturous slowness. Slowly, slowly, his hands slid up her arms, to her shoulders. Slowly, slowly—oh, he was killing her with his slowness!—his face moved nearer, his eyes heavy-lidded but still open, still looking straight into hers. The first brush of his lips on hers was soft, as soft as butterfly wings, a soft taunt of a kiss. He pulled back, still gazing into her eyes, then resettled his lips over hers, deepening and expanding the kiss. When he took her bottom lip into his mouth and softly suckled it, she was shocked to hear a moan escape from her throat, shocked to feel her arms reach up to encircle his neck. And then she was lost, swept up like Dorothy from The Wizard of Oz in the tornado, transported to another time and place. The world disappeared, gravity lost its power, and her grip on reality grew weaker and fainter and increasingly insignificant.

"Wow, Frannie," Austin murmured some time later. He pulled back and looked at her, his eyes glazed, and his breathing labored. "Where did you learn to kiss like that?"

"I think you just taught me," she whispered.

"Well, then, come back to class." Lowering his head, he pulled her close and reclaimed her mouth.

Eight

The moon shone through the pickup windshield as Austin drove down the tree-lined road an hour later.

"It's hard to tell without my glasses," Frannie said, "but I think you're about to drive past the house."

Sure enough, the truck's headlights gleamed on a wooden clapboard sign that marked the long drive leading to the Big Sky Bed & Breakfast. Austin braked harder than he'd intended, causing the tires to screech. He glanced over at her and grinned. "Sorry. Guess my mind is still on other things."

Like that amazing, incredible kiss.

Austin had kissed a lot of women, but he'd never felt anything like the high-voltage heat he'd felt with Frannie. It was good thing they hadn't been standing in water at the time or they probably would have electrocuted each other.

He'd never gotten so carried away in a public setting that he'd forgotten about time and place and decorum. If another couple hadn't wandered down the path, he would have made love to Frannie right there in the leaves. As it was, he'd had her sweater halfway off when they were interrupted.

After the startled couple beat a hasty retreat, Frannie had pulled away, straightened her clothes and asked Austin to take her home. He'd been aching to take her back to his ranch, but he hadn't wanted to pressure her.

Hell, who was he kidding? He would have been willing

to apply all kinds of pressure if he'd thought it stood half a chance of working, but he'd figured it would do no good. Especially after they got back to the truck when he sat down and heard a loud snap.

Her eyeglasses. In his back pocket. He'd broken them to smithereens.

"I'm really sorry about breaking your glasses," he told her now for the umpteenth time as he turned into the driveway of the Big Sky.

"Don't worry about it. It was an accident."

The pickup reached the end of the long drive. Austin flipped off the engine and turned toward Frannie. A light shone from the porch, dimly illuminating her face. He reached out a hand and sifted it through her hair. It was silky and soft and sweet-scented, and it aroused a fresh burst of desire. "When can I see you again?"

She brushed a strand of hair out of her face, her eyes downcast. "I don't know if that's a good idea."

"It's a great idea." He reached out and cupped her chin, urging her to look at him. "There's so much chemistry between you and me that we should probably wear rubber gloves when we touch."

He was glad to see he'd made her smile. "I know."

"So?"

"So that's why I'm not sure it's a good idea."

Oh, no. She wasn't going to start another one of those conversations where he didn't know what the heck she was talking about, was she? "I'm not following you."

"We're awfully different."

"Sure. But in a lot of ways, we're a lot alike. We're both loners, we share similar tastes in music and movies, we make each other laugh, and we're incredibly physically attracted."

"We want different things out of life."

The only thing I want right now is you. Austin sucked

in a deep breath, then let it out. What he was dealing with here was a case of stubbornness. He knew a thing or two about stubbornness. Next to a woman, the most stubborn creature on the planet was a horse, and he'd had plenty of practice with stubborn horses. The best way to deal with a balky horse, he'd learned, was to walk away before the creature dug in its heels. That left the door open to try a different approach at a later date.

"Well, it's late. I'd better get you inside. Sit tight and I'll get the door for you." He strode around the truck, opened her door and helped her down. "I intend to pay for your eyeglasses," he said as he walked her to the porch.

"That's very kind, but it's not necessary."

"But I want to."

Frannie grinned. "I really don't want to have to explain to my optician how they happened to be in your back pocket."

Austin grinned back. "Well, then, let me know how much they cost and I'll reimburse you."

"That's not necessary." She hurried up the porch steps and stopped, her hand on the door. "Thanks for dinner. I had a wonderful time."

"Me, too." Austin stepped toward her, intending to give her another kiss.

She stopped him by opening the door. "Good night," she said softly.

"Good night." Austin watched her slip inside and close the door behind her. With a sigh, he turned and walked back to his truck.

There was a warmth about Frannie that drew him like a moth to a flame. She was amusing and independent one minute, shy and defensive the next. She was sassy and sexy and smart as a whip, and he was determined to see her again.

* * *

Frannie sat bolt upright in bed and looked around the darkened room. She thought she'd heard a blood-curdling scream, but the only sounds in the quiet bedroom were the pounding of her pulse and the rustling of the leaves in the tall oak outside the window.

She must have been dreaming, she told herself, brushing the hair out of her face. A scream sure seemed out place among the dream fragments she remembered—dreams of Austin's face and hands and lips, dreams of his kisses and caresses. There was plenty of material in that dream to make her heart race, but none of it seemed connected to a scream.

Austin was turning her life upside down, she thought with a sigh, leaning back against the pillow propped against the mahogany headboard. Just thinking about the kisses they'd shared made her hot and restless. Throwing off the covers, she glanced at her bedside clock. Two in the morning. She'd be a wreck if she didn't get some shut-eye. She'd already stayed up far too late, reliving every luscious detail of the evening.

Punching her pillow, she lay back down. But she'd no sooner closed her eyes than another ear-splitting scream ripped through the air.

Aunt Celeste! The scream was coming from her room.

Grabbing her robe from the foot of the bed, Frannie dashed out the door and across the hall to her aunt's room.

The dim glow of a night-light revealed Celeste curled in a fetal position in the middle of her double bed. Frannie reached out and touched her. "Aunt Celeste?"

The older woman grabbed her hand as if it were a lifeline. "Oh, Frannie. Is that you?"

"Yes. Are you all right?"

Jasmine darted into the room, her white nightgown floating around her. "Mom? What's wrong?" Flipping on a bedside lamp, she helped Celeste sit up. The older woman's cheeks were wet and her hands trembled as she tried to brush away her tears.

"What happened?" Jasmine asked.

"I—I had a dream. Oh, girls, it was so awful!"

Jasmine and Frannie exchanged a worried look. Jasmine sat on the bed and put her arms around Celeste, hugging her for a long moment. Frannie fetched a tissue from the nightstand and handed it to Celeste. Her aunt took it and wiped her eyes.

"I'm sorry I awakened you. Oh, I hope I didn't disturb the guests."

"I doubt if they can hear anything from this wing of the house," Frannie reassured her.

"Do you want to talk about it?" Jasmine asked. "When I was a little girl, you used to tell me it helped to talk about nightmares."

Celeste took a deep breath and shuddered. "This was more than a nightmare. It was like a vision. It was so…so vivid. So real!"

"It was just a dream," Jasmine said soothingly. Celeste took another deep breath and dabbed at her eyes.

"What was it about?" Frannie urged.

Celeste leaned over to her nightstand and lit a white candle. It was her ritual after any of these nightmares. Her aunt rubbed some bergamot oil into her left hand, from a skeleton-shaped vial she'd brought back from Louisiana. Then, when she'd finished, she replied, "It was like a dream within a dream. I was in the house—you know, the one Yvette and Blanche and Jeremiah and I lived in."

"The old Kincaid mansion," Frannie prompted.

Celeste nodded. "I was in my old bedroom, in bed, in the middle of the night, and it started storming. Oh, it was a horrible storm! The thunder boomed like it was right overhead, and the lightning lit up the sky outside the window like it was high noon. And then I saw Blanche sitting at the foot of my bed, and she was like the ghost of Christmas past. She said she was going to show me something. And then she was gone, and I thought I heard Jeremiah yelling in another part of the house. So I went downstairs, and—'' Celeste's voice broke.

"And what?" Jasmine urged.

"And there was an intruder—a big man—and he was fighting Jeremiah. I walked into the room, and he had Jeremiah pinned to the floor. And then the fighting turned into the storm, and then the storm was inside the house. And the next thing I knew…'' Her voice trailed away and she covered her face with her hands.

"What?"

Celeste's hands moved to the side of her face. "Lightning struck the room and there was a horrible thunderclap, and then it was raining blood. Blood was everywhere. And I started screaming, and…'' She inhaled a ragged breath. "And I guess that's when I woke up.''

"How horrible,'' Jasmine murmured, rubbing Celeste's arms. "But it was just a dream. You're awake now and we're with you, and everything is nice and safe.''

"But it was so real—and so awful!''

"No wonder it woke you,'' Frannie remarked. "A dream like that would wake the dead.''

Celeste's gaze rested on her. Her eyes grew large. "I almost feel like that's what's happening.''

A shiver coursed through Frannie. She should have thought before she'd spoken, given her aunt's frail mental state. "I didn't mean that literally. It was just a thoughtless remark, just an expression.''

Celeste nodded, her eyes somber. "I know, dear. But I can't help thinking that Blanche is trying to help me get my memory back. I think that's what all these dreams are about. But they're in some sort of code, and I don't know how to break it." Celeste's expression grew determined. "Not yet, anyway. But I intend to. I intend to do a little investigating of my own."

Jasmine exchanged a long, worried look with Frannie. She patted Celeste's shoulder and gave her an encouraging smile. "Well, the thing we need to investigate right now is how we can help you get back to sleep. Would you like for me to make you some warm milk?"

Celeste squeezed her hand. "No thanks, dear. I feel much calmer after talking about it. I think I'll just watch a little television here in my room until I get drowsy again. You two go on back to bed. I'm sorry I woke you."

Frannie and Jasmine kissed Celeste good-night, then headed out the door. Frannie pulled it closed behind her.

"I'm worried about her," Jasmine whispered. "She hasn't been herself lately."

"Maybe she needs to see a psychologist," Frannie suggested.

"I tried to talk her into that. She refused. She said this is a spiritual quest. She said it needs to unfold as it's meant to, in its own time and its own way."

Frannie sighed. Her aunt had been heavily influenced by the bayou beliefs she'd picked up the year she and her late husband had lived in Louisiana, and she had a deeply spiritual nature. She wasn't a bit surprised that she would insist on letting things take a natural course. "You know, Jasmine, I'm growing more and more convinced that she heard or saw something traumatic the night Raven disappeared—something so awful that she's subconsciously blocked it out."

Jasmine nodded. "I think so, too. I think even Mom has come to believe that. Otherwise, why would she want to be doing any investigating? But the whole idea worries me."

"Why?" Frannie asked.

"She says she wants to get her memory back, but I think a part of her is still afraid to face whatever happened." Jasmine pulled Frannie further down the hall, away from Celeste's room, and lowered her voice. "Mom doesn't know it, but I discussed all this with a psychiatrist that Summer recommended."

"And?"

"And the doctor said that if Mom doesn't want professional help, it won't do any good for us to push her into it. We need to let her deal with this at her own pace."

"How can we help?"

Jasmine sighed. "The doctor said we need to keep doing what we're doing now—support her, encourage her to talk and hold her hand in the middle of the night."

It didn't seem like much, but it made sense. Frannie nodded.

Jasmine gave a big yawn and stretched. "Right now, though, I think the best thing we can do is to go back to bed and get some sleep." She looked at Frannie and grinned. "Unless you want to sit up and tell me all about your date with Austin. I'm dying to hear about it."

"No, thanks."

"Must have been some dinner. I was already asleep by the time you got home."

"Go to bed." Smiling, Frannie turned her cousin by the shoulders and pointed her down the hall.

"Only if you promise to tell me everything—and I mean everything—at breakfast."

"Okay." Frannie headed back to her bedroom, making a mental note to grab a fast-food breakfast on her way to work.

Frannie hoped to sneak out of the house the next morning without seeing Jasmine, but before she'd even finished dressing, she heard a soft rap on the door. She turned to see Jasmine slip inside her room.

Frannie finished buttoning the top of her black linen skirt and grinned at her cousin, one eyebrow arched reproachfully. "Most people wait to hear the magic words, 'come in.'"

"Sorry, Frannie. I'm too excited."

She looked it. The petite brunette was practically vibrating with excitement.

Frannie turned to her closet and pulled her suit jacket off a clothes hanger. "About what?"

"You've got a visitor." She paused melodramatically. "Austin."

Frannie was chagrined at how hard her heart began pounding. "At this hour? It's seven-fifteen in the morning!"

Jasmine nodded, grinning widely.

"What does he want?"

"He said he wants to see you."

Frannie tried hard to remain calm, but her hand shook as she picked up her hairbrush. She reached for an elastic band to pull her hair back, then changed her mind. What the heck. He'd liked her hair down. She'd wear it that way.

Jasmine's gaze raked her over from head to toe. "You look great. You're wearing your contacts. Frannie, you've even got on a little makeup!" Jasmine beamed, then narrowed her eyes suspiciously. "Did you know he was coming by this morning?"

"No."

Jasmine looked less than fully convinced. "So what happened last night?"

"We went to dinner at the Lakeside Inn."

"And?"

"And then he brought me home." Frannie fastened on small gold hoop earrings.

"That was it? No kissing?"

Frannie's palms started to sweat at the memory. She reached for her purse. "I'd better get downstairs. It's rude to keep him waiting."

"Oh, he's fine. He's drinking a cup of coffee." Jasmine peered at her closely as Frannie walked past her and opened the door. "You *did* kiss him! Oh, this is so exciting!"

"Shh! Don't broadcast it to the entire house!" Hoisting her purse over her shoulder, Frannie hurried down the stairs, Jasmine close on her heels.

Austin was waiting in the vestibule, wearing jeans and cowboy boots, his dark hair slightly damp, as if he were fresh from a shower. A hint of dark hair peeked out the unbuttoned neck of his denim shirt. The sheer masculinity of him made Frannie's breath catch in her throat.

"Good mornin', Frannie."

She fiddled nervously with the strap of her purse. "Good morning."

His mouth curved into a slow smile. "At the risk of somehow insulting you, I think you look mighty nice this morning."

Frannie could feel her cousin's curious gaze practically burning a hole in her. "Uh...thank you."

"It occurred to me that you might need a ride to work or to the optometrist's office."

Jasmine poked her head around Frannie's shoulder. "Why would she need that?"

Frannie suppressed the urge to strangle her.

Austin seemed unperturbed by Jasmine's flagrant eavesdropping. "Well, I accidently broke Frannie's glasses last night."

Jasmine's eyebrows rose. "While she was wearing them?"

"No. I'm afraid I sat on them."

Jasmine looked at Frannie, no doubt wondering why she'd taken off her glasses in the first place. Frannie could practically see her cousin's mind putting two and two together and coming up with five. Jasmine's face creased into a knowing grin.

"Don't you need to do something in the kitchen?" Frannie asked her.

"What?"

Frannie eyed her sternly.

Jasmine sighed. "Oh, sure. Nice seeing you, Austin." She gave Frannie a sly smile as she sauntered off.

Austin grinned at Frannie. "I was afraid you wouldn't be able to see well enough to drive without your glasses."

"That's very thoughtful of you." And it was, Frannie thought. Surprisingly thoughtful. A feeling of warmth flooded her chest. "But I'm wearing my contact lenses."

"Oh. Great." He gave a relieved smile. "Well, as long as I'm here, can I take you to breakfast?"

It had been awfully nice of him to drive all this way just to give her a ride, and she didn't want to appear ungrateful. Besides, she reasoned, if she stayed here, she'd be subjected to the third degree from Jasmine. Those were both valid reasons for saying yes—reasons that had nothing to do with the fact she was dying to spend more time with him.

"That sounds terrific."

With a little wave to Jasmine, who was watching with undisguised fascination, Frannie walked through the door Austin held open.

"You really do look nice this morning," he said as they walked down the porch.

"So do you."

Austin laughed as he opened the passenger door on his pickup. "You must not be able to see very well with those contacts."

"Actually, I can see better with them than with my glasses."

Austin shot her a puzzled look, then walked around the truck and climbed in. "So why don't you wear them more often?"

Frannie shrugged. "I'm more comfortable in the glasses, I guess."

"The contacts hurt, huh?"

"No. I'm just more at ease in the glasses. I feel more— I don't know—relaxed or something."

"Why?"

Why, indeed. Why had she opened her big mouth? Why was it that every time she was around Austin, she found herself saying something she had no intention of saying?

She gazed out the window as he backed out of the drive. "I guess I feel all exposed in my contacts. Kind of undressed and naked."

"I like your naked face." Austin shot her a wicked grin. "Wouldn't mind seeing the rest of you that way, either."

Frannie hated the way her face burned. She wished she were more at ease with sexual banter, wished she could take it more in stride the way other women did.

Austin didn't miss a trick. "Hey, I didn't mean to embarrass you. That was a crude and pathetic attempt at humor. Sorry."

I'm the one who's sorry. Sorry I get so nervous and tongue-tied around you.

He glanced over at her as he braked at a Stop sign. "Guess I need to brush up on my social skills. The talk at ranches and racetracks isn't as high-brow as what I'm sure you're used to hearing at the bank."

Frannie seized the opportunity to change the topic. "Speaking of ranches and racetracks, how did you get from horse ranching to car racing?"

"Natural progression, I guess. I've always liked speed and power, always liked taking on a challenge. The wilder and meaner the horses were, the more I liked taming them. And like most teenage boys, I also loved cars."

"How old were you when you started racing?"

"Seventeen. It was a year after my old man died. I was working at a ranch in east Texas, and the boss hired a new foreman who was into amateur drag racing. He invited me to the track one day and, well, I got hooked right from the get-go. I started spending all my free time at the track, helping him fine-tune his car, and sometimes he'd let me take a turn in it when no one was around."

She loved the way his face lit up as he talked about it. "I take it you liked that."

"Are you kidding? I loved it. When I was eighteen, he had a streak of wins, and he qualified for the championship finals in Oklahoma City. He got some sponsors to pay the way, and two other guys and I went with him to serve as his pit crew. Then, just two hours before the race, he got sick, really sick. Seems he'd eaten a bad turkey sandwich and gotten a big ol' case of food poisoning."

"Oh, no!"

"Oh, yes. And it was bad. He ended up in the hospital and everything. Well, the sponsors were in a pickle. They'd paid the entry fee and painted his car with their logo and coughed up a whole lot of cash for the trip, and they weren't too happy about pouring all that money out and not even having the car in the race. So I offered to drive, and they took me up on it. I guess they figured it was better than nothing. The car would at least be in the race, and they'd get some exposure for their money. "

"So what happened?"

"Well, I won."

Frannie liked the modest, simple way he said it. "And everyone was surprised."

"No one more than me. The next thing I knew, folks were calling me to drive their cars, and then sponsors started making offers, then I got my own car, and then I moved from drag racing to the NASCAR circuit. And, well, here I am."

"I'm sure that's an understated version of things."

"It's a pretty fair summary." He parked outside the Hip Hop Café. "Is this okay?"

"Great. They make the best pancakes in the county."

Austin watched Frannie pour cream into her cup, then add a teaspoon of sugar. Even her smallest gesture fascinated him, from the way she held the spoon to the precise way she stirred her coffee. Without a doubt, she was the most fascinating woman he'd ever met in his life.

He wasn't sure what it was about her, exactly, that held him so in thrall. Maybe it was the novelty of her buttoned-down appearance. Maybe it was her forthright way of speaking, or her unexpected dry sense of humor. Maybe it was all of those things, combined with a soft, understated beauty that seemed to grow more pronounced every time her saw her.

And then, of course, there was the memory of that kiss.

He couldn't remember ever responding so intensely to someone on a first kiss. She hadn't seemed exactly immune to him, either. There had been more heat in that kiss than in his car's radiator after fifty laps. Whatever it was that drew people together—chemistry or pheromones or vibrations or whatever—the two of them had it in spades.

He rested his forearms on the green Formica-topped

table and watched her take a sip of coffee. Lucky cup, he thought absently. It got to feel the press of her lips.

"How come a great gal like you isn't spoken for?"

Frannie set down her cup and lifted her shoulders. "Mr. Right just hasn't come along."

"Had any close calls with Mr. Wrong?"

"One. When I was in college."

"What was he like?"

Frannie's eyes grew somber, but her mouth twisted into a wry smile. "That depends."

"On what?"

"On whether you're asking what I thought he was like at first, or what I'd found out about him by the time we broke up."

"I'd like to know both."

Frannie sighed. "Well, when I met him, I thought he was wonderful. A few months later, I'd learned he was a lower life form than plankton."

She had a real way with words. Austin grinned. "What happened?"

Frannie toyed with the handle of her coffee cup. "He dumped me for my college roommate."

Austin shook his head. "What an idiot."

Frannie raised an eyebrow, her mouth pulled into a small grin that was half amused, half sad. "You wouldn't say that if you'd seen my roommate."

"Yes, I would. I've seen you."

Frannie stared down at her coffee cup, nonplussed. "Well, Ginger transferred to the university the second semester of my junior year. She was the blond, busty, golden-girl type. A dead ringer for Pamela Anderson."

Austin reached out and covered her hand. The contact of skin on skin caused a rush of heat to shoot up his arm. He saw her eyes grow wide, saw her pupils dilate, and knew she felt it, too. "Well, you're better than any old dead ringer. You're one of a kind. A real original. Not a second-hand version of anyone.''

She kept her eyes down, but he saw her swallow, saw the corners of her mouth form a faint smile. He ran his thumb over her knuckles. ''So this guy—he really hurt you, huh?'' he asked softly.

Frannie shrugged, but her eyes remained downcast. ''I'm over it.''

''Are you?''

''Yes.''

''Prove it.''

Frannie looked up, her eyes wary. ''And just how do you propose I do that?''

''Say you'll spend Saturday with me.''

''Oh, Austin…''

He leaned forward. ''I'm going to be hitting the road Sunday, and I'll be gone for about three weeks. I have races every weekend, and my sponsors have me booked with appearances in between. Saturday is the only day I'll have off for nearly a month, and I'd like to spend it with you, at my ranch. We can go horseback riding. I'll even cook for you.'' He squeezed her hand and smiled. ''If you say no, I'm going to figure you're not really over this guy.''

Her eyes were full of reproach. ''I don't have to prove anything to you.''

His hand tightened over hers. ''No. But maybe you need to prove something to yourself.''

Frannie's fingers tensed inside his palm. She looked at him, and he could see the wariness in her eyes. ''Austin, I don't think this is too wise.…''

Austin grinned. ''I've never been accused of being too wise.''

''You and I… We're complete opposites.''

"Then I guess what they say about opposites attracting is true."

A waitress in a green-and-white-striped apron appeared at their table with two plates of pancakes. Austin reluctantly turned loose of Frannie's hand.

Don't give her a chance to say no, he reminded himself. Instead of pressing the issue, he needed to figure out a way around her resistance.

Nine

Frannie was searching through a file cabinet behind her desk at the bank later that day when she heard a familiar voice. "Hi, Frannie. Ready to go?"

Startled, Frannie straightened and turned to see Austin standing in front of her desk. "Go? Go where?"

His smile warmed the air around her by at least twenty degrees. "On a picnic. I've got two boxes of fried chicken in my car, and I'm taking you to the park."

Frannie shook her head. "I can't. I'm supposed to have lunch with a customer who wants to discuss investment options. My boss set it up."

"I know." Austin's smiled widened. "Pretty clever on my part, don't you think?"

She stared at him blankly. "You mean…"

He nodded. "Yep. I'm your client."

A surge of alarm rushed through Frannie.

"Come on," Austin urged. "Let's go. Boss's orders."

Frannie frowned. She didn't like the feeling of being set up. "Austin, this is entirely inappropriate."

"Now, why is that? I have an account at this bank. Aren't I entitled to a little personal service?"

"Probably not the kind of service *you* have in mind. Besides, Mr. Billings is going to expect me to come back with a piece of business."

"And you will. You can tell him you talked me into investing another hundred grand in C.D.s."

"I thought you didn't make safe investments. You said the stock market was a lot more exciting."

Austin leaned across the desk and gave her a sexy smile. "Frannie, Wall Street doesn't have anything nearly as exciting as the assets this bank has going for it."

He was manipulating her, pulling her strings like a puppeteer. And just like a puppet, she was responding. She fought against it. "Now wait just a minute. Just because you're going to put more money into this bank doesn't mean I'm going to...to—"

His lazy grin grew wicked and sexy. "To what? Engage in customer relations?"

"Exactly."

"Ah, Frannie, I'm not asking for anything inappropriate. All I want is a little of your time, and your boss was kind enough to allow me to have it."

Frannie put her hand on her hip. "Austin, if you've already decided to make the investment, then we can do the paperwork right now and forget about lunch."

"Did I say I'd already made the decision?" His eyes grew round and innocent. "Oh, gee, I'm sorry if I gave that impression. I'm afraid you'll have to talk me into it. Over lunch." He flashed a devilish grin.

Frannie felt her resistance crumbling. The more time she spent around Austin, the more it eroded. She would have none left at all if she were exposed to much more of his charm. She decided to play the guilt card. "What I really need to do with my lunch hour is pick out some new glasses."

"Okay. We'll take care of that together, then we'll go on our picnic."

"That will take too much time."

"Oh, don't worry about that. Your boss expects it to be a long lunch."

Frannie tensed. "What, exactly, did you tell him?"

"Just that I trust your judgment and want your financial advice, and that I have a very complicated portfolio to discuss. I told him it might take two or three hours."

It was useless to fight against his appeal. He was incorrigibly charming, relentlessly persistent. He could charm the raisin out of a cookie—and the heart out of Frannie's own chest.

Which was exactly why she was worried.

Frannie shot Austin an irritated glare as they left the optical shop. "You knew I didn't want you to do that."

"Do what?" Austin flashed that annoyingly innocent look again as he opened the passenger door to his pickup for her.

"Pay for my eyeglasses." She'd practically created a scene, trying to pay for them herself. But Austin had been quick on the draw with his American Express card. The staff had been smitten at having a celebrity in their midst and had been more than happy to let him have his way.

Austin climbed into the driver's seat, checked the rear-view mirror, then carefully pulled the pickup out of the parking spot. "Now, Frannie, I was responsible for breaking your glasses, and I felt really bad about it. You don't want me to go around lugging a big old load of guilt, do you?"

It was maddening, how impossible he was to argue with. Frannie shook her head and sighed.

"Besides," Austin said, a mischievous grin curving his lips. "Maybe now you'll think of me every time you put them on."

That's exactly what I'm afraid of, Frannie thought ruefully. Austin was getting too close, too fast. And she was going to end up getting hurt. She twisted around on the leather seat to confront him. "Look, Austin, I don't like the way you're trying to take over my life."

"I'm not trying to take it over." His mouth was smiling, but his eyes were serious. "I just want to share a little of it with you."

Of all the things he could have said, why did he have to say that? The one thing she wanted more than anything else was to share her life with someone—someone she could laugh with and confide in, someone to have and to hold and to love. Someone warm and bright and funny. Someone just like Austin.

The thought sent a dart of terror zinging through her. Oh, dear heavens, was she falling in love with him? No. She couldn't be. She wouldn't let herself. It would be a terrible mistake. Falling in love with Austin was a guaranteed ticket to a heartache. She was looking for forever, and he wasn't in the market for commitment.

He'd said he wanted to share a little of her life, Frannie reminded herself. The operative word in the statement was *little*. A little of her life, for a little while.

To her chagrin, she realized Austin was braking in front of the city park. He killed the engine and grinned over at her. "If you'll bring the chicken, I'll get the blanket and drinks out of the back of the truck."

Before she knew it, he'd led her to a secluded spot by the duck pond. He'd evidently scouted the park before coming to the bank, because he led her without hesitation to a spot too private to be stumbled upon by accident. A thick stand of red cedar shielded the site from the west and north, and a sprawling caragana bush provided privacy to the east. Even the view of the pond was partially blocked by a flowering potentilla shrub.

Frannie helped Austin spread a large blanket on the ground, then sank beside him, gazing out at a narrow stretch of pond, feeling hidden from the world.

"This is a beautiful park," Austin remarked. "Is the pond natural, or did the city build it?"

"It's actually an old quarry," Franny said. "It gets really deep just a few feet from shore."

"That must be why the water looks so blue."

Frannie leaned back on her elbows, enjoying the view. Through the yellow-flowered branches, she watched a toddler in a pink jumpsuit giddily throw pieces of bread to three white ducks across the pond. The child looked to be about two years old. Frannie could see the child's mother sitting on a nearby bench, a newborn baby in her arms, calling encouragement to the child. The woman's hair was the same shade of deep gold as the little girl's. Lucky woman, Frannie thought wistfully—two beautiful children. She probably had a husband who adored her, too. That was what Frannie longed for—a family of her own, a life filled with love.

It was not the kind of life she was likely to ever have with Austin.

Why was she having such inappropriate thoughts about Austin? She needed to stop it, and stop it immediately. Frannie sighed.

Austin heard her. "What are you thinking?"

Frannie gazed up at the overhanging branch of a blue spruce and stared through the deep green needles at a deep blue sky. "About what a gorgeous day it is," she lied.

Austin nodded. "Summers in this part of Montana are about as perfect as weather can get. I'm not a big fan of oppressive heat. I remember a summer in southern Louisiana when I thought I was going to parboil. And I spent more than a few summers in Texas and Oklahoma where I dry-roasted."

Frannie looked over at him. "You've lived a lot of places."

"More than my share."

She was curious about his family, curious why he seemed so reluctant to talk about them. "You said the

other day that your dad started moving when your mother
left.''

''Yeah.'' Austin unzipped the padded red cooler and
pulled out a soft drink. He popped the top and handed it
to Frannie.

Her fingers closed around the cold can. ''Where did she
go?''

''She took off with another guy.'' A pop top hissed as
Austin opened another can of soda. He took a long drink.
''She'd always had a dream about making it big as a
country-western star. She wanted to go to Nashville, and
he evidently promised to take her there.''

''So she just up and left you?''

''Yeah.''

Frannie sat stock-still, stunned by the concept. The idea
of abandoning a child was as alien to her as the concept
of life on Mars. ''What was she like?''

Austin shrugged. ''My memory of her is kind of hazy.
She wasn't like other kids' moms. I mean, she didn't cook
or clean, and she wasn't much on playing with me or
taking me places. She didn't even want me to call her
Mom when Dad wasn't around.''

''Why not?''

''She said it was bad for her image. She wanted me to
call her Daisy.'' Austin took a long swig of soft drink and
leaned back on his elbows. ''That was her stage name.''

''Was she talented?''

''Who knows? I thought she was, but I was just a
child.'' He gazed out at the pond. ''I don't remember
hearing people talk too much about her talent, but everyone always raved about her beauty. She had long blond
hair and big blue eyes, and she looked like a movie star.''

''What else do you remember about her?''

Austin stretched out his legs. ''She loved having an
audience. She sang and played guitar in bars every chance

she got, whether she got paid or not. She and my father had a lot of arguments over it.''

He picked a rock off the ground beside the blanket and absently turned it in his palm. ''My dad was working two jobs, trying to give her all the things she wanted. While he was working, she'd go to the bars. Some nights she'd take me with her. I'd just sit in the corner and pretend I was invisible. I got pretty good at it. Sometimes I believed I really was.''

Austin expertly skimmed the stone on the water, making it skip three times. The toddler across the pond watched with wide-eyed delight.

''Daisy was a big dreamer. She loved to talk about what life would be like when she made it big. She said we'd have a big white-columned house like in *Gone With the Wind,* and it would have a big swimming pool. She said we'd invite all the neighborhood kids over for swimming parties. We'd serve ice cream and soda pop.'' Austin's mouth twisted into a tight smile. ''I used to believe her.''

Frannie's heart turned in her chest. ''Oh, Austin,'' she whispered.

''The night she left, she told me she had to go away so she could become a big star. She said she'd come back for me and when she did, we'd live together in that big white-columned house. I clung to her and cried. I told her I didn't care about the house. I just wanted her.''

He picked up another rock. ''She pried my hands from her neck, and she walked away. The man was waiting for her outside. I could hear his car engine running when she opened the door.'' A nerve worked in Austin's cheek. ''I remember the way that door sounded when it closed behind her. It made a real empty, hollow sound. It seemed like I could feel it in the pit of my stomach.''

The lump in Frannie's throat made it hard to speak. ''Did you ever see her again?''

Austin shook his head. "We got word less than a year later that she'd died in a car accident." Austin threw another stone. "Right after that, we moved. And we just kept moving. Dad never wanted to put down any roots. Said life was easier if you never got too attached to anyone or anything."

The story explained so much about this man. "Is that what you think, too?" she asked softly.

Austin shrugged. "It sure makes it easier to do what I do for a living."

"But you've bought a ranch. You must want some roots."

"Oh, yeah. I've always wanted a place with some permanence, a place I could go back to." Austin rolled his eyes. "Disgustingly typical, isn't it? People always want what they've never had. In my case, that's a home."

And love. It sounded like he'd never had love. Did he want that, too? Frannie gazed at his profile, her heart twisting. If he did, he wasn't likely to ever admit it, even to himself. His brief experience with love had hurt too much.

"What was your father like?" she asked.

Austin lifted a shoulder. "The tall, silent type. After Mom left, he got to where he hardly spoke at all. He took it hard. He tried to be a good dad, but I don't think he knew much about raising kids. He did the best he could."

What a sad, lonely childhood he'd had. Frannie reached out and touched his arm. "Austin, I'm so sorry."

"Hey, there's nothing to be sorry about. That was all a long time ago. It's water under the bridge."

But Frannie wasn't so sure. Abandonment by a mother—that wasn't the kind of thing a person was likely to ever get over. And from what he'd just told her about his father, his dad had been too deeply wounded to take up the slack. She couldn't imagine the kind of pain Austin must have felt. Must still feel in many ways.

Austin straightened and smiled. "Hey, I'm starved. Let's dig into that chicken."

Frannie passed him a box, and the conversation drifted to lighter topics. They were finishing their chicken and discussing a mystery novel they'd both read when a loud splash sounded across the water. Frannie looked through the veil of leaves and flowers to see a flash of pink flailing in the dark water.

"The baby!" She jumped up from the blanket and headed to the pond, but Austin was ahead of her, kicking off his shoes and diving in. Frannie looked for the child's mother. She saw the blond woman standing by a baby carriage several feet away from the pond, her face a mask of terror.

"Emily!" the woman called. She placed the infant in the stroller and raced toward the pond, her expression panicked, her blond hair flying behind her. "Emily!"

The mother jumped into the water and disappeared beneath the surface just as Austin reached the drowning child. Frannie's heart pounded hard as she watched him turn the toddler onto her back, put his arm around her and swim for shore. Just then, Frannie saw the mother bob to the surface in the same spot she'd disappeared, only to sink once more back under the water. Oh, dear heavens, now the mother was in trouble, too!

Without stopping to think, Frannie plunged into the cold water. It felt like ice, and it tasted like algae. Frannie kicked off her shoes and plowed through it, reaching the flailing woman just as Austin reached the shore with the toddler.

The woman was gasping and sputtering, her eyes wide with terror. "My baby!" The woman went under again, then resurfaced. "Help my baby!"

Frannie gulped a breath as she treaded water. "She's being helped. Let me help you."

The woman sank again. Frannie dove down to the spot she'd last seen the woman and brought her to the surface. The woman's arms whirled like a windmill. Her sneakered feet kicked Frannie in the stomach. "Can't swim," she spluttered.

Frannie spat out a mouthful of water, trying to remember the lifesaving training she'd taken as a teenager. "Put your arms around my neck. I'll take you to shore."

The woman frantically grabbed at Frannie's head, nearly drowning them both.

"Stop trying to swim," Frannie ordered. "Put your arms around my neck and just hang on."

The woman grabbed at her again. Frannie struggled to keep her head above water. "I can't help you if you're fighting me. Let me get you to your children."

The mention of her children seemed to calm the woman, and Frannie managed to haul her the few yards to shore. Austin reached them just as Frannie's feet touched bottom. Holding the toddler in one arm, he extended his other hand to pull Frannie and the woman ashore.

Gasping, Frannie helped the woman to her feet. The woman staggered forward, then reached for her bawling daughter, who was sobbing into Austin's neck.

The child grabbed her mother, and the woman clutched her as if she'd never let her go. "Emily," she murmured over and over. "Oh, Emily."

Austin hauled Frannie against his chest, his arms tight around her. "Are you okay?" he murmured.

"Yes. Is the child?"

"She's fine."

The mother looked up, her eyes filled with tears, her

voice thick with emotion. "Thank you. I don't know how to thank you. Both of you."

"We're glad you're okay." Austin ran a hand down his face, rubbing the water from his eyes. "Your girl didn't lose consciousness, but she swallowed a lot of water. It would probably be a good idea to get her checked out by a doctor."

The woman nodded. Her face was streaming with tears and pond water, and her eyes were full of gratitude. "I don't know how to thank you. I looked away for a moment while I changed the baby's diaper, and the next thing I knew, Emily was in the water."

"I'm glad we were here to help."

"How can I ever thank you?"

"You just did. Do you need a ride home?"

"Oh, thank you, but no. We live just a block away." After more effusive thanks, the woman and her dripping daughter traipsed toward home, pushing the baby carriage.

Austin looked down at Frannie. "Are you sure you're all right?"

Frannie nodded.

Austin's gaze latched on to hers. His eyes held a warm light that made it hard for Frannie to breathe. "You're really something, Frannie. A real-life hero."

"I was about to say the same about you. You saved that baby's life. You got to her in nothing flat."

"I didn't even see the mother, I was so focussed on getting to the child." His teeth gleamed as he smiled. "You handled that like a pro. Did you used to be a lifeguard or something?"

Frannie shyly grinned and nodded. "Or something. My dad made my brother and me take lifesaving training. He said that if we were going to live near a lake, we needed to know what to do in an emergency."

"Your dad sounds like a smart guy."

Frannie ruefully looked down at her sopping clothes. "I wonder what he'd say I should do about this."

"If he's as smart as I think he is, he'd probably say you should go home and change clothes." Austin tightened his hand around her arm. "Come on, let's go gather up our stuff."

They trudged around the grassy bank of the pond, back toward the heavy foliage that hid their picnic blanket.

"How am I going to explain showing up at the bank dressed in different clothes, after an extended business lunch with you?"

"Hmm. Guess I've put you in a compromising position, haven't I?" Austin rubbed his chin. "Well, maybe you should just take the rest of the day off."

Frannie lifted her eyebrows. "I go off to lunch with you, then call to say I'm not coming back?"

"I see what you mean." He suddenly snapped his fingers. "You could say you caught a sudden cold." He pulled her close to his side and ran his hand up and down her arm, causing Frannie to shiver. "You *are* cold, aren't you?"

She was actually growing quite warm, but she wasn't about to tell him that.

"On the other hand, honesty is usually the best policy," he continued. "Why don't you just tell them the truth?"

"That our business lunch was a picnic in the park? It doesn't sound very businesslike."

"Nonsense. We can discuss business here just as well as we could in a restaurant. But if it'll make you feel better, I'm perfectly willing to sit down and discuss investments now."

"That still won't explain why I changed clothes. And an explanation about getting wet during a lifesaving maneuver is going to sound pretty fishy."

"Not as fishy as we smell."

Frannie gave him a playful push. "Thanks a bunch, Austin. You're really helping a lot here."

"I pride myself on being helpful."

Frannie couldn't help but smile.

"Maybe I should pour a can of soft drink all over you," Austin suggested with a mischievous smile. "That way you can say I spilled a drink on your clothes and you needed to go home and change."

"Well, that's more plausible than the truth, but it's still going to look suspicious."

Austin stopped and lifted a branch of a red cedar tree. "Here's our blanket. You nearly walked right past it."

Frannie stepped into the secluded area and plopped down onto the blanket. "Face it, Austin. Whatever I say, people are going to think you and I are fooling around."

"Well, if that's what they're going to think anyway..."

Before Frannie knew it, he was beside her on the blanket, pulling her into his arms, his mouth slanting over hers. The kiss was playful at first, but it rapidly deepened into something more, something lusty and hungry and primal. A surge of heat pulsed through her as his lips mated with hers. His mouth was hot and demanding, his body warm beneath the wet cotton of his shirt. The feel of his masculine, muscular body stirred an urgent need to get closer. Frannie's arms wound around his neck and she pulled him down until he was lying on top of her on the blanket.

He rained kisses everywhere—her neck, her ear, her jaw—then returned again to her mouth, deepening the kiss. Frannie clutched at him, drowning in sensation, drowning just as surely as either of the victims they'd just rescued. She felt the weight of his body over hers, felt the warmth of his hand cupping her bottom, felt the hard length of his arousal pressed intimately against her. She moaned and arched against him, wanting more.

His hand moved up the inside of her thigh, pushing up her skirt and warming her skin. Heat shot through every muscle, every pore, every molecule of her being. The heat melted away all reason, all sense of time and place, leaving her with only a fierce, aching need.

His mouth slid down her neck to her chest, to her breast. He took her taut nipple in his mouth, through the silk of her blouse and the satin of her bra. The pressure was exquisite, but she wanted more. She longed for the feel of skin on skin.

She reached up and began unbuttoning her blouse, giving him access. One button, two buttons, three buttons…

A woman's voice broke the heady spell. "They came from over here somewhere."

Austin pulled back and looked at Frannie. Twigs snapped and leaves crunched. Someone—several some-ones—were coming.

Austin put his finger to his lips, then rapidly helped her refasten her buttons.

"Maybe they've already left," said a man's deep voice.

Austin pulled down Frannie's skirt and helped her sit up. Adjusting his khakis, he cleared his throat and slowly rose to his feet. "Are you looking for someone?"

Frannie saw the woman she'd rescued point to Austin. "That's him! That's the man who saved Emily. And there's the lady who saved me."

Frannie scrambled to her feet, self-consciously straightening her skirt. The woman had changed into a long denim jumper over a white T-shirt, and she was still pushing the baby carriage. She held the toddler, who was now wearing a yellow playsuit with Sesame Street characters on the front. Both of them still had wet hair.

Behind the woman stood two men. The tall one had a large camera dangling from a thick strap around his neck, and the other one was carrying a notepad.

The shorter man stepped up and stuck out his hand. "Hello. I'm Hugh Miller with the *Whitehorn Journal*. I understand you two just saved my wife and little girl."

Austin shook the man's hand. Hugh's face broke into an enormous smile. "Say, aren't you Austin Parker, the race car driver?"

Austin nodded.

"Oh, wow! This story is going to be huge! Do you mind if we get some pictures? Maybe of you holding Emily, and the lady here with my wife?"

Austin gave Frannie an apologetic smile. "Well, at least you won't have to worry about anyone not believing why you needed to change clothes," he murmured under his breath. "Now you'll have documentation."

But Frannie was too busy reeling from the impact of that kiss to worry about awkward explanations. It was alarming, how quickly and thoroughly Austin could turn her from a clear-headed, sensible loan officer into a panting, lovelorn vixen.

"Oh, dear," said the woman, gazing at Frannie's bare feet. "You've lost your shoes!"

She was afraid she'd lost far more than a pair of pumps, Frannie through ruefully. Somewhere between the rescue and the kiss, she'd completely lost her heart.

Ten

Summer walked into the kitchen of the bed-and-breakfast the next morning, carrying a stack of newspapers. She kissed Aunt Celeste's cheek, then plopped the papers onto the kitchen table and hugged Frannie. "I'm so proud of you!" She gave her a tight squeeze, then stepped back and beamed. "Imagine—our Frannie is a real, live, honest-to-goodness, front-page, news-making hero! She's famous!"

Frannie winced and hunkered down over her bowl of cereal. "The paper made entirely too much out of it."

Over at the stove, Jasmine grinned. "No, it didn't. You saved someone's life."

"Doctors like Summer save people's lives everyday," Frannie said.

Aunt Celeste smiled at Frannie. "Yes, but most doctors don't have the most popular race car driver in the country with them when they do it."

"And most of them don't rescue the wife and child of the local paper's news editor," Jasmine added as she turned out the last pancake onto a plate. She walked over and looked at the newspaper spread on the table.

Summer seated herself at the kitchen table. "I stopped by a newsstand to pick up some extra copies on the way here, and the story has evidently been picked up by a wire service. That picture of you and Austin with the baby and her mother is in just about every newspaper in the country!"

Celeste grinned. "You know what they say—everyone in the world will be famous for fifteen minutes. This is your time in the limelight."

"Great," Frannie said dryly. "My fifteen minutes of fame arrive, and I'm dripping wet."

"Oh, hey, get a load of this!" Jasmine looked up from her copy of the *Whitehorn Journal,* her eyes sparkling. "It says you're Austin's girlfriend!"

Frannie's heart pounded hard. "That just goes to show you can't believe everything you read."

"It says you were having a romantic picnic in the park when the accident occurred," Jasmine read.

"It was a business lunch," Frannie corrected.

Jasmine's gaze said she wasn't buying that for a moment. "Oh, come on! A picnic?"

"In the park?" Summer asked.

Celeste raised a questioning eyebrow. "Just the two of you?"

Frannie sighed. This was exactly the reaction she was likely to get from the staff at the savings and loan. She'd called the bank yesterday afternoon to explain that she needed to take the rest of the day off, but Mr. Billings had been in a meeting, so she'd left a message with his secretary. She wasn't looking forward to all the questions she was going to face this morning.

She glanced at her watch and sighed. It was time to head in and face the music. Her chair screeched on the wooden floor as she pushed back from the table. "I'd love to sit around and chat some more, but I've got to get to work."

"Not so fast!" Jasmine said. "I want to know about this romantic picnic."

"There's nothing to know." Frannie picked up her empty cereal bowl and carried it to the sink.

"Sure there is. Was it?"

"Was it what?"

"Romantic."

All three women turned and regarded her curiously. Frannie felt her face flame.

Jasmine and Summer looked at each other and smiled triumphantly. "It was!" they said in unison. They smacked their palms in the air in a high-five.

"You two leave Frannie alone," Aunt Celeste scolded. "Jasmine, you need to take those pancakes out to our guests."

Jasmine moved to comply. Summer glanced at her watch. "And I'm due at the hospital. I'd better get going, too." She rose and smiled at Frannie. "I just had to stop by to congratulate Whitehorn's newest heroine."

Frannie shot her aunt a grateful look as her cousins left the room. She rinsed her cereal bowl and placed it in the dishwasher, then glanced at Celeste. "I heard you up in the night. Were you having more dreams?"

The older woman nodded, her face solemn. "I dreamed Blanche visited me again."

A shiver chased up Frannie's arms. "Was it the same dream?"

Celeste shook her head. "Raven was with her. They were both sitting on the end of my bed and Blanche was trying to tell me something again, but this time I could understand what she was saying."

"What was it?"

"To look to the past. That old faces and old places would help jog my memory."

The chill on Frannie's arms moved to her spine. "What do you think that meant?"

"I don't know. But since Blanche has come to visit me a few times, I thought I'd return the favor."

"How?"

"I plan to visit the cemetery this morning."

The cemetery held the graves of both Blanche and Jeremiah. Given her aunt's fragile mental state, Frannie wasn't sure it was wise. What if she had a flashback and it was more than she could handle? Frannie's brows knit in a worried frown. "Are you sure you're up to that?"

Celeste nodded. "A part of my life is missing, and I want to get it back. I think Blanche is trying to show me the way."

"I don't think you should go alone."

Aunt Celeste smiled. "That's just what Jasmine said. She offered to go with me."

"Well, I hope you took her up on the offer."

"I did. We're going after all the guests finish breakfast."

"Good luck," Frannie said, kissing her aunt on the cheek. She lifted her purse from the back of the oak chair and slung the strap over her shoulder.

"You, too." Celeste smiled as Frannie headed to the door. "Enjoy your fifteen minutes of fame."

Frannie grimaced. "I think I'd enjoy a tooth extraction more."

Make that an unsedated tooth extraction, Frannie thought an hour later. She hated being the center of attention, and she found herself just that. She forced her mouth into a smile as Mr. Billings droned on about her bravery during an impromptu speech in the middle of the bank lobby following the weekly meeting of the bank's board of directors.

"...And since Frannie's brave actions yesterday exemplify this bank's commitment and dedication to the community, the board of directors has authorized me to give her this certificate of commendation." He handed Frannie an official-looking document. "Furthermore, Frannie, the board wants to use your picture and story in a new advertising campaign to promote the high standard of service we offer here at Whitehorn Savings and Loan.'' Mr. Billings turned and shook her hand. ''On behalf of all of us, thank you for representing us so well.''

All of the bank staff broke into applause.

''Would you like to say a few words?'' Mr. Billings asked.

A feeling of panic grabbed Frannie's stomach and squeezed it like a vise. She longed to just sink right through the floor. ''I'm…I'm not good at speaking in public,'' she murmured to Mr. Billings.

''Oh, come on.''

The panic escalated to terror. She couldn't. It was impossible. The last time she'd tried speaking in public…

The memory sent a surge of fear pulsing through her. She fought to tamp it down. ''No, really. I—I—''

To Frannie's relief, Mr. Billings's secretary whispered something in his ear, causing him to change the focus of his attention. Smiling broadly, he raised his hands to quiet the crowd. ''I've just learned that the Mayor of Whitehorn plans to present an award to Frannie and Mr. Parker tomorrow, and that a TV camera crew will be in town to film it for a segment of the show 'Celebrity Spotlight.'''

Another round of applause greeted Frannie. Frannie felt her face burn.

''What do you think of that, Frannie?'' Mr. Billings asked.

''I'm not a celebrity,'' she muttered.

''You are now.'' Mr. Billings beamed and patted her on the back.

Everyone else seemed to want to pat her on the back, too, or to shake her hand or to offer congratulations. It seemed to take forever for the crowd to disperse. When it finally did, she saw Austin seated in a chair in front of her desk, grinning at her. She would have thought she'd exhausted all of her emotion reserves, but her heart gave a wild, erratic little jump at the sight of him.

Trying hard not to let him see the effect he had on her, she walked to her desk, sank into her chair and gave him what she hoped was a calm smile. "How did you get in here without being carried on the shoulders of your adoring fans?"

"They were too preoccupied with you." And it was no wonder, Austin thought. She was adorable with her cheeks all rosy, her eyes as wide and bashful as a deer's. She was so different from the women he routinely met. Most of them were attracted to his fame. If it ever disappeared, so would they.

Not so with Frannie. She was shy and retiring and seemed to actively dislike the spotlight. He couldn't help but notice how pale she'd grown when Mr. Billings had asked her to say a few words. She wasn't ego-driven or self-involved, he reflected. She was low-key and warm and caring, and those were among the things he loved about her.

Loved? The thought alarmed him. No, that was the wrong word. He meant liked. Her unassuming demeanor was one of the things he *liked* about her, along with her soft shiny hair and gray-green eyes and that slim, shapely body she kept covered up like a race car under a tarp.

"It's ridiculous, all the fuss everyone is making," she was saying.

"Well, when a story involves the wife and child of a newspaper editor, it tends to get blown out of proportion." He eased himself out of the chair and perched on the edge of her desk. "Which is why I came by."

"What do you mean?"

"Seems the camera crew that Mr. Billings just mentioned wants to tape more than just the mayor's award.

They want to do a whole segment of their show about us.''

"Us?''

Austin nodded. "My chief sponsor, SeaBreeze Detergent, is thrilled about all the publicity our rescue is getting. They contacted the show and urged them to do a story. Under the terms of my contract, I'm supposed to cooperate.''

"Well, fine, but leave me out of it.''

"Hey, I'm not going on the air and taking all the credit. I won't do it without you.''

"No.'' Frannie shook her head. "No way. I hate public speaking.''

He reached across the desk and placed his hand over hers. "It won't be that bad.''

"I—I can't speak in front of a crowd. I—I freeze.''

"There won't be a crowd. It won't be like making a speech. It'll just be talking to a reporter, just like you're talking to me now.'' He lifted her hand from the desk. "Please, Frannie?''

He could see her reluctance, see the difficulty she had saying yes. He turned her hand over and stroked her palm. "Please?''

She sighed. "They're not going to ask me to stage a reenactment, are they?''

He laughed, an irrational sense of delight sweeping through him at the thought that she was doing this for him, despite her misgivings. "You won't have to get in the pond. I promise.''

"Well…'' She pushed a swath of hair behind her ear and sighed. "You're very hard to say no to, do you know that?'' Her lips curved up in a small smile that he found incredibly seductive.

"Glad to hear that.'' He squeezed her hand and returned her grin. "Since I'm on roll, I might as well go ahead and ask you for another favor."

"What?"

"Well, I have a new computer, and I don't know anything about setting it up. I'm wanting to get it up and running before I leave town, but I don't know anyone who's computer literate besides you." He gave her his most pleading gaze. "Would you come out to the ranch and help me get it set up on Saturday?"

Frannie sighed. "It seems to be my day for saying yes to you."

Austin smiled wolfishly. "Then maybe I should keep asking questions until I get to some really interesting ones."

Frannie grinned. "Maybe you should get the heck out of here and let me catch up on my work."

"All right. My agent arranged for the camera crew to come to my ranch early in the morning. I'll bring them here afterward—if you think that'll be all right with Mr. Billings, that is."

"Are you kidding? If it'll give the bank any publicity, it'll put Mr. Billings in seventh heaven."

"Well, then, I'll see you tomorrow. And on Saturday." He reluctantly turned loose of her hand as he rose from her desk. "And to pay you back for helping me out, I'll treat you to a horseback ride and a steak dinner."

He left the bank before she could voice an objection, pleased that his ploy had worked. He'd figured she'd have a hard time turning down a plea for help. Now all he had to do was buy a computer.

Frannie squinted against the afternoon sun as the female reporter angled the microphone toward her face. "How would you describe your relationship with Mr. Parker?"

Frannie shot Austin a look that reminded him of a horse

about to rear and run. "He's a…a friend. And a client of the bank where I work."

"Is that all?"

Austin stepped up, putting his arm around Frannie. "Our personal relationship is just that. Personal. And we intend to keep it that way."

The reporter's bright red lips curved in a knowing smile. She turned her attention back to Frannie. "I don't know if you're aware of it, but Austin was just voted the sexiest man in racing by female race fans. What do you have to say about that?"

Austin held his breath. He cared a lot more about Frannie's opinion than the public's.

He was relieved to see her smile. "Well, his fans obviously have excellent taste."

The reporter laughed, and the field producer signaled for the cameraman to turn off the camera.

"Good," the producer said. "We'll shoot the mayor's award, and then we'll be finished."

About time, Austin thought. It had been a long day. The TV crew had arrived at his ranch at seven that morning and had shot footage of his race car, his horses and home. Next they'd gone to the bank. As Frannie had predicted, her boss had been overjoyed at the publicity. The next stop had been the scene of the rescue, where the woman they'd saved, her child and her husband had all effusively thanked Austin and Frannie on camera. And now they were waiting outside city hall, where a large crowd had gathered in front of a portable stage.

"Here comes the mayor now," the producer said, raising his voice to be heard over the loud patriotic music of the Whitehorn High School band.

Mayor Ellis Montgomery, a tall, portly man with a self-important attitude, strode toward them. After a round of greetings and introductions, the producer asked, "What's the agenda for the ceremony?"

"Well, I'll make a few remarks, then I'll present the awards. After that, we'll ask Mr. Parker and Miss Hannon to each say a few words."

Frannie shook her head. "Oh, no. I can't."

"Oh, sure you can," the mayor said.

"No. You don't understand. I can't. Really. I—I freeze up in front of a crowd, and…"

"Oh, nonsense. You only have to say a few words."

Austin had never seen Frannie so pale. He put an arm around her and felt her tremble, and felt a surge of anger at the mayor's insensitivity. It took an effort to keep his voice even when he spoke. "You know, I don't much feel like talking, either, Mayor. Why don't you handle all the speaking duties, and Frannie and I will just come up and accept the paperwork."

The mayor immediately backed down. "Well, of course, if that's the way you want it. I just thought, with the cameras and all…"

"That's how we want it."

"Well, of course," the mayor sputtered.

Austin looked at Frannie and a surge of protectiveness shot through him, a fierce protectiveness he'd never felt before in his life. Her eyes were wide, her cheeks colorless, and her teeth were practically chattering. She looked scared to death—scared beyond mere bashfulness or stage fright. It was the look of a driver getting back into a car after a painful crash, the look of someone who'd had first-hand experience with terror.

Something in her past had hurt her, and hurt her deeply. He didn't know what it was, but he intended to find out. For reasons he didn't understand, it was important that she tell him, that she trust him, that she need him, be-cause…

Because what? Oh, no, he was going soft in the head, having such mushy thoughts about a woman. He'd never needed anybody, and he'd sure as heck never wanted anybody to need him. He liked Frannie and he wanted to help her, that was all. The only reason he thought about her day and night was that he had a raging case of the hots for her. It was a perfectly normal, perfectly natural case of hormones. He was making a big deal out of nothing.

The mayor mopped his brow. "Well, if you two are ready, I guess we'll get things underway."

Austin glanced down at Frannie and was hit by a fresh wave of emotion, warm and unexpectedly sweet. It socked him right in the midsection and felt suspiciously like tenderness.

It wasn't, of course. He didn't feel things like that. He didn't allow himself to. It was attraction—plain, pure, physical attraction, that was all.

"You ready?"

Her eyes were still wide and terrified, but she smiled bravely. "I am if you are."

"I've been ready for quite a while." And he wasn't just talking about the awards presentation, he thought grimly. He was more than ready to do something about this insane, obsessive attraction he felt for Frannie. It was unnatural, wanting someone so much and not being able to satisfy the craving. Playing the gentleman for this length of time had left him so addled he scarcely knew himself anymore.

He'd always been able to separate his emotions from his physical needs, and he was certain he'd be able to again. Once his relationship with Frannie progressed to the physical level, his emotions would surely settle down and he'd once again be able to think about something besides Frannie's smile, Frannie's scent, Frannie's voice, Frannie's touch and Frannie's sweet, sweet taste.

Eleven

Jasmine held up two padded satin hangers. "Which is better, the yellow dress or the green one?"

Frannie studied the dresses, her head propped on her hands as she sprawled on Jasmine's bed. It was Thursday evening, and she was trying to help her cousin decide what to wear to a wedding in Billings that weekend. "I don't know. Why don't you try them on?"

Jasmine had started to do just that when the phone rang.

"I wonder which of your many admirers this is," Frannie teased.

"It's just as likely to be one of yours," Jasmine replied from somewhere under the green dress. "You've had several men ask you out since the dance, but you've turned them all down." Jasmine's head reappeared at the neckhole. "Not that I blame you. No one can compare to Austin. Maybe that's him now."

Frannie's heart pounded at the thought. She reached for the telephone and lifted the receiver. "Hello?"

"Well, hi there, kiddo. How are you?"

"David!" Frannie sat up, startled to hear the unmistakable voice of her older brother. She swung her feet off the bed, her mouth pulling into a wide smile. "Long time, no hear! I'm great. How are you?"

"Proud as punch to have a hero for a little sister."

Frannie felt her face heat. "You saw that photo, I take it." Over the past few days Frannie had received phone calls from her parents and several distant friends who'd seen the picture of her and Austin in their local newspapers.

"Yep. In the *Atlanta Constitution*. Could have knocked me over with a feather. How the heck did you get involved with the likes of Austin Parker?"

A wave of apprehension shot through Frannie. "We're not involved."

"Uh-huh. Right." David's tone was more than a little dubious.

"And what do you mean, 'the likes of'?"

"Well, he's not the average, run-of-the-mill guy I expect to be dating my sister. But for the record, you have my complete approval."

"You know Austin?"

"Not personally, but I've heard about him. And after I saw that picture of you with him in the paper, I ran a little background check on him."

"A background check? You're kidding."

"Hey, you're the only little sister I've got. Anyway, he seems like a straight-up kind of guy. Everyone I talked to says he's as nice as they come. Runs a clean race, never tries any funny stuff with his car, pays his taxes, doesn't have any kind of a criminal record. Far as I can tell, the guy has never even gotten a traffic violation."

Frannie remembered how carefully Austin drove his pickup and smiled. "I'm not surprised."

"Yeah, well, he gets my seal of approval."

"He's just a friend."

"Yeah. Sure."

"He is!"

"Uh-huh. Hey, kiddo, what's with all the deaths on the casino construction site? I've been following the case about Raven, and I saw an article in the paper the other day that another body had been found at the construction site."

"Yes. They don't think the two deaths are related, though. They think the second one was an accident or suicide."

"Hmm. Pretty strange coincidence. Is Uncle Jeremiah still a prime suspect in Raven's death?"

"Yes. A couple of the pistols at the old house could be the murder weapon. They're running tests on them now."

"So how's Aunt Celeste taking all this?"

Frannie sighed. "Not too well. She's been questioned several times, but she can't seem to remember anything. She draws a blank about the night Raven disappeared. The detective in charge of the case thinks she might have blocked something out of her mind."

"Hmm. This is even more intriguing than I thought. Look, Frannie, I have some vacation time coming in soon. I thought I'd use it to come visit and take the opportunity to look into this whole situation while I'm there."

"It would be wonderful to see you."

"Well, you'll have that privilege in just a few weeks."

"Great!"

"Well, I just wanted to call and tell you I'm glad your lifesaving training didn't go to waste."

Frannie grinned at the phone.

"I'm proud of you, kiddo."

Frannie coiled the cord around her finger. "It wasn't that big a deal. The lady was just yards from the shore."

"Yeah, but if you can't swim, a yard is the same as a mile. Especially in an old quarry."

"Well, I'm glad I could help. But I didn't do anything that special. Anyone would have done the same thing in that situation."

"You're overestimating the human species. In my line of work, I see plenty of people who wouldn't have lifted a finger. Anyway, I'm awfully proud of you, sis."

Frannie felt her throat thicken with emotion. "Thanks."

"And not that it makes any difference, but Austin gets a thumbs-up from me."

"We're just friends," Frannie said.

"Right. Whatever you say." She could practically see his sardonic smile. "See you soon, sis."

"Okay. I'll look forward to your visit."

"David's coming for a visit?" Jasmine asked as Frannie hung up the phone.

Frannie nodded. "He's intrigued by all the news reports about a mystery in his hometown."

"Good. Your folks will be thrilled to see him, and Mom will, too. Maybe he can help get her mind off ghosts and nightmares and murders."

"Maybe." Frannie watched Jasmine as she looked at herself in the mirror. "I'm hoping this wedding in Billings will do the same thing. I'm glad you're going with her."

"Oh, I love weddings. You can meet the cutest men at them. Are you sure you don't want to come with us? Mom said her friend invited all of us."

"I can't. I've got plans."

"With Austin?" Jasmine fixed her with a keen gaze.

Frannie shrugged and looked away. "He needs some help setting up a new computer."

Jasmine's eyes twinkled. "A likely story."

Frannie threw up her hands. "Why does no one believe there's nothing going on with Austin and me?"

"Because it's obvious that something is. Anyone who's seen the two of you together can feel it in the air."

"He asked for help, and I told him I'd help. That's all there is to it."

Jasmine smiled at her. "Well, if your help requires you to stay overnight, you won't have to answer to me or to Mom. We're spending the night in Billings, and Mom is putting the No Vacancy sign on the door of the bed-and-breakfast for the weekend.''

"Don't be ridiculous, Jasmine. Things aren't like that with Austin."

Jasmine's eyes narrowed as her lips curled into a knowing, catlike smile. "Maybe not yet. But I can't wait to get an update on Sunday."

Saturday dawned bright and clear, a perfect day for an outing. The bed-and-breakfast's three guests checked out early, and Celeste turned the sign on the front door to Closed as soon as Tommy and the elderly couple's cars left the driveway.

Frannie stood in the foyer with Celeste as Jasmine lugged two suitcases down the front stairs. "Are you only taking one bag, Mom?"

"Yes. It's just an overnight trip." Celeste turned to Frannie. "Are you sure you don't want to come with us?"

"I'm sure."

"She's got better things to do than go to a wedding," Jasmine volunteered. "She's spending the day with Austin."

Celeste smiled and patted Frannie's arm. "How nice. I really like that young man."

Jasmine grinned. "Frannie does, too, but she won't admit it."

Celeste looked at her watch and moved toward the door. "Come on, Jasmine. If we want to get there by noon, we'd better get started."

Frannie helped Celeste carry her bag to the car. "You two enjoy yourselves." A change of scenery ought to do Celeste good, Frannie thought.

She watched them drive off, then climbed into her white Camry and drove to Austin's ranch. He'd wanted to come pick her up, but Frannie had wanted the independence of having her own transportation. It gave her a sense of control, and heaven only knew she needed as much of that as she could muster whenever she was around Austin.

He'd given her detailed instructions, and she found her way easily. She turned onto a gravel road off a two-lane highway, traveled two miles, then came to a large stone entry gate. Above it hung an iron sign proclaiming The Range.

Austin had a home on the range. Smiling at his sense of humor, Frannie turned her car onto the narrow gravel drive. The road wound around a densely forested hill, then took two more turns before a house came into view. It was a large, rambling, one-story house made of rock and natural wood that blended in with its surroundings. It had a deep, covered porch supported by large cedar beams, and the tall, multiple windows were all framed in rough-hewn wood.

Not a white column anywhere in sight, Frannie noted. She had secretly wondered if Austin's house would resemble the one his mother used to promise him. It made sense that it wouldn't, she thought as she pulled the car into the circular drive. That house had been his mother's dream. Austin was the kind of man who would have dreams of his own.

She braked and turned off the engine, still looking at the house. It suited him, she thought, unfastening her seat belt. Like him, it was rugged and handsome and larger than life.

Austin stepped out of the heavy wood entry as she shut the car door. Her heart seemed to slam in her chest, as well, as he walked toward her. "Did you have any trouble finding your way?"

"No. You gave excellent directions."

He gave her a friendly peck on the cheek. Frannie inhaled the faint scent of shaving cream and soap, and found it strangely hard to breathe.

"Good," he said, casually looping an arm around her shoulders. "Well, I hope you can do the same on my computer."

Her short leather boots clattered on the wooden porch. He held the front door for her, and she walked into an enormous room filled with oversize pine furniture, colorful Navajo rugs, Native American pottery and artwork. A massive stone fireplace sat against one wall. The back of the room was largely glass and looked out over an immense outdoor pool.

"This is beautiful," Frannie breathed, looking around.

"Thanks. I like it."

"I remember you saying you were in the process of remodeling. Is this room part of that?"

Austin shook his head. "No. Just the bedrooms. The family that lived here before me had four daughters. All of the bedrooms except for the master one had flowered wallpaper, pink carpeting and dainty little chandelier-type light fixtures. Since most of my guests will be members of my pit crew, well, it just didn't seem fitting somehow."

Frannie grinned. "It *is* kind of hard to picture Tommy sleeping in a room with pink carpeting."

Austin grinned. "Yeah. He might start showing up for breakfast in a lacy pink robe and curlers. I couldn't risk that."

Frannie laughed.

"You want some coffee?"

"Sounds good." Frannie followed him through the living room into a large sunlit kitchen with hardwood flooring, granite countertops and custom-made pine cabinetry. Best of all, there was another fireplace in the kitchen, next to a large old farm table. "What a wonderful kitchen! It must be a real pleasure to cook in here."

"I'm afraid I really wouldn't know."

"You don't cook?"

He pulled two brown mugs down from the cabinet and gave a sheepish smile. "My culinary skills don't extend much beyond steaks and salad, but I've got those down to an art. I'll show you tonight."

What else was he planning to show her tonight? The thought sent a shiver running through her. His fingers brushed hers as she accepted a mug of coffee from him. Sexual awareness hung thick in the air, giving it an electric charge. Frannie looked around nervously, wanting to break the tension. "So where is your computer?"

He waved his hand toward a room across the living area. "In the study."

Frannie followed him through a pair of open French doors into a well-lit, pine-paneled room lined with bookcases. A large old desk stood in the center of the room, and piled in the center of it was a brand new computer, its cords still wound and wrapped with wire. Its empty box sat on the floor.

"I started to try to assemble it, then figured I'd just wait for you. I figured it would be easier for you to start from scratch than to undo my mistakes."

"This won't take long," Frannie said. She got busy and ten minutes later, the computer was assembled. She turned it on, watched the screen flicker, then studied the menu. "It's loaded with software. Which do you want me to show you how to use?"

Austin stood behind her and gazed at the screen. "I don't know. Something that'll let me keep track of my finances, I guess."

Frannie seated herself in the cordovan leather chair behind the desk and clicked an icon for an accounting program. Austin pulled up a matching chair and scooted it close beside Frannie's.

It was hard to concentrate on the computer screen with him sitting so close to her. His shoulder was several inches from hers, but she could practically feel the heat emanating from his body. She forced herself to focus on the program and carefully explained it to him.

"That's all there is to it." Frannie slid the mouse and pad over to him. "Here. Try it for yourself."

He hesitated, and it occurred to her that he might not know anything at all about computers. "Do you know how to use a mouse?"

"Why don't you show me?"

His hand looked intimidatingly masculine. Tanned and large, with a smattering of dark hair across the top, it completely covered the mouse. A wayward thought rushed through her mind. What would it feel like to have that hand on her body, moving across her skin?

But this was not the time for erotic conjecture. Taking a deep breath, she placed her palm on top of his hand. A shock wave of sensation flashed through her, making her stomach tighten. He seemed to feel it, too, because his long fingers curled around the mouse.

She forced her thoughts back to the computer. "Have you ever used a computer before?"

"Yes. This is a different type, though."

"Well, the mouse is for moving the cursor." She clicked it and guided his hand. He leaned forward, his face close to her hair. She heard him inhale deeply, as if he were smelling her shampoo. There it was again—that incredible awareness, that tension that stretched like a high wire between them. She pulled back. "You try it."

He guided the cursor across the screen.

"Very good. Now, see if you can open the program."

He hit the wrong icon. "Oops."

"Try again."

"I think I need some more help."

Frannie moved her hand back over his. He leaned in close again, so close she could feel his breath on her neck. "That's better," he murmured. He cut her a sideways glance as she helped him guide the mouse. "I guess you took all kinds of computer courses in college."

"A few."

"I've always wished I had more formal education." He clicked the mouse, and the program opened.

Frannie looked at him. "It's never too late to go to college."

"Maybe I will someday."

"What would you study?"

"I don't know. Literature, science, history. All the stuff that an educated person knows. I'd just like to feel more educated."

As famous and successful as he was, he had an inferiority complex about his education. The realization touched her. "You know, being educated isn't really a matter of having a college diploma. It's a matter of having knowledge and knowing how to use it. It seems to me that you know an awful lot about a lot of topics."

"I'd like to know more."

"About any particular topic?"

"There's one that's really got my interest."

"What?"

His gaze latched onto hers and wouldn't let go. "You."

Frannie swallowed, her throat suddenly dry. She stared at him for what must have been several seconds. She should change the subject, she should move, she should do anything but sit here and stare at him, letting the heat between them intensify. She should, but she didn't. Instead she found herself asking in a voice so low she could barely recognize it as her own, "What do you want to know?"

"Everything."

The air was charged with an almost palpable tension. Frannie tried to pretend it wasn't. "There's not much to know."

"Sure there is."

Pull back. Pull back, or it will be too late. Oh, dear Lord, maybe it already was. She swallowed hard. "Ask me one question and I'll answer it. Then we'll get back to the computer."

"All right." He reached up and touched her face, his finger soft as a feather. "What are you thinking right now?"

"Well, uh, I, uh…" *I'm thinking how much I want to kiss you. I'm thinking that your mouth is the sexiest, most sensual thing in the world. I'm remembering how it felt on mine and thinking about how much I want to feel it again. I'm thinking that I've fallen head over heels for you, that I have no defenses against you, that I want to feel your arms around me, your hands upon me, your skin against mine. I'm thinking that fighting something I want so desperately is impossible. I'm thinking that if I had a shred of an instinct for self-preservation, I'd stand up and leave right now.*

She jerked her gaze back to the computer and forced a lightness she didn't feel into her voice. "I'm thinking that I should probably show you the word processing program next."

Austin let out a long sigh, then rubbed his jaw. "Frannie, I've got to admit something."

"What?"

"Well, don't hate me for this, but I already know how to use a computer."

"You do?"

He nodded, his expression contrite. "I already have one. It's a different type, and I'm no great whiz at it, but I already know how to do the basic stuff."

Frannie stared at him. "So why did you act like you needed my help?"

"Well, I did need some help in setting this one up. And I've never used an accounting program before."

Frannie didn't like the feeling of having been duped. "If you're familiar with computers, you could have figured it out yourself."

"I know." Austin's chest rose and fell as he inhaled and expelled a deep breath. His gaze was direct and remorseful. "The truth is, I didn't think you'd come if I just invited you to spend the day with me. Knowing what a nice person you are, though, I figured you wouldn't be able to turn down a plea for help."

She knew she should be angry, should feel some measure of outrage, but she couldn't seem to muster any. "Let me see if I've got this straight. You deliberately took advantage of my good nature?"

"Pretty much." His blue eyes were doleful. "I guess I wouldn't blame you if you decided to leave."

If she had any sense, she would. It was obvious where all of this was headed. The attraction between them was clearly out of control. The problem was, her feelings for him were out of control, as well. She was head over heels in love with him.

She loved him. The realization broke over her like a freshly cracked egg, pouring slowly down around her, revealing the bright yellow center of truth.

She loved him. She could suddenly see it, could suddenly see it with sparkling clarity. She could also see that she was kidding herself, trying to keep from getting involved with him. She was already involved. It might not be wise, but it was too late for wisdom.

"Please don't leave," he murmured.

How could she? How could she leave, with the discovery that she loved him fresh on her heart? She'd waited all these years to feel this way about a man. She might never get another chance to experience real, heartfelt love. She couldn't leave. Not now.

Besides, he was going to do the leaving for both of them. He was going leave tomorrow.

Frannie looked into his blue, blue eyes.

"Don't leave," he whispered again.

Her mouth pulled into a soft smile. "I won't. I intend to stay and make an honest man of you."

One dark eyebrow lifted quizzically.

"You promised me a horseback ride and tour of your ranch, and I'm going to hold you to it."

His eyes sparkled as he grinned. "I also promised you a steak dinner."

"Well, then, I'll hold you to that, too."

"I'd rather just hold *you*." There was no mistaking his meaning. His gaze deepened and darkened, and ran caressingly over her face.

Frannie strove for a light tone, but her voice came out so low and soft, she was afraid she sounded like Mae West. "Pay off your promises, and then we'll see."

But it was no longer a matter a question of "if," Frannie thought. It was merely a question of when, where and how.

Twelve

Frannie walked beside Austin as they strolled down a path through the woods for about a quarter mile. The dense forest around the house had given way to rolling pastureland. He'd taken her hand as they'd left the house, and he was still holding it. Frannie reveled in the sensation. All of her senses seemed heightened, and the world somehow seemed more intense—the sky looked bluer, the pines smelled crisper, the sun felt warmer. She felt as if she could stroll hand-in-hand with Austin forever.

As they rounded a bend in the path, a large rusty-red outbuilding loomed ahead. Austin gestured toward it. "There's my shop."

"Your shop? I thought you were going to show me the garage where you keep your race cars."

Austin grinned. "It's one and the same."

"It looks like an old-fashioned barn," Frannie commented as they approached the building. She looked out over the rolling pastureland, where two similar buildings sat on separate hills. "In fact, it looks like you have three old-time barns."

"Glad you think so. It's supposed to look that way." Austin pulled out a set of keys and unlocked the wide, sliding door of the building. "When I bought the place, I had to build a shop and a stable, but I didn't want them to be eyesores. The architect suggested that we keep them all in the same style as the existing barn."

"It looks great," Frannie commented. "Like something from a postcard."

Smiling, Austin rolled up the door to reveal am enormous automotive garage.

He flipped on bright overhead lights as they stepped inside.

Frannie looked around and marveled. It was larger and better equipped than any service station garage she'd ever seen—and definitely cleaner. "This looks more like an operating room than a garage," she murmured.

It was true. The shop had two car lifts and all kinds of computerized testing equipment, and all of it gleamed as brightly as Aunt Celeste's freshly polished silver. So did the tools lined up on the shelves and in the rolling toolboxes. Even the concrete floor looked as if it had just been pressure-washed.

She turned to Austin in amazement. "I've never seen a garage so spotless!"

Austin grinned. "I like a clean shop."

Two low-slung, red-and-yellow race cars covered with decals and logos sat at the back of the shop. Frannie headed toward them. "You have two race cars?"

"Actually, I have four. These two are for use on short and intermediate tracks—tracks that are just a half mile to two miles. The other two are for use on superspeedways—tracks that are two and a half miles around."

"Where are they now?"

"On their way to a studio in New York City. Tommy and another member of the crew left yesterday to haul them out there."

"Why are they going to a studio?"

"I'm supposed to shoot a TV ad for SeaBreeze on Monday. Then the cars and I are scheduled to make an appearance at a big automotive show in New Jersey. After that I'll do some appearances in Philadelphia, then I'll head to Atlanta on Thursday for a qualifying race on Friday.''

Frannie shook her head. ''I had no idea there was so much involved in racing.''

''There's a lot that goes into it.''

''I guess you don't just drive the cars to the racetracks, huh?''

Austin grinned. ''Nope. I have a special truck for hauling them.'' He pointed to a large empty spot at the back of the garage. ''It's usually parked there. And the motor home is parked beside it.''

Frannie's eyes widened. ''You have a motor home?''

''Yep. It's home base when we're at a track.''

''Is that where you sleep?''

''Sometimes. I usually stay in a hotel and let the crew stay in the motor home.''

Frannie looked around, trying to absorb it all. She pointed to eight immense, shiny motors. ''What are those?''

''Extra engines.''

''You change them out?''

Austin nodded. ''After every race.''

Frannie shook her head at the incredible expense of it all. A truck, a motor home, extra engines... It was mind-boggling. ''It's amazing, what it takes to operate one race car.''

''It's a pretty pricey enterprise,'' Austin agreed. ''That's why we have sponsors.''

''SeaBreeze Detergent pays for all this?''

''Well, they're my main sponsor. I also have a soft drink company and a tire chain. Sponsorship's the name of the game.''

Frannie looked at the decals that covered the cars. ''How does a sponsorship work?''

Austin grinned. ''It's pretty simple. A company pays

me a huge amount of money, and I let them put their logo on my car and clothes. I also agree to do a certain number of public appearances and ads for their product. That's what SeaBreeze was holding over my head about that TV show.''

Frannie had no idea that racing was so involved. ''Can I get a closer look at the cars?''

''Sure.''

He walked with her to the far end of the garage. Frannie stared as they neared the vehicles. ''They don't have any doors!''

Austin nodded, his face creased in a huge grin. ''It makes them more streamlined. We crawl in and out through the windows.''

Frannie leaned down and peered through the window. ''There's no passenger seat, either!''

Austin smiled. ''Nope. That's where we put the primary and secondary ignition systems.''

Frannie gazed at the sparse interior. It looked stripped down, just dials and controls and foot pedals. ''They don't exactly look like luxury vehicles.''

''They're strictly built for speed,'' Austin agreed.

''What about safety?'' Frannie asked.

''Oh, there are lots of safety features.'' He leaned in beside her and pointed to the black dashboard. ''The gauges are all extra large and easy to read. And we have a built in fire extinguishing system, padded roll bars and a shock-resistant seat.''

''How fast do you drive?''

''About two hundred miles per hour.''

Frannie felt as if he were talking at that speed as he explained about engine components, using foreign words such as ''bulkhead'' and ''crankshaft'' and ''bearing bosses.'' Frannie didn't understand half of what he was talking about, but she loved the way his eyes shone as he talked about the cars.

"Do you keep track of all the publicity you get?" she finally asked.

"Yep." Austin led her to the side of the garage, pulled open a large drawer and extracted an enormous black folder that looked something like an artist's portfolio. Placing it flat on a workbench, he unzipped it to reveal large, plastic pages with laminated newspaper articles inside. "My publicist sends me these. There are some great shots of the cars in action."

Frannie thumbed through the pages, less interested in the cars than the photos that clearly showed Austin. The book was full of them. Austin in a one-piece scarlet racing suit, holding his helmet. Austin seated inside the car. Austin holding a trophy. Austin standing between two gorgeous girls, each one kissing his cheek.

An unfamiliar flash of jealousy stabbed through Frannie as she gazed at the photo. "I guess you have a lot of fans."

Austin nodded amiably. "We've got our share."

Frannie pointed to the photo of the two women. "Looks like some of them are pretty enthusiastic."

Austin grinned. "I guess you could say that."

"Do you have a lot of women fans?"

Austin nodded and shifted his stance. "There are quite a few ladies who follow the races."

"Like groupies follow rock bands?"

"Sort of."

"Do women throw themselves at you?"

Austin rubbed his chin. "Some of them can be pretty persistent." He took a step toward her, his eyes warm. "But, hey, Frannie, you've got nothing to worry about."

Frannie's heart pounded hard. Were her thoughts so transparent that he could read them?

He lifted a strand of her hair and twirled it around his finger. "I have no interest in being a notch on some bimbo's bedpost."

The statement was so blunt and outrageous that Frannie couldn't help but laugh.

"It's true," Austin said, and his eyes looked as though he meant it. "I did my share of cattin' around a few years ago, but not anymore. It's not worth the risk, physically or financially."

"What about emotionally?"

"That has never been an issue."

At least he was honest, Frannie thought. She wondered if his emotions would be involved as far as she was concerned. He probably wouldn't want them to be.

Frannie swallowed around an unexpected lump in her throat. She didn't want to ruin today by worrying about tomorrow. She loved him, and she wanted to experience that love to the fullest.

She flipped another plastic page, and saw a photo of Austin pouring champagne over the heads of five smiling men. "Your crew?"

Austin nodded and grinned. "They're the best in the business. Those guys do all the real work. I just do the fun part."

"The risking-your-life part," Frannie reminded him.

"Yeah, but still, I just sit behind the wheel and drive. Those guys change out the tires, gas up the engine and service anything else that needs it in just sixteen seconds flat."

"Sixteen *seconds?*"

Austin nodded. "Amazing, isn't it?"

"I'll say." Frannie flipped through more pages. "What actually happens at a race?"

"Well, on Fridays, we have the qualifying rounds. The top finalists in that are the only ones who get to enter the real race. Along with the actual racing, there's a lot of mandatory schmoozing that goes on. The sponsors bring their top clients, and we have to mingle with them at dinners and parties and what-not.''

"Do you do something special before the race to psyche yourself up?"

Austin shook his head. "This is the only sport where the participants don't get much time to mentally prepare. There's usually a big sponsorship breakfast, then photos beside the cars and last-minute schmoozing with the sponsors." He closed the portfolio and zipped it. "There is a drivers's prayer meeting, though, right before the race. I always go to that."

"Do you pray to win?"

"Nah. I pray that nothing I do ends up hurting another person. That's my worst fear about racing." He put the portfolio back in the drawer, then turned back to Frannie. "And I pray to drive my best so I don't let my team down. That's it."

Frannie's heart opened like a morning glory at dawn. She loved him, all right. How could she not?

"You said you've been in some accidents."

Austin nodded. "It happens."

"An accident at two hundred miles an hour must be pretty serious."

He gave a short nod, then looked away and shifted his stance. "Hey, what do you say we head back to the house, pack a lunch, then saddle up a couple of horses?"

He didn't want anyone to care, she reminded herself, just as *he* didn't want to care. He'd told her as much. His detachment was his winner's edge. If she didn't want to drive him away, she couldn't let him know how deeply she'd grown to care about him.

"Whoa, there, Charlie Horse." Frannie pulled on the reins and leaned back in the saddle as the large roan gelding hurried toward the corral.

Austin watched her hair gleam in the last rays of sunlight and grinned. He couldn't remember when he'd spent a more enjoyable day. He and Frannie had ridden up a winding mountain trail and picnicked on a flat ledge that offered an expansive view of the ranch. They'd laughed and joked and talked, then talked some more. He didn't know when he'd talked more freely, or enjoyed a woman's company more. They'd covered anything and everything—everything, that was, except the incredible sexual attraction sizzling between them.

Jumping down from his mount, Austin tethered his horse to the fence, then turned to help Frannie dismount. She didn't really need the help—he'd been pleased to discover she was an experienced horsewoman. All the same, Austin wanted to be there to catch her as she climbed off her horse, simply because he wanted the excuse of feeling her warm, soft body against his.

He was acting like a schoolboy, he thought ruefully, trying to find sneaky little ways of getting close to her. He'd wanted to kiss her all day, but he'd restrained himself, afraid he'd scare her off if he came on too strong. He needed to take his time. If he were smart, he'd let her make the first move.

He'd never known waiting could be so hard. He couldn't remember ever wanting a woman as much as he wanted Frannie.

Austin put his hands on her waist as she swung her leg over the horse and jumped down. The scent of her soft perfume filled his nostrils for a sweet, short moment, then she pulled back and rubbed her leg.

"I haven't been on a horse in a while, and I'm starting to feel it," Frannie said, massaging her calf. "I think Charlie Horse has given me one."

"I've got just the cure for that. A long soak in the hot tub."

Frannie's eyes grew large and round. "I—I didn't bring a swimsuit."

"That's okay. Tommy bought me half a dozen women's swimsuits as a housewarming present."

He enjoyed the way Frannie's mouth fell open. "Why?"

"He said I needed to be prepared if company dropped by."

"Yes, but half a dozen?"

Austin uncinched the saddle on Frannie's horse and hauled it off the animal's back. "I'm afraid he's got some warped fantasies about bachelor life." Austin shot her a grin. "He said he didn't know what size to get, so he ended up buying every size the store carried." Austin grinned at the memory. "He said it was his proudest moment. The salesladies were all whispering behind his back that he must have a harem."

The vision of the stocky, grizzled man surrounded by a bevy of bathing beauties made Frannie laugh. "So have any been worn?"

"You'll be the first."

Frannie slid the saddle blanket off her horse's back and draped it over the corral fence. She turned and did the same with the blanket from Austin's mount as he removed the saddle, then picked up the blankets and headed for the tack room. He followed her with the saddles.

"Where are your curry brushes?" she asked, putting away the blankets.

"Over there." He indicated a shelf off to the side. Frannie picked up two of them and headed back to the horses. Austin followed, trading out the horses's bridles for soft harnesses while Frannie groomed the horse she'd ridden.

He liked the way she just pitched in and helped. He

liked the way she talked to the horse in low, soothing tones and brushed its coat in long, smooth strokes. Heck, he liked everything about her. And the more he was around her, the more he found to like.

He realized he was standing there like an idiot, watching her do all the work. He picked up the second brush and quickly groomed his own mount, finishing just as she did.

"Let's give these fellas some oats and put them out to pasture," he said.

He led the horses through a gate on the far side of the corral, unhitched the lead ropes and turned them loose. They ambled over to the water trough. Austin grabbed a bag of oats from inside the stable and poured it into two feed buckets. The horses eagerly trotted over and were soon head-down in the feed.

Frannie followed Austin back to the stable as he put the oats away. "Who takes care of the horses while you're gone?"

"I have a husband and wife caretaker team. They're terrific. She cleans the house, and he sees to the grounds and horses."

Austin and Frannie returned to the tack room to put away the brushes and hang up the bridles. Austin locked the door as they left, then turned to Frannie.

"How's your leg? Can you walk back to the house?"

"Oh, sure. It's just a little stiff, that's all."

Austin stifled his disappointment. He'd been hoping she'd need to be carried. "Well, a soak in the tub should fix that right up."

"Considering that I now smell like Charlie Horse, a soak is probably a good idea."

The thought of Frannie in a swimsuit made Austin break a sweat. He was already in hot water where she was concerned, and he wasn't anywhere near the hot tub.

* * *

The sun was setting behind the mountain ridge out the west window as Frannie stood in the yellow guest room, holding the can of beer Austin had handed her as they'd passed through the kitchen. She gazed at the assortment of tiny bikinis in the dresser drawer in dismay. "Oh, dear," she murmured, lifting out a tiny white thong.

Austin had guided her to the guest room and told her where to find the swimsuits. He'd shown her where the towels were kept, and pointed out the adjacent bathroom. He'd told her everything she needed to know, except that Tommy's taste in ladies' bathing suits ran from skimpy to barely there.

Frannie pulled out a hot pink bikini top and stared at it. The bra cups were approximately the size of her head. Oh, dear, she certainly hoped these sizes didn't indicate Austin's usual taste in women, or he was going to be sorely disappointed.

Frannie took a long swig of beer, then pawed through the drawer until she found a black string bikini that appeared to be her size. It was far more daring than anything she'd ever worn—just two little triangles of fabric up top, and a scant amount of cloth on the bottom that tied together at the hips. The only good thing about it was that at least it wasn't a thong.

Taking another long draught of beer for courage, Frannie scrambled out of her clothes and into the swimsuit. It took two more long sips before she worked up the nerve to look at herself in the mirror.

"Oh, my," she murmured. It was a shock, seeing herself so scantily clad. And the really shocking thing was, she looked…great.

She turned to one side and then the other, staring at her image. Maybe the beer was blurring her vision—after all, she wasn't much of a drinker. Or maybe it was her new haircut, or the fact she was wearing her contacts. Whatever it was, she sure didn't look like the plain Jane she'd always assumed herself to be.

She looked attractive. And desirable. Seductive, even.

The thought sent a rush of heat coursing through her. Oh, dear. What would Austin think? She was too shy to just stroll out there in front of him, wearing only this! It was scantier than her most daring underwear. Looking around, she grabbed her denim shirt and put it on over the bikini, buttoning it nearly to the neck. Rapidly swallowing the rest of her beer, she took a deep breath and headed down the hallway.

She found Austin standing in the kitchen, wearing a pair of blue swim trunks. Her mouth went dry at the sight of his shirtless chest. Good heavens, his body was even better than she'd imagined. His biceps were large, his pectorals well-defined, his chest covered with dark hair that narrowed to an enticing line that disappeared into his waistband.

She suddenly realized she was gawking at him. She pulled her eyes away from his chest to find him gazing at her with amusement. "Want another beer?"

She probably shouldn't, Frannie thought. She was already feeling a little tipsy from the first one, but it was helping to take the edge off her nervousness. "Sure," she said.

Austin popped the top on the can and handed it to her, his eyes on her legs. He glanced up, his gaze appreciative. Frannie fiddled self-consciously with the top button of her shirt, feeling practically naked.

He picked up a stack of towels he'd placed on the kitchen counter, then led the way through the French doors of the living room out onto the deck. He'd turned on the whirlpool as soon as they'd headed back to the house, and now steam was rising in the cool twilight air.

He set the towels on a padded chaise longue. "Can I take your shirt?"

She folded her arms across her chest, feeling as skittish as a colt. "I—I think I'll keep it on for a while. It's starting to get chilly."

"The tub is heated," he pointed out.

"I'll wear it anyway."

Austin looked at her as if he were wondering if she was wearing anything under it. "Didn't you find a swimsuit that fit?"

"Yes. If those tiny scraps of fabric actually qualify as swimsuits."

Austin grinned. "I'm afraid Tommy belongs to the less-is-more school of thinking when it comes to women's apparel."

"What about you?"

His grin deepened. "It depends on who's doing the wearing."

A shiver chased through her. He seemed to notice. "Let's get in the water where it's nice and warm." He stepped into the tub and held out his hand. She gingerly took it and stepped in with him.

The water was warm, very warm, and turbulent. Just as he made her feel inside.

Austin stepped down further, then motioned to the ledge. "Have a seat."

She sat where a water jet bubbled against her back. With water covering her up to the chest, she felt herself relax. "Oh, this feels great."

Austin held out his hands. "Give me your sore leg."

Frannie turned sideways and gingerly placed her calf in his lap. His thigh felt hard and muscular, and his fingers on her skin sent quivers of heat racing up her leg. She nervously took another long pull on her beer.

He gently kneaded her muscle. "You have beautiful legs."

"Thanks. Yours are pretty nice, too."

Mortified at what she'd just said, she took another long drink. Austin laughed. "Frannie, are you getting tipsy?"

"I'm getting a bit of a buzz," she admitted. "I'm not much of a drinker."

"Well, now is not the time to turn into one." Austin took her beer and placed it on the deck, out of her reach, then shifted closer so that both of her thighs now rested on top of his. "I want you to know exactly what you're doing tonight."

"What am I going to do?"

"Darned if I know." He slowly massaged her calf, his fingers both strong and gentle. "But I want you to be in complete control of your faculties."

It was hard to be in control of her faculties around him—especially when she was wearing practically nothing under her shirt, and his hands were rubbing her leg so erotically. Yet he said he wanted her to be.

"You're a really different kind of guy," she found herself saying.

"What do you mean?"

"Oh, I don't know—decent. Straightforward. Honest."

"That hasn't been your experience with men?"

Frannie leaned her head back against the side of the tub and rolled her eyes. "Ha!"

"Tell me about the guy from college."

"He was a jerk. End of story."

"So how did you meet him?"

She hadn't talked about Joe in a long while. There were parts of the story she'd never talked about at all. Maybe it was the beer, maybe it was the deepening twilight, maybe it was just Austin. Whatever the reason, she found the words just spilling out. "Joe was in my junior calculus class. He was having trouble with the course, and he asked if I'd help him." Frannie stared up at the sky, at the enormous orange moon hanging low over the mountains. "One thing kind of led to another. I was crazy about him. I thought he was The One." Frannie gave Austin a wry smile. "And then I got a new roommate."

Austin's eyes looked silver in the moonlight. "The Pamela Anderson look-alike."

Frannie nodded. "She was new to Montana, and she didn't know anybody on campus. I invited her to go out with Joe and me a few times because I didn't want to leave her sitting alone in the dorm room. Like an idiot, I missed out on all the signals that anything was brewing between them."

Austin's hand continued to rub her calf. The muscle didn't hurt anymore, but she decided not to tell him just yet. His fingers felt delicious, and she didn't want him to stop. "Anyway, about that time, a professor talked me into running for class treasurer. He said it would look good on my résumé. All of the candidates had to make a speech to the junior class the day of the homecoming ball. I was nervous about it, but I had it all prepared. I'd practiced and practiced and practically knew it by heart."

The memories were getting uncomfortable now. She took a deep breath. Seeming to sense her anxiety, Austin shifted closer and started rubbing her neck.

"What happened?"

"Right before I was supposed to give the speech, I went to lunch with a friend at a pizza place. The restaurant had high-backed booths where you couldn't see who was seated behind you. Anyway, my friend went to the restroom, and while she was gone, I heard a familiar voice from the booth behind me."

"Let me guess. Joe and Pamela."

Frannie gave a mirthless smile. "No. That would have

been a lot easier.'' She leaned her head back as Austin's fingers massaged her neck. "It was Joe, all right, but he was with a new pledge to his fraternity. Each upperclassman was assigned a freshman fraternity member that he was supposed to mentor—sort of a big brother, little brother arrangement.''

"I get the picture.''

"Anyway, Joe was talking to his plebe, giving him the lowdown on life, as if he were some kind of all-knowing, experienced man of the world. It probably would have been funny, listening to him, if the topic hadn't hit so close to home. Joe was explaining that women are like currency. 'You use them to get what you want,' Joe said. 'Take Frannie, for example. I used her to get through a couple of tough math classes.'''

"What a jerk,'' Austin muttered.

"Oh, it gets better. This freshman—I think his name was Nathan—said something like, 'I thought you and Frannie were kind of serious.' Joe laughed and said I didn't know it yet, but we were seriously finished. He'd already found my replacement.''

"Man.''

Frannie's mouth twisted into a wry smile. "Joe said he was ready to trade up. He said being seen with a beautiful woman was a status symbol, like driving a fancy car, and if a guy wanted to be looked up to by his peers, he'd better find—and I quote—'a real show dog.'''

"Ah, honey.'' Austin's voice poured over her like a balm. He ran his hand up and down her arm, and the words began to pour out faster.

"Joe said that women were always competing in a big beauty contest. He said I was nice and smart and everything, but I didn't rate very high on the head-turning scale. He said he wanted a woman who made other guys think,

'Wow! Joe must really be cool if he's got a gal like *that.*'"

"The idiot must have been blind," Austin muttered.

"Nathan asked him who he had in mind to replace me, and Joe said, 'Frannie's new roommate.' And then he went into a crude description of the size of her chest. He said he planned to dump me after the dance that night."

Frannie glanced over and found Austin's gaze resting on her, his eyes warm and troubled and filled with concern. "Did you ever let the moron know you were sitting right behind him?"

"No. They left soon after that, and then my friend came back to the table." Frannie gazed out at the sky. The moon was higher now, but still incredibly large and orange. A sprinkling of stars twinkled around it.

"Did you tell your friend what you'd heard?"

"I tried, but I couldn't. I just couldn't bring myself to repeat the words. I—I just kind of sat there. I can't tell you how bad I felt. How inadequate. And then it was time to go give my speech."

Austin's hand stilled on her arm. He pulled her closer.

"It was in a big auditorium," Frannie continued, "and it was nearly filled. Most of the people running for office were in fraternities and sororities, and their whole houses had come out to support them. It was kind of a rowdy crowd. I pulled myself together as best I could. The first candidate for treasurer gave a really good speech. He ended it by throwing candy that looked like little coins out into the crowd.

"And then it was my turn. I walked out on stage, stepped up to the microphone and looked out at the crowd, and then, there in the back, I saw them. There was Joe, standing right beside my roommate."

Frannie's throat started to close up at the memory. "I froze. I couldn't talk. I couldn't move. I just stood there like a statue, paralyzed with fear and hurt. And the room fell completely silent.''

Frannie fell silent now, just thinking about it. ''And then someone laughed.'' Her voice came out barely more than a whisper. ''And then some more people. And then a guy yelled, 'You want to be class treasurer? Show us how you count money!' And he threw a piece of the candy money at me. And then all of a sudden, everyone was throwing it. I just stood there, getting pelted.''

''Ah, Frannie,'' Austin's hand ran from her neck down her back, then up again.

''It was awful. I finally managed to run off the stage. I felt like the biggest loser in the world.''

Austin pulled her close, his arm around her. ''But you know you're not, right? You know that this Joe creep is the real loser, don't you?''

Frannie swallowed hard. ''That's not how I saw it. I felt like the homeliest, stupidest female on the planet. I decided that if life was a beauty contest, well, I just wouldn't enter it. I wouldn't even *try* to look attractive. I figured that if you don't try, you can't fail. So for years, I refused to do anything to call attention to myself. I tried to just blend in with the background.''

Austin gazed at her, his heart heavy, his chest tight. This explained so many things about her. The prickly way she'd acted when he'd told her she'd looked beautiful the night of the ball, her fear of public speaking, the way she liked to hide behind her glasses even though she could see better out of her contacts. And it was all because of a conceited, air-headed jerk who obviously had no taste in women.

A surge of rage pulsed through Austin. He wasn't a violent person, but he'd give anything to be able to smash his fist through the creep's stupid face right now.

Frannie was staring up at the moon. ''...And then my

cousins started giving me a hard time about turning into a hermit," she continued. "They wanted to make me over and fix me up with a blind date for the Whitehorn Ball. And then I met you, and..."

Austin's heart thudded hard. "And what?"

"Oh, nothing." She looked away, and her voice lowered until it was barely audible over the swirling water. "That's just the beer talking."

"One beer can't say very much."

Frannie stared at the bubbling water. The color in her cheeks might be the result of the hot water, but the way she avoided his gaze spoke of embarrassment.

The ache in his chest tightened. He shifted closer toward her, and gently rubbed her arm. "Let me guess. You were about to say that then you met me, and you could tell I didn't see you the way you saw yourself."

She turned toward him, her eyes wide.

"In fact, you could tell that I thought you had the sexiest legs...." Austin ran his right hand from her calf up her thigh, and was gratified to feel her tremble. "And the most beautiful, kissable lips..." His wet finger drifted to her mouth and softly traced its outline, carefully following the curve of her upper lip.

Frannie's lips parted. Austin leaned closer. "And the softest, warmest, most intriguing eyes..." His hand feathered up her cheek and worked its way into her hair. He was whispering now, his mouth close to her ear. "You could probably tell that I haven't been able to get you off my mind since we met, and that I've lain awake nights fantasizing about you."

His face was close now, very close to hers, close enough to see that her pupils were dilated, her eyes filled with desire. A rush of need throbbed through him, hot and hard.

"Austin," she breathed. Her arms reached up and circled his neck.

And then he was kissing her, devouring her sweet, salty mouth, and she was kissing him back, kissing him with a fervor that was hotter and wilder than the swirling water—hotter and wilder than the last lap at Daytona the time he was three abreast and fighting for the lead. She shifted onto his lap, pressing her bottom against his arousal, and he moaned at the sweet torture.

The denim of her shirt rasped against his chest, making him ache to feel her skin against his. She must have felt the same need, because she reached for her top button. Austin covered her hand with his.

"Let me." He slowly unbuttoned her shirt, one button at a time, trailing kisses on her flesh as he exposed it. He eased the shirt down and off her arms, then tossed it on the deck behind them.

She was wearing a tiny black bikini, and her nipples pushed at the wet fabric in hard, erect peaks. He took one of the tips into his mouth, fabric and all.

"Austin," she murmured. "I want…"

He circled her breast with his palm, reveling in the soft weight, and kissed the peak again. "Yes, sweetheart?"

"I want…"

"Tell me what you want." He ached for her, ached to do anything, anything at all that she wanted.

"You," she whispered. "I want you."

The blood roared in his ears. He put one hand under her knees, the other under her arms, and lifted her as he stood. He carried her out of the steaming tub to the chaise longue where he'd placed the stack of towels.

Propping her on his knee, he picked up several towels, then carried her to a pair of French doors on the west wing of the house. Balancing her again, he turned the doorknob and carried her across the threshold, not setting her down until he reached his bed.

Thirteen

Frannie felt the give of a mattress beneath her, then felt Austin's mouth settle softly upon her lips. She shivered, and he pulled back to settle a towel around her. "You're cold. Let me light a fire."

"You've already lit it," she murmured.

He grinned as he leaned over her in the dimly lit room, rubbing her arms with the soft ends of the towel. "Well, let me light another one."

Frannie hugged the terry cloth around her and watched him stride across the room to a large stone fireplace, where logs were already neatly stacked, just waiting to be set afire. He squatted in front of it and touched a match to the kindling. Flames blazed and crackled, illuminating the room. Frannie glanced around. It was large and masculine and handsome, with taupe adobe walls, oversize Southwest-style furnishings and animal-skin printed fabrics. Frannie picked up the other towel Austin had laid on the bed beside her and padded across the thick cream carpet to the faux fur rug in front of the fireplace, where he was crouched to adjust a screen.

He looked so masculine, so manly in the flickering firelight. A fresh rush of desire pulsed through her as she draped the towel over his muscled shoulders.

He turned and looked up at her, his gaze hotter than the flames leaping in the hearth. "Come here," he growled, pulling her to him.

The next thing Frannie knew, they were lying on the

thick, soft fur rug, and Austin's mouth was working its magic, coaxing sensations from her that she never knew existed. She arched toward him, straining for every point of contact her body could make with his, intimately pressing against the rock-hard proof of his desire. She was on fire, aflame, ablaze with wanting, and she moaned softly against him.

His mouth moved to her neck, to her throat. He slid the straps of her bikini top off her shoulders and pushed her top down around her waist. His gaze moved over her breasts, as warm as a caress, making the hardened tips swell still more. "Frannie… You're even more beautiful than I imagined."

Beautiful. Austin thought she was beautiful. The thought hazily filled her mind and her heart. The words freed something inside of her, something she had always held back, something she had always been afraid to give. She wanted to give everything, everything in her heart and soul, to Austin.

He bent his head and kissed her breast, pulling the sensitive flesh into his mouth. Sweet, hot arrows of pleasure shot through her, firing connections all over her body, pooling into throbbing need at the center of her being. Her hands played over his back, into his soft hair. "Austin," she murmured.

His mouth traveled down, down to her bikini bottom. His fingers toyed with the strings that held the fabric on her hips. "Just like a present, all tied up with bows," he murmured. He tugged at the string with his teeth, unfastening one side, then slowly trailing kisses across her lower belly to the string on the other side.

"Please," Frannie moaned.

"Not just yet."

His fingers moved lower and his kisses followed. Frannie lost all sense of place and time, all sense of anything but an aching, melting need.

"I want you," she whispered. "I want to touch you. I want…"

He slowly slid up her body, trailing kisses across her belly and breasts. He pulled away for a brief moment and shucked off his swim trunks, then returned to reclaim her lips.

He hovered enticingly above her. She reached out and closed her hand softly around the hard length of him, and was gratified to hear him moan. She arched against him, fitting herself against him. Austin gazed at her for a moment, his eyes dark and tender. "Frannie," he whispered, then buried himself inside her.

And then she was flying, racing through space and time, weightless and free, aware of nothing but the lusty, primal, urgent pleasure of loving Austin. She felt the love well up inside of her, felt it fill her to bursting, and when she finally shattered, she wasn't sure if the words spilled out of her lips or were just shouted in her heart. "I love you, love you, love you."

And it was true. With all her being, she loved him, as completely, as fully as any woman had ever loved any man.

She heard him gasp, felt him shudder, and held him close as he followed her into the star-strewn place they had created for each other.

She loved him. And if he couldn't love her back, well, she would just have to love him enough for both of them.

Austin was dreaming of Frannie, dreaming that he was following her alongside a mountain stream. The stream magically turned into a waterfall. Frannie stepped under the water and started taking off her clothes, beckoning for Austin to follow. He reached out for her, and…

Austin's hand reached out, but instead of touching Frannie, it fell on an empty mattress. Opening one eye, he saw that the pillow next to him was empty. A feeling of loss fell over him like a painter's drop cloth. He'd known the waterfall part had been a dream, but had the rest of it been unreal, as well?

He pushed up from the pillow and opened his other eye. The bathroom door was closed, and the sound of running water was faintly audible through the wall. The shower. Frannie was in his shower. He leaned back against his pillow, an immense sense of relief pouring over him.

It was strange—he normally couldn't get women out of his room fast enough the morning after, but with Frannie, he'd felt panicked at the thought she'd left without saying good-bye.

The shower shut off. A minute later, the door opened, to reveal Frannie in her jeans and one of his SeaBreeze Detergent T-shirts.

She gave him a shy smile. "Good morning."

"Mornin'."

She crossed the room and stood by the bed. "I hope you don't mind my borrowing your shirt. Mine was still wet."

Austin grinned. "Well, I sure as heck do mind."

Her eyes widened. "You do?"

"Yeah. I think you should take it off immediately."

Frannie gave him a playful push. He grabbed her and hauled her back onto the bed.

"You're insatiable." She laughed.

"Me? Who kept me up till all hours in the kitchen?"

"You promised me dinner. I was hungry."

"Yeah, well, so was I. And our steaks were just about cooked to perfection when you lured me away from cooking duties."

"You didn't seem to mind at the time."

"Oh, I didn't mind." Not at all. He smiled at the memory of making love to her in the kitchen while she'd been perched on the countertop. "But our steaks burned to a crisp, and I had to start all over with fresh ones."

"Well, maybe I'm responsible for the kitchen episode. But who woke who up in the middle of the night?" She arched an eyebrow. "Not once, but twice?" She wagged two fingers at him.

He was incapable of even pretending remorse. His grin widening, he pulled her down and gave her a thorough kiss.

She reluctantly pulled away. "I need to go." She rolled off the bed and ran a hand through her hair. "I want to get home before Aunt Celeste and Jasmine so I won't have to make any awkward explanations."

Austin nodded. He understood, but the prospect of her leaving made him feel as empty and deflated as a punctured hot-air balloon.

She picked up her purse and slung it over her shoulder. At some point in the night, all of her belongings had ended up in his bedroom. "What time do you leave for New York?"

"I have to be at the airport in Bozeman at three."

"How long will you be gone?"

"Three weeks, if we qualify for all the races. Then I'll have a week off before the final race in Denver. I hope to spend at least part of that here."

Frannie adjusted the strap of her purse. "I'll miss you."

Ah, hell, he didn't want things to get all heavy and serious. That wasn't his style. He swallowed hard. "Look—I'm, uh, not very good about calling. I mean, I don't like to have any distractions while I'm focused on a race, and, well…" He let his words trail off. Damn, this was awkward. He felt like a heel. He cleared his throat. "I'll call you when I get back to Whitehorn, okay?"

"Okay." Her mouth smiled, but her eyes looked hurt. "I understand."

He was afraid she did. A funny ache settled in his chest as she looked away.

She pulled her car keys out of a side compartment on her purse. "Well, I'd better be going."

"I'll walk you out." Austin flung back the covers.

To his surprise, Frannie blushed at the sight of his naked body. After all they'd shared, she still blushed. He grabbed a towel and wound it around him, feeling oddly touched and more than a little guilty. Why did everything about her this morning have to remind him that she wasn't the type of woman who made love lightly?

He walked her through the main house. She stopped at the front door and gave him a quick kiss. It would have been no more than a peck if he hadn't grabbed her shoulders and deepened the kiss. He immediately regretted it, because he felt an undeniable surge of fresh desire.

She did, too. He could see it in her eyes, see it in the way she backed away and smoothed her hair. When she spoke, her voice was breathless. "Well, thanks for everything."

"The pleasure was all mine."

She opened the door and gave him a Mona Lisa-type smile over her shoulder. "No, it wasn't. Not entirely."

A slight drizzle was falling. He watched her walk to her car, her keys in her hand. She opened the driver's side door, then paused. "Good luck at the races."

"Thanks." He tightened the towel around his waist and watched her duck down to enter her car. "Hey!" he called. She turned and straightened. "The roads are wet, so they'll be slick. Drive safely."

She looked directly at him, and her gaze hit him like

something tangible, something with weight and warmth and depth, something that socked him right in the chest. "You, too."

And then she was in her car, driving away, and he was more alone than he'd been in years.

Drive safely. Hell's bells—he didn't want to drive safely. He wanted to drive as though he had nothing to lose. Furthermore, he didn't want to give a damn about how safely somebody else drove, either. What the hell was the matter with him?

He slammed the door harder than necessary and strode into the living room. Through the floor-to-ceiling windows, he saw a cream-colored towel sitting on the chaise longue, a taunting reminder of how he and Frannie had begun their lovemaking the night before.

Mumbling an oath, he turned away and stalked into the kitchen, only to face the dirty dishes left over from their midnight feast.

He heaved an exasperated sigh. Maybe he should just go back to bed and get some more shut-eye. He started toward the bedroom, then stopped. Hell. If the kitchen made him think of Frannie, the bedroom was bound to be ten times worse. Dad-blast it, even the thought of taking a shower brought Frannie to mind.

He fell heavily on his leather sofa. What the devil was the matter with him? He didn't feel at all like himself. He'd been with women before, lots of women, and none of them had ever left him feeling this way—mooney-eyed and sad and forlorn, missing her like crazy when her scent still hovered in the air.

Well, it was a darn good thing he was leaving town this afternoon, he thought. Time and distance were just the ticket to cool things down. The sooner he put some miles between himself and Little Miss Hap, the better off he'd be. He'd take a shower in another bathroom, throw his things together, then get the hell out of Dodge. He'd leave the kitchen mess and rumpled bed for his house-keeper to deal with.

There was no room in his life for sentimental soggy-headedness, he told himself, rising to his feet. No room at all.

Across town, Lyle Brooks stood as a tall, silver-haired man strode toward his table in the dining room of the Whitehorn Country Club. At seventy-two, Garrett Kincaid still cut an intimidating figure. Lyle swallowed down his nervousness and pasted on what he hoped was a warm smile. "Grandfather. So glad you could make it."

"It's good to see you." The athletically built older man seated himself at the table. "You could come out to the ranch once in a while, you know."

Lyle lowered himself back into his chair, trying not to let his grandfather's chastisement rattle him. "I'm afraid I've been very busy lately, what with the construction project up in the air."

Garrett's blue eyes cut across the table like the blade of a hunting knife. "What do you mean, up in the air?"

Lyle shrugged. "The Indians are all upset about the two deaths at the construction site. Seems they've gotten it in their heads that the location is cursed." Lyle took a sip of water, trying to play it cool. "There was even an article about it in today's paper." Lyle had planted the story himself by making an anonymous call to the business re-porter.

"I haven't seen the paper yet." Garrett spread his nap-kin in his lap and took a menu from the white-jacketed waiter who'd silently materialized at their table.

Lyle accepted a menu, as well. He paused until the waiter had filled both of their cups with coffee and moved away. "Well, it has to with the fact that the land is the burial ground of ancient Cheyenne warriors. The Indians think their spirits will return to bring death and destruction to anyone who disturbs their graves.''

''You don't say.'' Garrett took a long slurp of steaming coffee, his face inscrutable. Lyle nervously took a sip of coffee, too. Damn, but the old man gave him a case of the jitters! Sometimes it felt as if the old goat could see right through him and somehow read his mind.

Lyle leaned forward, trying hard to look earnest. ''Some of the Indians are really up in arms. They think the land is sacred. It could bring all sorts of problems for us if the tribe decides to stop the project.''

''Are they threatening to?''

''Well, not yet. But you know how these things spread like forest fires, especially if any more accidents happen. That's why I want to bring up another option for your consideration.''

Garrett squinted at him. ''And just what might that be?''

Lyle carefully added a packet of sugar to his coffee. ''Well, we're not too far into this project yet. It's not too late to move the site to another location.''

Garrett's jaw twitched. ''And would that location happen to be on your land?''

Lyle squirmed. Damn, but the old man was shrewd. ''Not exactly. Under my proposal, the land would no longer be mine. It would be Gabriel's.''

Garrett's gaze fastened on his face like a bear trap. ''What are you sayin', boy? You're going to give your land to Gabriel?''

''Well, no, not exactly.'' Lyle picked up another packet of sugar, wanting an excuse not to look his grandfather in the eye. ''It wouldn't be an outright gift. I would simply swap my land for his.''

The old man's eyes turned cold. ''We've already covered this ground, and I've told you no. I'm not trading your land for Gabriel's."

"But this curse business puts everything in a whole new light! If the resort is moved, then the northern land becomes the more valuable property."

"And you'd want Gabriel to have the more valuable property out of the goodness of your heart?" Garrett snorted. "Pardon my skepticism, son, but I wasn't born yesterday. What's in it for you?"

Damn. Lyle inwardly squirmed. "A guarantee that the project won't be held up indefinitely by some legal injunction."

The hard set to Garrett's mouth softened, but he still looked less than convinced. Lyle decided to try to appeal to the old man's emotional side. "There's another reason, too. A couple of them, actually."

"I figured there was." The old man drummed his fingers on the table. "Well, let's have it."

"Well, I've, uh, gotten real interested in Indian history lately. And the fact is, I hate to disturb the burial grounds myself."

"Is that a fact." Garrett looked as if he'd have an easier time believing the table in front of him would sprout wings and fly. "What's the other reason?"

Lyle swallowed nervously. "This is kind of embarrassing to admit because it's not very business-like, and I pride myself on being business-like, but, well, I spotted a bear and a couple of cubs. I hate to destroy their home."

"That's funny." Garrett's voice was curt. "I don't recall you bein' much of a nature lover. In fact, I don't recall you havin' much use for the wildlife at all."

"Well, I don't let most people see my softer side." Lyle reached for yet another sugar packet, trying hard to appear confident and chipper. "So, what do you say? If I can convince the Indians to move the resort to the land up north, will you let me swap that land for Gabriel's?"

"No."

The old man was impossible. A burst of rage shot through Lyle. He tried to tamp it down. "It would be in the child's best interests. How can you possibly object?"

"Because you're up to something." Garrett stared at him hard over the rim of his coffee cup. "But I'll be damned if I know what it is."

Lyle sat back and did his best to look wounded. "Granddad, how can you think that? I'm your own flesh and blood. It hurts me that you distrust me."

"Yeah, well, it hurts me that you'd try to pull the wool over my eyes."

"I don't know what you're talking about."

"Don't you?" Garrett slammed down his coffee cup, making the saucer rattle. Coffee sloshed over the sides as he leaned forward over the table. "That land's no burial ground. If you were half as interested in Cheyenne history as you say you are, you'd know they used to place their dead up on tall stilts, not bury them in the ground."

Oh, hell. Why hadn't he checked his facts? He should have known the old goat would know all about the customs of the Cheyenne. Lyle's hands knotted into sweaty fists under the table. "Well, maybe a lot of them were put on stilts on that land. Or..." Lyle thought fast. "...Or perhaps they died in battle there. I don't know all the details. All I know is the Indians are saying the land is cursed."

Garrett stared at him across the table, his eyes as cold as the eyes of a trout. "I've got good friends among the Cheyenne. My own grandmother was Cheyenne, and I've never heard that tale before now." Garrett plopped his napkin onto the table. "I don't know why you want that land, boy, but I've designated it for Gabriel, and that's not going to change. Cursed or not cursed, that land is his." Garrett scooted back his chair and rose.

"Granddad, wait a minute." Lyle stood and reached out his arm, wanting to restrain the old man. "Where are you going? We haven't even ordered."

Garrett shrugged off Lyle's hand. "I seem to have lost my appetite. I'll talk to you later."

The old man stalked out, leaving Lyle to stare after him. Lyle slowly sank back into his chair, his spirits sinking with him.

Hell. He'd been sure the curse approach would work. Instead of convincing his grandfather to give him the deed to the land he wanted, he'd only managed to make him suspicious.

The waiter stopped at Lyle's table and gave a solicitous smile. "Are you ready to place your order, sir?"

"Yeah. Bring me a bloody Mary. Make it a double. Hell, bring me two doubles."

"Yes, sir."

He watched the waiter scurry away, his dejection hardening into anger. He'd have to come up with another plan. He wanted that land, and by damn, whatever he wanted, he got. He could do anything he set his mind to. Hell, he'd already gotten away with murder.

And it had been surprisingly easy, Lyle thought, drumming his fingers on the table with satisfaction. Peter Cook had met him at the construction site that night, just as Lyle had asked him to. The heavy equipment operator had been excited at the prospect of getting his hands on some money. When Lyle had asked him to point out exactly where in the pit he'd found the sapphire, he'd been more than eager to comply. The unsuspecting construction worker had crept close to the ledge and bent to point out the location. By the time he realized Lyle was about to shove him in, it was too late. He'd put up a fight, but Lyle had been on solid footing, and Peter had been too close to the edge. After a brief struggle, the sucker had lost his balance and fallen to his death.

Lyle had no intention of giving up his quest for the land now. No, sirree. His grandfather wasn't buying his story about the curse, and Jackson Hawk hadn't believed it, either, but that didn't mean they couldn't be persuaded to change their minds. It might take another accident to do it, but it could be done.

Somehow, some way, Lyle Brooks always made sure he got what he wanted.

Fourteen

"Frannie, come quick!" Celeste's voice called from the hallway. "The sports news is coming on, and they're about to interview Austin."

Just the mention of Austin's name was enough to make Frannie's heart pound. Lately it seemed as if everything elicited an emotional response from her—the ringing of a phone, the delivery of the mail, the opening of a door. He'd been gone for two and a half weeks, but instead of becoming accustomed to his absence, she felt it more deeply with every passing day.

He'd told her he wouldn't contact her until he came back to town, she reminded herself. It made no sense that she should feel so awful about not hearing from him when he was only keeping his word.

He'd said he didn't want to be distracted from concentrating on each race, but she knew it was something more. He was deliberately keeping his distance. He didn't want to be attached to anyone or anything.

"Hurry, Frannie! They're almost back from the commercials!"

Putting down her book, Frannie rose from her bed and padded barefoot into Aunt Celeste's room to watch the end of the ten o'clock evening news.

"Austin Parker was today's top finisher at the qualifying race for the Daytona 500 in the Winston Cup series," the dark-haired newscaster said. "We have a reporter at the track who talked with Austin after the race."

Frannie sank onto Aunt Celeste's bed, her hand over her stomach, as Austin's face filled the screen. The reporter thrust a microphone toward him. "Austin, you've been on a roll here lately—a win last week in Atlanta, and now finishing first here in the qualifier. To what do you attribute your winning streak?"

Frannie's heart jumped in her chest as the camera zoomed in on Austin. "I have the best crew in the business. All the credit belongs to them."

"Well, your driving is certainly a major component," the reporter said.

"I just try to do my best."

"Austin, we were all touched to read about how you and your girlfriend saved a baby and her mother from drowning in a cold Montana pond this summer."

"Did you hear that?" Aunt Celeste said, squeezing Frannie's hand. "He called you his girlfriend!"

Would that it were so, Frannie thought. She watched Austin tuck his helmet under one hand and run a hand through his hair. "We, uh, just happened to be at the right place at the right time."

"Well, I understand our network is airing the story about that rescue on next week's 'Celebrity Spotlight' show." The reporter grinned. "What does your girlfriend have to say about your performance at the tracks lately?"

"I, uh, haven't had a chance to talk to anyone except you and my crew since finishing here today."

"Well, I'm sure she'll be proud. Have you got a strategy for the race on Sunday?"

"Just to make sure that the car's in top shape and to drive my best. There are a lot of excellent drivers here. It's a tough race, but I'm looking forward to it."

"We are, too. Best of luck to you, Austin. Steve, back to you."

Celeste hit the remote control, turning the TV set off,

then turned to Frannie, her eyes glowing. "They talked about you nearly as much as they talked about Austin."

Frannie traced a rose in Celeste's floral comforter with the tip of her finger, trying to blink back the tears that threatened her eyes. "I noticed he managed to change the subject every time that interviewer brought it up."

Celeste's hand landed on Frannie's shoulder. Frannie could feel her aunt's eyes on her. "Honey, are you all right?"

Frannie nodded. "Sure. Why wouldn't I be?"

"There's just something about you…" Celeste regarded her silently for a moment. Her voice grew soft and low. "Frannie, are you pregnant?"

Frannie looked up, startled. Her eyes filled with tears. "How did you know?"

"Oh, Frannie." Celeste reached out and hugged her.

"How did you know?" Frannie asked again.

Celeste slowly released her. "Your hand. You put it on your stomach just the way Blanche always did. I remember doing that myself with Cleo and Jasmine." Celeste patted Frannie's hand. "Oh, Frannie, is it Austin's?"

She nodded. The tears she'd held back so long came pouring out, along with a rush of words. "I just found out this morning. I did a home test, and it was positive, so I called my doctor. She worked me in on my lunch hour, and when she checked me, she confirmed it. It's very early—I'm just a few days late. But I'm definitely pregnant."

"Well, honey," Celeste crooned, stroking her hair, "don't cry. This will all work out. A baby—why, that's wonderful."

"I'm not sure Austin will feel that way." Celeste reached over and pulled a tissue out of a box on her nightstand. Frannie blew her nose into it. "He hasn't even called."

"When he left, you said you didn't expect him to," Celeste reminded Frannie.

"I know. But on some level, I—I kept hoping." Frannie twisted the tissue until it looked like a paper tornado. "I wanted to believe he feels about me the way I feel about him."

"You love him."

Frannie nodded miserably. "And he doesn't want to love anyone. He told me so."

"What a person wants to feel isn't always what he ends up feeling," Celeste said matter-of-factly. "Besides, love has a way of changing the things people think they want."

Frannie sighed. "If he cared about me half as much as I care about him, I would have heard from him by now."

Celeste patted her hand. "Men have odd ways of dealing with their emotions. For some reason, most men don't want to show them. Not at first, anyway."

That was true. Frannie knew from her cousins's experience how easily that could be the case.

"When will Austin be back in Whitehorn?" Celeste asked.

"The race is Sunday. I guess he'll be back Monday or Tuesday."

"All right. You'll see him then, and you'll talk. This will all work out. I know it may not feel that way now, but it will. Just wait and see."

Frannie took a deep breath. "Waiting seems like the hardest part."

Celeste smiled, her eyes full of empathy. "It always does, honey. It always does."

The phone rang Sunday evening as Frannie was loading the dishwasher after dinner. She picked up the kitchen phone, her other hand holding a dirty plate. "Hello?"

"Frannie?" said a deep, familiar voice.

The plate nearly slipped from her fingers. Frannie grabbed it, her heart pounding hard. "Austin! Are you already back in town?"

"Not yet. But I should be there late tomorrow."

"Congratulations on the race."

"You heard, huh?"

"I watched it on TV."

She could almost hear the smile in his voice. "Don't tell me you're turning into a NASCAR fan."

"Well, I'm a fan of one particular driver." She swallowed around a lump in her throat. "You were great."

"Thanks."

Silence beat between them. Frannie felt a current of electricity racing through the phone line.

"I was calling to see if you'd have dinner with me Tuesday night."

"Gee, I'll have to check my social calendar to see if I'm scheduled to dine with any other race car drivers that evening. If not, well, I suppose I could find time."

"Good."

I've missed you, Frannie thought, willing him to say the words. *I love you.* "How long will you be in Whitehorn?" she finally asked.

"Just a couple of days. And I'm afraid it's going to be crazy while I'm there. Five members of my crew are coming out to rework the suspension on the cars, my main sponsor wants to see the ranch and I'm being trailed by a bunch of sports media."

She shifted the phone to her other ear. "Where's your next race?"

"In Denver. I leave Thursday morning for the qualifying race on Friday."

He'd be here for just two days—and he'd be surrounded by a throng of people the whole time. Somehow, in the midst of all that, she'd have to find a way to talk to him.

"Well, I'll look forward to Tuesday."

"Me, too." In the background, she could hear laughter and loud voices. She heard Austin's muffled voice call, "Keep it down a second, guys!" She could picture him pulling his hand from the mouthpiece and turning back to the phone. "Listen, I've got three separate schmoozing events I have to go to tonight, so I'd better get going. See you Tuesday evening. I'll pick you up around six-thirty, okay?"

"Okay."

"Oh, and Frannie, that show about our rescue airs Wednesday. I thought you'd want to know."

Frannie was fully aware of the air date. Mr. Billings, all her co-workers and half the population of Whitehorn had mentioned it to her, telling her they couldn't wait to see it.

"I'll try to watch."

"Me, too."

Frannie hung up the phone, her emotions jumbled and raw. He'd called before he'd come home—that was something. In the back of her mind, she'd secretly harbored the notion that if he called before he said he would, it meant she'd broken through his wall, that he cared for her more than he wanted to.

On the other hand, the call left her feeling more disconnected from him than ever. This was a man who drove race cars at two hundred miles per hour, who had thousands of devoted fans, who regularly got doused with champagne on national TV. He inhabited a world of fame and excitement and endless parties about as far removed from her own quiet life as she could imagine. Could a man with such a thrilling, exciting life ever find happiness with an ordinary, everyday kind of woman such as her? Could two people so dissimilar ever build a life together?

She didn't know about building a life, but they'd already created one. Frannie placed a protective hand on her stomach and prayed that she'd find the right time to tell him in the right way.

Jasmine peered out the front parlor window Tuesday evening as a car pulled into the long drive. ''He's here, Frannie! He's here!''

Frannie smoothed her new black dress, wishing she knew how to smooth her nerves, as well.

''You look wonderful,'' Jasmine told her.

''Thanks.'' She'd pulled out every trick in the book to look her best, but she still didn't feel equal to the task in front of her. How was she supposed to tell a man who didn't want any emotional involvement that he was about to become a father?

''I can't wait to see how he greets you. I bet he's going to kiss you the moment he sees you.''

Frannie shot her cousin a meaningful glance. ''Don't you have something to do in another room?''

Jasmine grinned. ''No, not really.''

Celeste stepped into the hallway and firmly took her daughter's arm. ''Come on, Jasmine. Let's give Frannie a little space.''

Frannie cast a grateful smile at her aunt as she ushered Jasmine out of the room. She was nervous enough about seeing Austin without having an audience.

The doorbell rang. Frannie silently counted to three before crossing the foyer to open the door, not wanting to look too eager.

The impact of seeing Austin face-to-face nearly took her breath away. He was taller and more handsome than she remembered. Her voice came out low and breathy. "Hi."

"Hi, yourself." Grinning widely, her pulled her into his arms and gave her a hard kiss. He held her at arm's length and let his gaze run over her. "Wow. You look terrific." He kissed her again, and this time it was a slow, lingering kiss that made her blood tingle. "Taste good, too."

A shiver coursed up her spine. In all of her thoughts about seeing him, she'd underestimated the power of the physical attraction she felt for him. "I've missed you," she whispered.

"Me, too." Sexual energy surged between them. They stood there, just looking at each other. "You make me want to skip dinner and head right for dessert."

Frannie's heart pounded.

He grinned ruefully. "I wanted to take you to my house for a nice quiet dinner, but my place is crawling with people."

"This place is, too."

"Well, then, I guess we'll just have to go to a restaurant. Maybe we can form a plan for dessert over dinner."

He walked her to his truck, and the drive to the restaurant passed in a flurry of conversation. From watching the races on television, Frannie was filled with questions. She asked about restrictor plates, fabricators, and drivetrains. She asked about the problems he'd had with a tire in the qualifying race at Atlanta, and about the two-way communication system between him and Tommy at Daytona.

"You've really been following the races, haven't you?" Austin said.

Frannie nodded.

He smiled in a way that made her think it pleased him. Her spirits soared. Maybe, just maybe, he cared more than a little.

Before she knew it, he'd pulled the truck into the parking lot of the Lakeside Inn. "I didn't know where to take you, but I have great memories of this place."

"So do I."

They walked to the door and were promptly escorted to a lakeside table. "It feels great to have a night off," Austin said. "The last few weeks have really been hectic."

"It's good to have you back." Maybe I should just go ahead and tell him, Frannie thought. Get it out in the open, and get it over with.

Austin leaned his elbows on the table. "You know, as great as racing is, sometimes it just feels like an endless series of decisions. Should we put more air in the tires? Tighten or loosen the steering? It feels really good to be with someone who's not going to expect me to make a major decision in the next few minutes."

Uh-oh. Now was evidently not the time. After dinner— after they'd had a chance to reconnect—she'd find a way to tell him about the baby.

He reached out and covered her hand with his. "I missed you."

Frannie swallowed. "I missed you, too." She looked away. "I kept hoping you'd call."

"I started to. I actually picked up the phone a few times, and then I put it down."

"Why?"

Austin lifted his shoulders. "I didn't know what to say."

"Hello would have been a nice start."

"I wasn't sure what to say after that."

A flash suddenly went off in Frannie's eyes, momentarily blinding her. She blinked, startled, and as her vision cleared, she saw a tall, wiry man with a large, professional-looking camera standing beside the table. A shorter, heavier man stood beside him, holding a small tape recorder and a flash attachment connected to the camera.

"Hey, Austin, can you give us a smile?" the photographer asked.

Austin scowled. "We're out for a private evening here. Do you mind?"

"Ah, come on. I've got to make a living."

Austin raised his hand and signaled the waiter. "Could you get the manager, please?"

"Hey, Frannie, how 'bout a smile?" the photographer wheedled.

"How does he know my name?" Frannie asked Austin.

The photographer answered before Austin got a chance. "Saw your picture in the paper, sweetheart. And after that episode about your rescue airs on TV this week, you'll be even more famous." He clicked another picture. "The readers of the *National Reporter* will want to know all about you." He clicked another photo.

The reporter held the tape recorder close to Austin. "Are things getting serious between you two?"

"Frannie and I are just friends," Austin said flatly.

"Any chance of wedding bells?"

Austin looked around, obviously searching for the manager.

"Any chance at all?"

Austin tried to ignore him, but Frannie saw a muscle flex in his jaw.

"You've been quoted as saying you're not the marrying kind. Is that an accurate statement?"

Austin hissed out an impatient breath. "Look, I have nothing further to say."

"So your statement stands?"

"I have nothing new to say."

The reporter turned to Frannie. "What do you think of

that, sweetheart? Must be pretty disappointing to hear. Think you can get this confirmed bachelor to change his mind?''

Frannie looked down at the tablecloth, trying to follow Austin's lead, trying to ignore the man.

''I'll bet you want to be more than just his friend, huh?'' the reporter persisted.

To her horror, Frannie's eyes filled with tears. The photographer snapped another picture, blinding her. And then another. And another.

''Hey!'' Austin's mouth grew tight and his eyes spat fire. He was halfway out of his chair when a man in a dark suit strode up and bent to talk to him.

After a brief exchange, the man turned to the reporter and the photographer. ''Excuse me. I'm the manager here, and I'm going to have to ask you to leave.''

The photographer fired off one last shot of Frannie, then waved his hand in a little salute. The reporter gave a smug smile. ''Well, I think we've gotten all we need. Nice meeting you, Frannie.''

The two men left the restaurant, escorted by the manager. Frannie was mortified to realize a tear was still drizzling down her cheek. She quickly rubbed it away with the back of her hand.

Austin regarded her, his eyes worried. ''Hey, are you all right?''

''I'm fine.''

''I'm really sorry about that. I know how much you hate being in the spotlight.''

Frannie nodded, grateful to have an excuse. Anything would be better than explaining she was heartbroken at the quick way he'd described their relationship as ''just friends.''

She'd claimed the same thing, she thought ruefully— up until they'd made love. It had been her way of mitigating her emotions, of trying to avoid the fact that Austin had stolen her heart. But she'd been deluding herself, denying what her heart had secretly known all along.

Austin, on the other hand, was simply stating the truth. Friendship was casual. It made no demands, it wasn't exclusive, it didn't require commitment. If it ceased to be mutually beneficial, friends could drift away and fall out of touch.

Friendship was all he wanted, she thought forlornly. She was a friend—someone he liked, someone he was even romantically involved with, but nevertheless, just a friend. A friend didn't hold your heart in the palm of his hand. A friend didn't promise to share a lifetime, to be there through good times and bad, to create children and raise them together. A friend was just...friendly. Like a dog.

Frannie blinked back a fresh onslaught of tears. She'd known Austin wasn't interested in a serious relationship. So why did it hurt so much to hear him say it out loud?

Somehow, in the time he'd been gone, she'd started believing in dreams and fairy tales. Somehow she'd fooled herself into imagining that once she told Austin she was pregnant, he'd do a complete one-eighty. In her mind's eye, she'd pictured him being happy and excited, eager to take on marriage and an instant family.

How had she deluded herself so thoroughly? She was usually so logical and practical. It must be the hormones. Pregnant women were notoriously emotional and sentimental. Austin had said he didn't want commitment, and it didn't come in any bigger packages than with a wife and child. What had she been thinking?

The manager returned to the table, his mouth creased in an apologetic smile. "I'm very sorry, Mr. Parker. I've given instructions to the staff not to allow any more photographers in. And I'm sending a bottle of wine to your table with my compliments.''

''Thanks. I appreciate it.''

Frannie struggled to pull herself together. ''Does that happen a lot?'' she asked when the manager left.

Austin grinned ruefully. ''It's starting to, now that I've won a few races. And our little tag-team rescue at the lake really sped things along publicity-wise. My sponsors are thrilled. I'm sorry I had to drag you into it, though.''

Frannie managed a weak smile. She was grateful when the waiter arrived with the wine, and took their orders.

''So what's been going on in Whitehorn while I've been gone?''

Frannie played with her napkin, trying to compose herself. ''Nothing nearly as exciting as the things in your life.''

''Oh, I don't know about that. I read about the controversy concerning the casino site in some of the Atlanta newspapers.''

Frannie nodded, grateful for the neutral topic. ''That's been front-page news around here. I don't think the Cheyenne really want to move the site, though. Jackson Hawk was quoted in yesterday's paper as saying that everything is going to go ahead as planned.''

''What's new with you?''

Frannie's heart thudded hard against her ribs. She stared at the tablecloth. She couldn't tell him. Not now. ''Nothing much,'' she managed.

''Have you mailed off those manuscripts of your children's books?''

Frannie looked up. ''As a matter of fact, I did.''

''Good for you!'' A soft, high-pitched ring sounded. Austin frowned apologetically and pulled a phone out of his jacket pocket. ''Excuse me.'' He opened the cell phone, punched a button and spoke into the receiver. "Yes?"

Frannie watched his mouth tighten as he listened. His eyes grew dark and troubled.

"Is anyone hurt?"

Frannie's stomach clenched. Something had happened—something bad.

"Is there much damage?" Austin asked curtly.

His forehead eased a bit. "All right. Get on the phone and see of you can locate another dyno. Then give Buddy a call and get him out here by tomorrow morning. I'll be there as soon as possible."

Austin gave a heavy sigh as he clicked off the phone and folded it.

"What happened?" Frannie asked.

"An engine blew while Tommy was testing it on the dyno. No one was hurt, thank God. And the cars and engines are all okay. But I really need another engine to take to Denver, so that means we're going to be working around the clock to build one by tomorrow night."

"Dyno? What's a dyno?"

"It's a machine that records engine performance. It tells us where in the powerband the engine is making its power." Austin looked at her ruefully. "I hate to run out on you, but I'm afraid I need to go. The shop is in shambles, and they need me there."

Frannie forced a smile she didn't feel. "Go ahead. I'll call Jasmine to give me a ride home."

"No. I brought you. I'll take you home."

"You'd lose forty-five minutes running me to the Big Sky, then turning around and going back to your ranch."

"But I don't want to abandon you here."

"I'll be fine." She leaned forward and placed her palm on his hand. "Go on and take care of things at your shop."

"Are you sure?"

"I'm sure."

He rose from the chair, circled around and kissed her soundly on the lips. "I'm really sorry about this."

"It's not your fault. Stuff happens."

"Thanks for being so understanding." He gave her another quick kiss, then strode for the door, stopping to talk to the manager on the way.

Understanding. Her eyes filled with tears again as she gazed out at the lake. Oh, she was understanding, all right. She understood that Austin didn't have the time or the inclination for a relationship. She understood that she was just a diversion in his very busy, very full life. She understood that he might like her and even care for her, but he wasn't looking for marriage or parenthood. He was looking for an escape from pressure and problems, not a whole new set of them.

But she also understood that he was a good-hearted man, the kind who would want to do the right thing. If she told him she was carrying his child, he would no doubt ask her to marry him out of a sense of duty.

Did she really want a husband who'd married her as an obligation? Did she really want a loveless marriage—one that left Austin feeling trapped, one that was sure to breed resentment, one that sooner or later would almost certainly end in divorce?

Wouldn't everyone be better off—her, Austin and their child—if she dealt with the situation by herself from the very beginning?

Her heart knew the answer, but it hurt, letting go of her dreams and hopes. It hurt, accepting the truth.

And the truth was that Austin's abandonment issues ran too deep. He didn't want to get close, didn't want to commit. Even if he married her, he'd never let her close enough to truly share his life, to truly know his heart. And

Frannie was certain that a loveless marriage would leave her feeling more lonely than she'd ever feel on her own.

No. Marriage was out of the question. She would make a life for herself and the child without him. And it would be easier on everyone involved if she made it somewhere besides Whitehorn.

Austin pushed through the door of the Hip Hop Café early the following afternoon, scanning the room for Frannie. He'd stopped at the bank looking for her, and the receptionist had told him she'd come here to have lunch with Summer.

He spotted Frannie in a corner booth, and a feeling of delight welled up in his chest. She was wearing a sky-blue dress that reminded him of the day they'd spent together at his ranch. Good grief, but he was crazy about her! Just seeing her across the room made his heart seem to swell.

He'd been wanting to tell her as much, but he'd wanted to do it in an appropriate way. That was why every time he'd picked up the phone to call her over the past few weeks, he'd abruptly put it down without dialing her number. He was afraid he'd just blurt out "I love you" the moment she answered the phone, and he didn't want to tell her that way.

He'd never felt this way about anyone. The need to tell her he loved her was burning a hole inside of him, but he wanted to do it in a romantic setting, when the two of them were alone. He guessed he'd have to wait until he returned to Whitehorn.

But he couldn't wait that long to see her again. That was why he'd tracked her here.

He strode up to the booth, and both women turned toward him. From the grim looks on their faces, they were in the middle of a serious discussion.

He looked from Frannie to Summer, then back again. "Hi. Is everything okay?"

Frannie's face went pale at the sight of him. Her cousin blanched, too, but she quickly recovered, pasting an unnaturally bright smile on her face. "Why, Austin! Good to see you again." She scooted out of the booth. "Here, take my seat. I was just about to leave and go back to work." She patted Frannie's hand, gave her a long look, then quickly headed to the register, the bill in her hand.

Austin slid across from Frannie into the booth and looked at her questioningly. "You two looked like you were having a serious discussion. I hope I didn't interrupt something important."

"Oh. N-no. We were just finishing up. I have to get back to the bank in a minute."

"Well, I didn't want to leave town without seeing you again. I'm awfully sorry about last night. I hated running out and leaving you like that."

"Is everything under control?"

"More or less. A swarm of contractors is buzzing around repairing the shop. When that engine blew, it took out half a wall that held a lot of our spare parts. My engine specialist is nearly finished building a new engine for an intermediate track, and Tommy is beating the bushes getting all the extra parts that we need. But it looks like it'll all come together in time to make it to Denver."

"Good."

Austin reached out and covered Frannie's hand with his. "I'm sorry I couldn't spend more time with you this week. After this race is over, I'll be back for three weeks in a row, and then…"

Frannie's chin tilted up slightly. She pulled back her hand and swept a strand of hair behind her ear. "I, uh, won't be here."

Austin's heart seemed to stop. "What do you mean?"

"I won't be here. I'm moving to Billings."

"But, Frannie—what for? Where did this come from?"

"The bank has a satellite office there, and they've been after me to transfer for some time. I finally decided to do it."

"But, Frannie…" Austin ran a hand through his hair, completely bewildered. "When did this come up?"

"I made the decision to accept the offer this morning. It will be a big step up. I'll be in line for a vice presidency."

Austin stared at her, dumbfounded. "I thought you were more interested in staying near your family and writing children's books than climbing some corporate ladder."

Frannie shrugged. "Circumstances change. It seemed like too good of an opportunity to pass up."

It struck Austin as mighty odd, but if it was what she wanted, he'd support Frannie's decision. More than anything, he wanted Frannie to be happy. "Well, then, I'll come to Billings and see you there."

Frannie looked down at the green-flecked Formica-topped table. "I don't think that would be a good idea."

"What do you mean?" Austin leaned forward. She was acting distant, not at all like herself. He tightened his clutch on her hand. "Frannie, what's going on?"

Frannie sucked in a deep breath. "I don't think we should see each other anymore."

Austin's stomach knotted hard. "Why the hell not?"

She looked up at him. Her eyes were filled with pain. "I'm not cut out for this. I don't want a part-time, long-distance relationship. I can't make love with my body and keep my heart out of it. I'm an all-the-way, in-over-my-head, till-death-do-us-part kind of woman. I'm not what you need."

"Frannie—"

She put up her hand. "Your life is too different from mine, and I can't handle it. I never should have gotten involved with you in the first place."

Hurt. It burned through him, hot and fierce, cutting into his chest. This was what happened when you let someone get close. His father had been right. "So you're blowing me off? Is that what's happening here?"

"Don't put this all on me." She looked up at him. "You're the one who left for two and half weeks and didn't call or drop a note or send an e-mail."

She had no idea how many times he'd nearly done just that. "Now, look here, Frannie," he began.

But she was in no mood to listen. She shook her head. "Don't give me excuses or tell me what you think I want to hear. I prefer being straightforward about this. We never should have gotten involved in the first place. It'll never work. And I don't want to pretend that it will." She gathered up her purse and slung it over her shoulder.

"Can't we talk about this?"

"There's nothing to talk about, Austin. We want different things out of life. You want to risk your life on a racetrack every week, and I want a man who'll be around to raise children and grow old with me."

Her words hit him like a sledgehammer, the weight of their meaning pounding his heart. She was right. He wasn't very good marriage material, and a woman such as Frannie was cut out for having a family.

She gazed at him pleadingly. "If you care for me at all, even a little bit, you'll leave me alone. Please don't make this any harder than it already is."

He watched her slip out of the booth and hurry away, taking his heart with her.

He banged his fist on his thigh, hard enough to leave a bruise, but he hardly felt it. The pain in his chest was too all-consuming, too hot, too fierce.

Damn. The last thing he'd ever intended to do was to hurt Frannie, and it looked as if he had. And the way she'd left things, if he tried to make amends, he'd only hurt her more.

Damn, damn and double damn! He'd never felt about a woman the way he felt about Frannie, and she hadn't even given him a chance to tell her.

Not that telling her would make any difference. She wanted a home and marriage. And he wanted…

Hell. Just what the heck *did* he want? He no longer knew. He used to think he just wanted to win races. But now he was winning, and he'd never been more miserable in his life.

He propped his elbows on the table and sank his face in his hands. It wasn't fair. He was at the top of his career. By all rights, he should be on top of the world. If he did well at the race in Denver, he would win the Winston Cup. It was the granddaddy of all wins, the dream of every race car driver out there. He should be thrilled and excited, chomping at the bit for that checkered flag to drop. So why did the prospect of heading to Denver leave him as flat as a can of cola that had sat open overnight?

Because all he wanted was Frannie, and all she wanted was to be left alone.

His father had been right, he thought bitterly. He could almost hear his old man's voice, low and rumbly, barely audible over the rusty engine of his ancient pickup as they'd headed down the highway one hot day in June. Austin had been eight years old, and he'd tried hard to keep the tears from rolling down his cheeks as he waved goodbye to his best friend out the dusty rear window of the truck.

"If you let someone close, you give 'em the power to hurt you," his father had said. "Don't give away your heart, boy, unless you're willin' to live without it."

Austin hadn't meant to let it happen, but he'd given his heart away to Frannie.

The old man had been right, he thought grimly. It hurt like hell.

Fifteen

"You didn't tell him?" Summer stared at Frannie incredulously.

"I never got the chance." Frannie pulled a stack of folded knit shirts from her dresser drawer, then turned and placed them in the open suitcase on her bed. She was packing to move to Billings tomorrow. She didn't yet have a place to live, but that was all right. She'd stay in a motel until she could locate an apartment and at least minimally furnish it. The important thing was to make a clean break, and the easiest way to do it was as quickly as possible.

Aunt Celeste sat beside Summer and Jasmine on Frannie's bed, watching her pack.

"He's the father of your baby," she said, her face lined with concern. "He has a right to know, a right to be a part of his child's life. You can't just run away."

"I know. I intend to tell him." Frannie opened another drawer and pulled out a stack of underwear. "And I will. But right now, I just need some time to get over him."

"Frannie, you're making no sense."

"I'm making perfect sense." She placed the undies in the suitcase. "All my life I've wanted one simple, old-fashioned thing—marriage and a family. I want a loving, faithful, committed relationship with a man who loves me just as much as I love him. And Austin can't give me that."

"You're not even giving him a chance!" Jasmine exclaimed.

"Yes, I am. I'm giving him a chance to live his life the way he wants to live it." Frannie crossed to the closet and pulled a pair of slacks off a hanger. "That's the best I can give."

Aunt Celeste's eyes were warm with concern. "But, Frannie, why do you have to move? You need the support of your family at a time like this!"

"Don't you see? The media is constantly following Austin. He lives under a microscope. And because of the publicity from that rescue, I'm linked with him. If I stay in town and start sprouting a pregnant belly, well, it won't take anyone very long to put two and two together. And a scandal would ruin his career. He's a spokesman for a detergent company, for heaven's sake. He needs to keep his image squeaky-clean in order to keep his sponsors."

Summer eyed her soberly. "You really do love him, don't you?"

Frannie nodded.

"But, Frannie," Aunt Celeste said, "if Austin knew you were pregnant, I'm sure he'd want to marry you."

Frannie plopped onto the bed and sighed. "I don't want him marrying me out of a sense of obligation. It would kill me, living with a man I'd trapped into marriage. No. I won't do that. Not to Austin, and not to myself." Frannie picked up the slacks and started folding them. "For the first time in my life, I feel like I deserve to be loved. Austin helped me see that. He helped me put that whole college episode behind me, once and for all. And I'm not going to throw away all that hard-won self-esteem by entering into a one-sided marriage where I love a man and he doesn't love me."

"Marriages don't always start off even," Summer said gently. "In time, Austin might grow to love you."

"It's more likely he'd just grow to resent me. No, thanks." Frannie shook her head. "It's not an option."

"But you shouldn't be alone at a time like this," Jasmine said, her brow furrowed with concern.

"I know." Frannie looked into Jasmine's warm eyes. "Promise me you'll come see me often. And after some time has gone by and the baby's born, I'll come back and visit here, too. But I can't for a while. Not until this whole media thing has died down."

The telephone rang in the hall. Celeste rose to go get it. She returned, her forehead puckered. "Frannie, it's Tommy. He says he needs to talk to you right away."

"Tommy? Austin's crew chief?"

Celeste nodded.

Frannie felt the blood drain from her face. "Has something happened to Austin?"

"I don't know."

Frannie dashed to the phone, her heart in her throat, and grabbed the phone. "Yes?"

"Frannie, it's Tommy."

"Is Austin all right?"

"Well, not really."

Frannie's heart skipped a beat, then drubbed madly. "What happened? Was there an accident?"

"Nothing major. He crunched the nose of his car, but he's all right. And he managed to qualify for the race, but just barely."

"So, what— Why—"

"Frannie, he's not himself. He's drivin' reckless. Makin' stupid mistakes. I'm worried about him."

"Why…why are you calling me?"

"Well, because it's kinda your fault."

"My fault?"

"That didn't come out right. What I mean is, he's all torn up over you breakin' up with him."

"Tommy, Austin's the one who didn't want a relationship."

"That's not what he told me."

Frannie couldn't believe her ears. "What?"

"He got pretty loaded Wednesday night, drank more than I ever saw him drink. We sat up, talkin'. An' he told me he loves you, but he doesn't know how to handle it. Says he's never loved before, and he acted like a jackass, and now he's gone and lost you. An' he hasn't been himself ever since."

He loved her? Austin loved her? The concept whirled around her brain, then spun into her chest, where it grew and expanded like a hurricane, gaining force and strength, until her heart felt as if it would explode.

"He...loves me?" Frannie's voice was just a whisper.

"Yes, ma'am. That's what he said. I tried to get him to call you, but he tol' me some nonsense 'bout you sayin' that if he tried to call you, it would mean he'd never cared about you at all."

That was what she'd told him, all right. She'd said as much just before she walked out of the café.

"Now, I don't know what this is all about," Tommy continued, "but I know this—if you care the least little bit about him, why, you'll get your tail down here to Denver as fast as you can. 'Cause the frame of mind he's in, he's not drivin' worth a damn. I'm not worried about him not winnin'. I'm worried about him crashin'."

Frannie didn't hesitate. The words were out before she knew she'd even said them. "I'll come."

"Thank heaven!" Relief flooded the older man's voice. "Now, listen—I've already got you booked on a plane. It leaves from Bozeman tomorrow mornin' at six. Can you make it?"

"I'll be there."

"I'll send someone to meet you at the Denver airport and bring you straight to the track. Austin will already be racin' by the time you get here, but we'll get you seated where he can see you, and hopefully that'll pull him out of this black state of mind.''

"Okay." Frannie hung up the phone and turned to find Celeste, Summer and Jasmine staring at her in fascination.

"Well?" Jasmine said.

"He loves me. Austin loves me!"

Amid war whoops and squeals of delight, the women hugged Frannie. "Come on, I've got to pack," she said abruptly.

Summer frowned. "But, Frannie, surely you're not still planning to go to Billings!"

"No." Frannie smiled so wide her face hurt. "I'm going to Denver."

"One more lap, and it's time to hit the pit." Tommy's voice crackled in Austin's ear over the headset. During the race, the two men were in constant communication. "How's she runnin'?"

"The car's fine, but I'm about half speed."

"Roger that. You're down a lap, but you're still in the runnin'. I've got a little somethin' to perk you up when you stop."

"Oh, hell. Not more of your coffee."

"Nope. Not coffee."

"What is it, then?"

"Come on in and see. You're clear to change lanes. Atta way. Bring it on down."

Tires squealing, Austin expertly pulled into the pit. Half a dozen men ran out and started working on the car—one on each tire, one refueling, one checking under the hood. Austin leaned out the window.

"Take a look in the stands," Tommy shouted. "Front row."

Austin scowled. "Hell, I'm in no mood to play babe watch.''

"That's not what this is. Take a look, damm it! Right behind the pit."

Austin had never heard Tommy so worked up about anything other than the car in all the years he'd known him. Unfastening his seat belt, he reluctantly pulled himself through the window and sat on the frame, lifting his eyes to the spot the Tommy had indicated.

He blinked, then blinked again. *Frannie.*

It couldn't be. But it was.

She stood and shyly waved. Austin waved back. She broke into a grin, and a weight seemed to lift from Austin's chest. The feeling was so strong, it almost seemed as if the law of gravity had just been repealed. His heart was floating, flying to the sky, soaring higher than the Goodyear blimp hovering overhead.

Frannie. Here. Waving at him and smiling. And her eyes held everything that felt as if it were about to burst wide open inside him.

She was wearing red and yellow—his race colors—and she looked as bright as a ray of sunshine. Seeing her warmed him like sunshine. Her smile was a golden ray, beaming down like a benediction. He stood there and basked in it, smiling back, and suddenly everything was clear, as clear as a cloudless sky on a sunny day.

His father had been wrong. Love wasn't something to be avoided. Love was something to be embraced, to be nurtured, to be cherished. It was something to be accepted, something to be given.

From Frannie. To Frannie.

How could he have been such an idiot? He didn't need to worry about giving her his heart. It was safe in her keeping, safe and cared for. It belonged to Frannie. It always had. He just hadn't known it.

Not until this second.

"Four more seconds, and you're ready to roll," Tommy said.

His eyes on Frannie, Austin touched his chest and mouthed the word "I." He crossed his hands across his heart, and his lips formed the word "love." Then he pointed right at Frannie. "You."

Even from this distance, he could see tears glitter in her eyes. She rapidly returned the hand signal, adding two fingers at the end. *I love you, too.* She blew him a kiss.

Austin pretended to catch it and clutched it to his heart.

"Okay," Tommy said. "Time to go, Romeo. The sooner you finish the race, the sooner you'll get to kiss her."

Austin climbed back in the seat, switched on the ignition and roared back out onto the raceway. He might be a lap down now, but he wouldn't stay that way for long. No, sirree. No one on the track had a bigger incentive to get across that finish line than he did.

"And the winner is...Austin Parker!"

The black-and-white flag dropped in a blur as Austin zoomed past. His pulse was racing harder than his car's engine and his adrenaline level was somewhere near the ozone. But it wasn't the joy of winning the race that had him lit up on the inside like the sky on the Fourth of July. It wasn't the wildly cheering crowd, or his jubilant crew jumping up and down in the pit. It was the thought of the woman in the grandstand, the woman he loved with all his heart and soul.

He steered his Monte Carlo around the curved end of the track on his slow-down lap, his eyes searching the stands. He reluctantly drove a victory lap, then headed into the winner's circle.

And that was where he saw the face he'd been searching for. The face he'd been searching for his entire life, but hadn't known until now.

He jerked the car to a stop and hauled himself out the open window. "Frannie."

She hurled herself into his arms, her eyes shining, her cheeks wet, her face ablaze with love. Around him the crowd roared, but Austin only heard the roar of the blood in his own ears as he kissed the woman he loved.

At long last he pulled back. "Frannie, Frannie, I love you."

"I love you, too."

"I can't live without you. Will you marry me?"

Frannie's smile would forever be etched in his memory, would forever be burned on his heart. The moment was golden, as gold as the sun on her light-brown hair, as gold as the ring he longed to put on her finger.

Her eyes twinkled in that impish way he loved.

"Well, that depends."

"On what?"

Her gaze grew serious. "On whether you're willing to take on a baby as well as a wife."

It took a few seconds for the words to sink in. He would have thought he couldn't feel any happier, thought his heart couldn't contain any more joy, but he was wrong. His hands tightened over hers. "You mean…you're…"

Frannie nodded.

With a wild whoop of joy, Austin picked her up and swung her around in a wide circle. He abruptly set her down and leaned over her. "Oh, hey, are you all right? I didn't hurt you or the baby, did I? Oh, Frannie, I don't ever want to hurt you."

"I know. And I'm fine. The baby's fine. We've never been finer. And, Austin, I don't ever want to hurt you, either. I love you so!"

Austin gathered her into his arms, a feeling of love,

overwhelming and complete, filling his chest, choking his throat, pulsing through his veins. He'd do anything, anything at all, to keep from ever hurting her.

"This is my last race," he murmured abruptly. "I'll quit NASCAR."

"No, you won't. I love you just the way you are. I want to add to your life, not detract from it. The baby and I will come to the races with you and cheer you on." Looping her arms around his neck, she pulled him down and gave him a kiss that all but made him forget his surroundings.

Tommy's elbow dug into his ribs. "Uh, boss, the cameras are rollin'. Everybody's waitin' to see what you have to say."

Austin reluctantly ended the kiss, but kept an arm firmly clenched around Frannie, pinning her to his side. Six separate microphones were thrust in his face. "Folks, I've won something far more important than a race today." He glanced down at Frannie, his throat swelling with tenderness. "I've won the heart of the most wonderful woman in the world, and she's just agreed to become my wife."

The crowd went crazy. Flashbulbs and strobes went off his face. He looked down at Frannie, worried that she'd be overwhelmed, but she beamed like the sun, bright and steady.

"What are your plans?" called a reporter.

"Well, the first thing we intend to do is get back to Whitehorn and get married as soon as possible."

"Hey, Austin," another reporter called. "Will you keep on racing?"

Austin opened his mouth to answer, but Frannie beat him to it. "Yes," she said emphatically. "I wouldn't dream of asking him to give up his first true love."

The crowd burst into cheers and applause. Someone

threw paper money all over the car, and someone else popped the cork on a champagne bottle. "I thought you couldn't speak in public," Austin murmured in her ear.

Frannie smiled up at him. "As long as you're by my side, I feel like I can do anything."

Austin's heart was so full, he thought it would burst from his chest. "That's how you make me feel, too. But you've got one thing wrong."

"I do?"

"Yeah. Racing's not my first true love. You are."

"I am?"

"My first, and my last."

He heard another cork pop.

As a shimmering spray of champagne rained down, he drew her near and lost himself in the intoxicating sweetness of her lips.

* * * * *

Don't forget to look out for
Just Pretending *by Myrna Mackenzie,*
the next book in the MONTANA BRIDES
spin-off series on sale June 2002.

▼™ SILHOUETTE®
SPECIAL EDITION™

AVAILABLE FROM 17TH MAY 2002

MY LITTLE ONE Linda Randall Wisdom

That's My Baby!

Prim Dr Gail Roberts never thought she'd still be with her gorgeous blind date, Brian, come morning. And she definitely didn't expect the little bundle of joy that was soon to follow!

CONSIDERING KATE Nora Roberts

A Brand-New Stanislaski Novel

Brody had never come across a woman as gorgeous, sensuous, provocative...and utterly irritating as Kate. But Brody was determined to resist her—even though he longed to make her his...

JUST PRETENDING Myrna Mackenzie

Montana Brides

Pretending to be engaged to beautiful police detective Gretchen Neal was the only way Agent David Hannon could investigate the murders in his home town. He could cope...after all it wasn't real—was it?

MOTHER IN A MOMENT Allison Leigh

Runaway heiress Darby White thought she knew nothing about family. But suddenly she was answering gorgeous new dad Garrett Cullum's pleas for help and caring for his motherless children...

SOMETHING TO TALK ABOUT Laurie Paige

Windraven Legacy

Kate realised that getting involved with devastatingly attractive Jess Fargo and his little boy wasn't wise. But then she was forced to trust Jess with her life. Could her heart be far behind?

GRAY WOLF'S WOMAN Peggy Webb

After spending one night of passion with single mother-of-three Mandy Belinda, loner Lucas Gray Wolf discovered she was pregnant with twins! But how would this wanderer cope with becoming a husband and father?

2 Books
and a surprise gift!

We would like to take this opportunity to thank you for reading this Silhouette® book by offering you the chance to take TWO more specially selected titles from the Special Edition™ series absolutely FREE! We're also making this offer to introduce you to the benefits of the Reader Service™ —

- ★ FREE home delivery
- ★ FREE gifts and competitions
- ★ FREE monthly Newsletter
- ★ Books available before they're in the shops
- ★ Exclusive Reader Service discount

Accepting these FREE books and gift places you under no obligation to buy; you may cancel at any time, even after receiving your free shipment. Simply complete your details below and return the entire page to the address below. *You don't even need a stamp!*

YES! Please send me 2 free Special Edition books and a surprise gift. I understand that unless you hear from me, I will receive 4 superb new titles every month for just £2.85 each, postage and packing free. I am under no obligation to purchase any books and may cancel my subscription at any time. The free books and gift will be mine to keep in any case.

E2ZEB

Ms/Mrs/Miss/Mr ....Initials ....

BLOCK CAPITALS PLEASE

Surname ....

Address ....

....

....Postcode ....

Send this whole page to:
UK: The Reader Service, FREEPOST CN81, Croydon, CR9 3WZ
EIRE: The Reader Service, PO Box 4546, Kilcock, County Kildare (stamp required)